Totally Bound Publishing books by Landra Graf

Bad Boys of Space
A Talent for Trouble
A Gamble Among Sheep

I0680940

Bad Boys of Space

A TALENT FOR TROUBLE

LANDRA GRAF

A Talent for Trouble
ISBN # 978-1-83943-822-6
©Copyright Landra Graf 2019
Cover Art by Erin Dameron-Hill ©Copyright January 2019
Interior text design by Claire Siemaszkiewicz
Totally Bound Publishing

A TALENT FOR TROUBLE

Dedication

To all the space shows I've loved before —
Farscape, *Firefly* and *Dark Matter*. May there be
more of them in my future.

Chapter One

The room held the hint of lemons, tropical essence and money. That meant opportunity, and Emilio Morales lived for the next leg up, like having intercepted the invitation to his boss, Manolo, from the Coco Cartel, out of the blue two weeks prior, to meet here on Ganymede at the Chateau Phillipe.

The chateau spanned several acres, with multiple buildings trimmed in gold with tile roofs, fancy materials he'd seen available only to those on the upper planets, not this close to the asteroid belt. Fresh fruit trees in the gardens, fine furniture without holes or tears, guards at every door with automatic weapons, not wheel gun pistols or ceramics. This was what money got a person—whatever they wanted. And Emilio wanted.

Walking in a tight circle, he took in the meeting room. These kinds of fancy surroundings beat the villas and homes of the cartel leaders on Earth by a long shot. Anything was better than sleeping on those hard, wooden cots kept in some drafty room off a main Earth house.

"Do you think they'll feed us any of that?" Emilio asked, motioning to a table behind him. It was covered in sandwiches, fruits, vegetables and a few other more traditional Earth meals, like enchiladas. The last time he'd shoved an enchilada in his mouth had been the day before his partner had offered him a job. Since then, it'd been food cubes, the occasional good meal and plenty of bootlegged booze.

The other group who had received an invitation—a pair of bald-headed men with matching spider tattoos on their hands—stood side-by-side, glancing out of the floor-to-ceiling window. Emilio recognized them as part of the Web Spinners, another drug-runner crew. They mainly worked with cartels in the Western Hemisphere of Earth, whereas Emilio had connections across the globe but did a lot of work in the Eastern Hemisphere.

The skinnier one piped up first. "Feed us? To sharks maybe—did you see that water? Besides, we're here to talk business."

A gong sounded somewhere, echoing through the room. A heavy-set shirtless man, positioned by a white door lined in painted gold roses, announced in a deep bass voice, "The Honorable Alfonso Grecia arrives."

Emilio would normally have shrugged off the elaborate entrance, something he'd seen before during previous business meetings. But, this time, Grecia wasn't doing one-on-one business. He'd opened up to competitors. As the only cartel boss who didn't reside on Earth, choosing to live on the outskirts of the uppers, Grecia was rumored to have ties to Earth royalty from 'before-the-nuke'. Over the years, Emilio's admiration for the man's amassed wealth and power, the way he commanded his organization, had grown. This was something he aspired to have for himself, the reason he'd chosen to attempt putting this deal together on his own…without his cokehead partner.

"Greetings, runners. Join me at my table." Grecia, with his low voice and expressionless face, stood an inch taller than Emilio and wore a floor-length black tunic. He'd already moved to the large cherry-wood table set up in the center of the room and flanked by matching leather upholstered chairs. Damn things even had little rolling wheels on the bottoms, an unexpected, luxurious touch.

Emilio was the last to sit, and Grecia turned his soulless eyes on him. Emilio pushed the gut twinge away, the one that said this man ate bullshitters for breakfast and that Emilio would never get away with his plan.

"Did you have a good trip?" Grecia asked him.

"As expected."

"Why is your partner Manolo not here?"

"He's not allowed on the planet anymore. A disagreement with your local law enforcement." In truth, Manny didn't know anything about this meeting, and nor would he. If all went well, Emilio's mentor might remain in a coke-induced haze while this deal was brokered and executed. "I can speak for both of us."

"Good. Good." The kingpin's attention moved to the Web Spinners, whom he'd ignored so far — possibly a good sign. "And welcome, Recluse. I've brought you both here because I have a proposition for you. My growers have developed a new product called Kiss Kiss. There's nothing like it anywhere on Earth, and I've got buyers waiting on the pleasure moon, Callisto.

I don't trust easily and have recently ended my short-term arrangement with the Hermes service."

Hermes had been an established group, with a handful of ships, and according to the latest wire reports, they'd been wiped out. Shot down by law, ships stalled in space with everyone on board dead due to exposure, top lieutenants killed in a poker game gone wrong—the list went on. It appeared Grecia ended things in a permanent fashion. Not a common practice, but accepted if the runners had been acting against their contract.

"You offer us business, but it's not really an offer. More a demand." This crap came from the crossed-armed Recluse in his unexpectedly high-pitched voice, and his skinny, bald companion nodded in agreement.

"What demand? I'm giving you both a chance to prove you're fit to run my exclusive product to the upper planets. If you meet my requirements, then you get this product and all my others. Once I contract with you, my allied cartels will follow suit. You'll control all Eastern Hemisphere running."

Emilio did his best to school his features at Grecia's reply. The benefits and possibilities were too numerous to even list, but the potential to retire from this shit in a matter of months versus years ranked high among them. "What are the requirements?"

Manny would have walked away already, spouting inanities and paranoid theories, whereas Emilio believed in analyzing all facts before making a decision. He hadn't kept their entire enterprise afloat by making half-baked choices.

Grecia smiled and motioned to the man from the door. The lackey dropped a memory disk in the center of the table and up popped a visual projection. It held several images of Earth, Grecia's product and a map.

The best part was the way the projection held steady and bright, no fading or flickering, with everything being one hundred percent triggered by touch. A display table almost as good as the ones on Emilio's ship, and a sight better than Manny's.

The drug boss swiped through the images, all smaller versions of what they could be, and selected Earth first. "You'll take your ship to the third planet, retrieve a shipment of my herb, Kiss Kiss, then transport the product to Callisto in six days from receipt."

He selected a map, pulling up the proposed trajectory and fastest route. It took them past all the major hotspots, places runners usually avoided unless they were stupid or suicidal. But the fastest route rode the currents with ease, putting less pressure on a slip drive, using less fuel. Emilio respected Grecia's presentation. It came with a plan.

"If you don't get caught, make it past the checkpoints and no harm comes to the shipment in transit, the contract is yours."

"Ridiculous." Recluse slammed a hand on the table. "No one runs or bootlegs along that route. It's a death trap and a sure-fire way to get your ship and crew pinched."

Attitudes like that get people killed. Emilio piped up fast. "Now, hold up a minute. If His Honorable wants this route run, then his people must know where there may be gaps in security. And if not, my folks would be happy to figure it out. There's nothing like exploring new travel routes." One more lie added to the couple he'd already launched made no difference.

Grecia's mouth twisted. On most people, it would look like a smile, but on his... "I like your thinking. Emilio, right?"

It irked him a bit that the big drug boss knew his partner's name and had to check his, but after this run, he'd make sure this guy always remembered him. They'd be contracted business partners. "That's correct."

"I like your style. You've got—how do they say it on Mars—steel stones?"

"Nuggets, sir. They call 'em steel nuggets."

This provoked a full grin, with teeth this time, and Grecia raised his hand above his head before bringing it down in a forward motion. The visuals on the table disappeared and a slicing sound rent the air. Emilio had been looking at Grecia but heard a gagging sound from the skinny guy and Recluse's head rolled onto the table.

There was no time to react before a blade shoved through Skinny's torso, razor-sharp and lined in red. Emilio took in a steadying breath, low and slow.

"Those men, they have no creativity, no passion. I can tell you do." Grecia walked around the table and sat next to him, steepling his fingers under his chin. "We're going to make this deal between us. You do the job, you deliver the goods and you get all my business."

People died every day, sometimes at his hands. He'd taken lives, almost lost his before. *The nature of the beast, the business.* Emilio could only be thankful his blood wasn't on some assassin's blade. An assassin who'd disappeared into the shadows of the room once more. Staring at Recluse's head, his stomach grumbling with unease, Emilio replied, "Sounds like a plan."

"No." Grecia shook a single finger in the air. "You haven't heard the rest. I determine pricing and you mark up twenty-five percent on this shipment. If you win the business, I'll let you mark up thirty percent."

Emilio whistled low. Yes, the deal wasn't perfect, but no deal was, not in his years of experience. Someone always came out on with the stems on a marijuana plant, as the saying went. But negotiations never got old. "Then I can't guarantee we go the route you want. It's not easy unless there's money to grease the wheels. I have to replace depleted funds."

Markups were always the runner's game, never the cartel's. The cartels made their money on the front end, with the runners assuming all the risk on the backside. That was the way Earth's economy worked. Cartels rarely owned ships, let alone wanted to bring the fury of the United Allied Planets down on them. This boss wanted to change the game—and for what purpose, Emilio didn't need to know. He did need to make sure he earned a profit.

"You, nuggets of steel." Grecia glanced around at his doorman and the guy Emilio hadn't seen, the one responsible for the dead bodies in the room. "Nobody talks to me like this."

"I don't believe in making commitments I can't keep. A man is as good as the deals he honors."

"Have you heard the one about no honor among thieves?" Grecia waved his hand in the air, and two seconds later a door shut behind them. The assassin had been dismissed.

"I'm a runner, not a thief. Soon, the sole runner for the Eastern Hemisphere of Earth."

This made Grecia laugh. A good sign, Emilio hoped.

"I'll tell you what. I'll include twenty-five kilos of Opium Dust and several cases of brandy on the pickup. You sell those and mark them up for whatever you need to cover the expense. I give these to you at cost."

The cost wouldn't do him. Emilio leaned up, propping his elbows on the table. "You give them fifty percent off."

Grecia's smile disappeared. "At cost."

"At cost." He'd settle in order to keep his life and the assassin with his sharp sword out of the room. "Do we shake on it?"

"I don't touch hands, but I'll remember your face, and your ship has already been scanned. Where it goes, I'll know." The boss leaned in close, giving Emilio a good look at the tiny scars running across the older man's cheeks. "If you fuck me over, you won't get the quick treatment disrespectful Recluse received. No, I'll hang you up by your arms and ensure you die slow. Now, let's eat."

Chapter Two

The airlock sealed and the door beeped then rolled out of the way to let Emilio onto his ship, *Gina*.

Once he passed through the entry, a light rail running through the middle of the walls lit up in yellow and a female voice greeted him. "Welcome back, sir. Was the meeting fruitful?"

"Get us off-world, then we'll talk." The entrance sealed shut behind Emilio.

"Heading, sir?"

He stopped right outside the entrance to the cockpit and sighed. "Open space? Just start moving the ship in the direction of Earth at a slow speed."

"Speed and course set, sir."

Mother Mary! Does she have to work so fast? "Great. I'm off to change."

Crossing through a room of windows, screens, an empty captain's chair and several stations to get to the captain's quarters was simple enough. His room was the second along a wall of seven cabins, six of them empty since he had no crew. *Don't need one.* People always gummed things up, made a mess. Like Manny, which Emilio cleaned up after. This time, this deal, meant no more Manny, no more messes.

"Can you tell me about the meeting, sir?"

Though a crew of people might be preferable to this damn ship.

"Can you wait until I get out of these clothes?" He'd eaten with blood spatter on the sleeve of his jacket. *A jacket I loved now ruined forever.* The door to his cabin slid sideways, granting entry, and Gina's yellow light followed him like a brilliant, talented, annoying sister.

"It went fine."

"Fine? This word is not an accurate description. I don't compute fine."

Artificial intelligence at its best. "Gina, I don't need sarcasm right now. In fact, you should focus on running basic diagnostics and inventory for your upcoming trip to Earth."

"My technological distinctiveness allows me to multitask multiple projects. But, if you'd rather be alone, all you need to do is say so, sir."

"Joseph's balls! I want to be alone."

"As you insist." The light rail turned blue, and Emilio sighed. Gina could be a regular pain in the *culo* sometimes. He'd won her from some dandy on Callisto, where dreams were made or destroyed. She was by far his most prized possession.

He'd become dependent on her for myriad things from probability programming to the cooking system she operated. A regular little homemaker, and like any sister, nosy and in constant need of attention. Her multitasking capabilities alleviated the need for actual people on ship, though some days he'd have loved to talk to a real person. Someone to bounce ideas off and who could understand his moods.

Part of his ongoing excuse for continuing to hang around Manny and his never-ending party attitude was a desire for human companionship—even if those companions weren't getting him anywhere.

Emilio grabbed a few of his tri-color coconut candies from the bowl next to his bed and popped one into his mouth. The others went into his pants pocket, for later. The candies were a slice of home, like those enchiladas he'd enjoyed earlier at Grecia's. *Home isn't complete without death, right? The blood on my jacket sleeve is evidence of that.* For a man constantly in a position as witness or killer, blood shouldn't have bothered him, but he found the sight abhorrent. Emilio stripped off the jacket and threw it onto the floor.

"Are you done being alone, sir?" Gina's light shone yellow once more.

"I was looking for a few more minutes. To freshen up, change my jacket." He pulled at the collar of his dull red button-down shirt. "Seems like I'm not going to get it, though."

"Sorry, sir, but I'm a little nervous about not having a clear heading. You are also eating candy. You only eat candy when things are bothering you." *The damn ship.*

"We got the deal."

"But you're not smiling."

"Correct, because we have to do some fancy maneuvering, and we'll need help. And the candy…I can eat whenever I want, for whatever reason."

"There is a ninety-five percent probability your consumption of candy is related to stress. What is our heading?"

"Earth." His home, the land of drugs and booze. "Eastern Hemisphere, Grecia cartel stronghold."

Except, not there. No, his birthplace lay in the west, the previous home of the United States, before-the-nuke. Imagining home brought the smell of marijuana on the breeze, the crazy wind storms, the taste of iron in his mouth after being whipped by the foreman.

Emilio opened his closet door and pulled out another jacket, identical to the first except this one was green, instead of brown. "The plan is we go to Earth and get Grecia's product. Then we head to Callisto, along this prescribed route." He produced a small chip from his pants pocket and held it up for Gina. The steady hum of her infrared scanner echoed around him.

"Based on this proposed route, there are approximately seven checkpoints between Earth and Callisto. I recommend an alternative route. There are four additional options."

"Yes, but to earn the contract, we need this route."

"It's impossible, sir."

Oh ye of little balls.

"Not impossible. Not for what I have planned. Gina, have we received a message from Johnny?"

"Yes, would you like me to read the message?"

Mother Mary, save me from this ship. "Of course I want you to read it."

"Johnny states, 'I have the software you need. It would provide engine cloaking for your AI.' An interesting upgrade, sir, but I don't think it's necessary."

"It is if we're going to get past all those checkpoints." The investment would cut into Emilio's savings, the money he kept putting away for when he could take a step back from running and start investing in his future—a house and roots. Now they needed the cloaking software and, in the long run, it would benefit them both.

"I can't believe you're outfitting me with some upgrade from those stoners?"

Emilio slid into his jacket then sat on the edge of his bed. "Those stoners are geniuses. They sit around in their bunker on Luna, thinking shit up then developing it out of a pile of scraps. Who do you think came up with your technology to begin with? Not a bunch of pompous asses on the Uppers."

"I'm still not comfortable working with them. They smoke on my ship, look at me funny."

"Oh." Emilio chuckled. "They admire you, Gina. Can't you appreciate a little adoration?"

"Maybe if I could trust them to keep their hands off my parts—" A ringing noise cut off what Gina planned to say next, saving him from another retort. "Incoming call from Manny."

Tugging on the cuffs of his jacket, he sat up a little straighter before replying, "Put it through."

"Emilio." Manny's voice, weathered and rough, came through Gina's wave cast crystal-clear.

"Hello, my friend."

"*Friend?* I'm not so sure, not with some news I just received." The censure behind those words, the tone, flashback to all those times Emilio had been scolded. Whether bodyguarding, providing transport, acting as muscle and sales delivery boy… *No more.*

"There a problem?" A small widget of fear rolled in his gut, deep inside. *If Grecia called Manny. If Manny called Grecia.* A dozen possibilities, but no sense in working himself up.

A laugh rippled through the sound system. "No, *mi hijo.* Just want to see you. It's been solar days. We need to talk about next steps, next runs. You have time?"

"Sure. I can be there in a couple days."

"Now, today…hours." The jovial sounds were replaced with stern, stubborn words. Manny wouldn't let him have a shot at picking up the shipment beforehand.

"I'll see you then," was the best response he could give without raising suspicion.

"See you soon, Milio." Then the call ended, evidenced by Gina's light going from red to yellow.

"Looks like you'll have to hit the moon and Earth without me, Gina."

"We could abort."

"No!" Emilio jumped up and started pacing. "This is a guaranteed shot of wrapping our hands around so much crinkle we'll be able to buy what we want, go where we want... These dreams—they're within our grasp. The only thing we're doing is splitting up for a short bit. I'll take care of Manny and you take care of getting the product safely to its destination."

Fifteen minutes later, he stood in front of the shuttle door. He hated leaving his ship. It was home. The one place he at least gave two shits about. The last few years he'd found more peace on this metal boat than he'd ever experienced anywhere else, except it seemed lonely without someone to share it with. Not his partner, a deadbeat druggie who needed to be dealt with. The kind of sharing he wanted to do involved the female type, one he could trust. Women like that didn't come cheap. Men paid lots of flash to guarantee loyal followings. He needed all the profit from this Grecia deal to come to him.

And, if his partner did talk to Grecia, then things wouldn't be all crinkle and champagne.

"Gina, tell me it's going to be okay."

"I can't lie, sir. My ethical programming prohibits it."

Emilio shook his head. "One day we're going to give those things an upgrade. Get you a sense of humor, too.

Speaking of upgrades, that glitch in the shuttle—did you fix it?"

"All shuttle readings show everything is fine. You have less than five percent chance of surviving until we meet again. I would like you to survive."

"I'd like to live a bit longer, too."

Exactly why it was high time he flew solo. A runner tied to someone else's bank account wasn't someone capable of providing for a woman. Though once he got the flash, he'd need to find the right one.

Chapter Three

If his family consisted of Gina and Manny, then Manny qualified as his sorry sack-of-shit father, though he wasn't a blood relation. Manny had found Emilio, an orphan, when Emilio had been a soldier for a drug cartel and had given Emilio the opportunity to get off the backward-ass planet he called the place of his birth. But, over the years, Manny had become less of a mentor and more of a partner. The good years hadn't been that long ago—four years of bliss, huge sums of flash and parties that never ended—and only within the last year had things started to sour.

His partner had stopped worrying about making money and broken his own rules, deciding that drugs were as good as the flash. In some cases, they'd lost funds because Manny had gotten too busy snorting up the profits.

"Gina Shuttle One, requesting permission to dock," Emilio radioed on the standard channel.

Compared to Gina, Manny's ship looked like a clunker, rust visible in some parts, different-colored panels where quick repair jobs had been completed. This had been the main smuggling ship in their operation until Emilio had come into possession of Gina. Now, they used Manny's vessel for reduced entertaining and living off Emilio's hard work.

"Permission to dock approved. Approach the starboard shuttle port," came the response from Manny's pilot. There were other differences between this ship and his, mainly that Gina handled all the shuttle nonsense and communications while Manny still needed a small crew to cover essentials.

There were a few creaks and groans as his bay door lined up, the hiss of the compression seal, then, "Your docking clamp is secure, Emilio. Come on board."

He exited the shuttle, which would also serve as his quarters for the duration of his stay. Trusting his safety to this death trap wasn't ideal. Outside the shuttle door stood his escort, one of Manny's bodyguards, Alfie.

"Welcome back to Casa Manolo." Alfie stood a few inches taller than he did. Teenaged Emilio had believed naming a ship after yourself and possessing bodyguards to be a sign of wealth. Now, it sounded silly, when compared to the opulent chateau belonging to Grecia and the presence of one lone assassin.

"Happy to be here. How's the boss holding up?"

"High as a kite and excited for your meeting. He said he needed to use the facilities, but he'll meet you in the lounge area." The nightclub bouncer turned bodyguard had been on the ship for less than a year, and his laissez-faire attitude and free manner of speaking worked in Emilio's favor.

"I can find my way." Emilio left Alfie behind and walked down the corridor, a stretch of steel, carpet and plastic reminding him of his youth and his first time on the ship. He'd barely been past twenty, soldiering for one of the cartels in the Western Hemi and surviving the last big battle, while earning a vicious-looking scar on his cheek, when Manny had spotted him. Had offered for him right up, even paying more for the shipment of marijuana he'd come to get.

Emilio's eyes had been wide open back then, and posters and relics from Earth-before-the-nuke had adorned his walls. Now, most of those were gone, gambled away or sold off to reimburse the business accounts for Manny's coke habit. Emilio didn't know the day Manny had become addicted, but at least a year ago the drug had taken over his life. His love for the rush that the coke gave him had canceled out everything else and once it had affected business, Emilio had decided things had to change. He'd tried to get Manny to quit like he'd begged his mother to stay. She'd abandoned him on Earth. Manny had ditched him for drugs... He could only trust his ship. A person who wanted to survive in this shitty world trusted loyalty earned with the flash.

He came to a halt in front of a set of double doors, and they hissed open to the lounge room. Red and gold were the primary colors divided among all the furniture, wall paint, carpet and curtains. The soft deep-colored plush seats and gold-flecked tables called to him with memories of their own, though now those things were chipped, the colors faded and the fabric threadbare. *Manny used to throw insane parties here...* The bar, once fully stocked, held a couple of bottles of whiskey. Emilio headed there first.

He poured himself a glass. Turning it slowly, spreading the liquid up the sides and back down, he noticed he wasn't alone. "Can I offer you a drink?"

"No," a sultry feminine voice responded. "There's nothing over there isn't made in the still or fermented in a barrel."

"Suit yourself." Emilio turned and took in the view. *Mother Mary.*

The woman, a vision of sin, stood angled toward the fancy window display where three floor-to-ceiling panels showcased the twinkling view. She wore a glimmering red dress, which sparkled even more as she turned toward him. Her hair was a pale-white blonde, short and framing her face, giving it a distinct diamond shape. She'd be labeled gorgeous, more than the word could construe, with her eyes the color of whiskey — and not the cheap stuff in his glass. No, the full-bodied swirling amber and caramel colors.

"What brings you to Casa Manolo?" He swallowed a little more whiskey than he intended and did his best to sound suave, but the words came out more like a croak.

"Nothing that concerns you." The dismissal paired with a smile, a little thing revealing flawless teeth. He glanced down at her one note of defiance — boots. Grav boots to be exact, black and fierce. A deep, soul-encapsulating need clamped onto his brain, a need he'd waited years to experience. *This* was the woman he'd been waiting for. The type he'd always wanted. The one he'd call his.

He walked closer, eager to see if she took a similar interest in him. "Oh? Well, I'm happy to make this visit less business and more pleasure. Your name is?"

The words escaped his mouth as he glanced at her lips — expressive, full and waiting for his kiss, even when those same lips uttered, "Too expensive for you."

"You'd be surprised what I can afford." Even more surprising was Manny paying for this pretty bit. His partner would be seriously cutting into their funds when there were better ways to get laid. She should be doing dirty deeds with Emilio. "Besides, do you want a coked-out bed partner when you can have someone who can handle two rounds of strenuous physical activity?"

She frowned at him. "I don't need someone capable of feats of strength. I need someone who knows his way around the place."

That was what he imagined as he eyed her entire form again, now mere inches from him. "Honey, I'll pay whatever you want for a grand tour, and believe me, I know how to treat a woman."

"You damn runners are all the same." She stuck out an index finger and poked him in the chest. "Thinking with enough flash you can buy your way to anything." There, that spark in her eyes, an inner fire—if she unleashed similar emotions in the bedroom, he'd find heaven. Though her general distaste alerted him to the fact that she might not be a space whore.

Before she could pull away, he circled her wrist with his fingers, finding her skin warm and soft. "Crinkle talks. Anyone will tell you that. I haven't found a thing I couldn't buy with it."

"Even love?" The question came on a breathy whisper. A tone he could imagine she used in the bedroom.

"Love? Who said a thing about that? Love's as bad as the drugs I run. The day you love something is the day you've signed your own death sentence, because someone saying the words equals saying goodbye. I'll take loyalty over love any day." He'd also take her, any way he could have her…to start.

The woman wrenched herself free and took two steps back. "You have a twisted way of thinking."

contacted me a few solar hours ago, it was to confirm I liked the arrangement."

Emilio sighed before downing the rest of his drink. Hands down this was the worst news of the day, next to getting blood on his jacket.

"Nothing to say?" Manny asked. He slapped his hand against the table before glancing at the girl. "Toni, any thoughts?"

Call me stupid, but Emilio hoped she did say something. He wanted to know her opinion, to see if the subtle banked heat in her eyes flared at the mere mention of his predicament. Instead, silence. Not even a shrug of shoulders or a shake of her head.

"See, if this dumb broad knows when to take the high road and keep her mouth shut, then you'd think *you* might have been smarter than trying to sneak something like this past me."

Manny's words got a rise from her and those amber eyes flashed with fire. As fast as her angry reaction emerged, it disappeared, replaced with a semi-smile. She went to sit in a chair at one of the gambling tables, faced them and shuffled a deck of cards.

Emilio slid out of the booth and to a standing position, watching the bodyguards circle the room in slow, measured steps. "I'm afraid I don't see the point." This beating around the slip drive engine shit had to stop.

"The point is, it's my way or the highway. Grecia doesn't trust you not to muck this up. He's worried about the agreement, how you'll try to change things or fuck up. You've got no space cred, *mi hijo*, at least not on your own."

"Why did he call you?" Emilio asked before he poured his third drink. A light tingling sensation had started to course through his body, but the buzz wasn't enough to cover the growing rock in his gut. Or that niggle in his brain, reminding him of Gina's ominous predictions before he came here.

"Your ignorance. Cartels don't get to control the markups and you allowed him to. You let him set rates, which is unheard of—not that he's unhappy with the deal. He won't let me renegotiate. I'm stuck in the same crappy situation as you are. Except now, you'll be splitting the profits with me."

Shit. He should have pushed Grecia more in the negotiations. Turning and leaning against the bar, Emilio slid a finger around the rim of his glass, feeling the smooth surface. All eyes were on him and he hated himself for not figuring this mess out sooner. "What if I refuse?"

The sounds of gun hammers cocking echoed around them, along with the incessant shuffle of cards from Toni. Manny slid out of the booth. "You don't understand, and you never did. This game we play, *mi hijo*, is as much for safety as it is for security. No one does business with people they don't know, people who can't be vouched for. Not with the Unis and Allied government trying to sneak in and learn about our operations. This isn't a get rich quick scheme—running is a way of life. You walk away from this and not only will Grecia not do business with you, but no one will."

Emilio looked at Toni, the way her long fingers warped and bent the cards, tumbling them together. She represented what he needed from life. To reach someone like her he had to have influence. "I think I can convince them otherwise."

Manny frowned, his voice turning from soft to low and harsh. "They don't deal with trash like you...no, you would be stripped of everything. Then you'll be crawling back to Earth on your hands and knees begging to be a soldier again, if you get that far. Cartel leaders don't like liars. I don't like liars. Take the deal."

No fucking way. Emilio refused to give in. This was his shot, his one chance to break away from yet another toxic relationship. To be the master of his own destiny, the path he wanted to take that would set him on the track of power. If Emilio played this right, he could work this game for the next four to five years, save back the crinkle and retire. By then it'd be easy to find another sucker to work for Grecia. He'd been twenty-one, and standing on Manny's ship, he'd promised himself he'd never be hungry, shoeless or homeless again. Manny's ideas and addictions were in direct opposition to this.

"Too late. Gina is already en route to Earth." Emilio set his now-empty glass down and stepped away from the bar, letting those words sink in.

"You make it sound like you can't cut me in, as if I won't be a part of this."

The hard echo of cards hitting each other got Emilio's attention. But Toni never acknowledged either of them, just started dealing out a game.

"Maybe you don't get it. It's too late to cut in. I made the deal with Grecia, not you. At the end of the day that's what matters. Whoever has the flash has the power, and who's got the power will rule the currents."

Manny downed his entire drink, a rough cough following, before throwing the empty glass at the wall. As it shattered, he shouted, "Fuck! I brought you into this world, gave you a place to grow, to be safe. This is how you repay me, repay the years of me teaching you how to survive out here."

"At some point all little boys have to grow up."

"I love you, Emilio," Manny replied, motioning his bodyguards over to him. "But I'm going to need a damn good reason why I shouldn't kill you now."

"I say, put your crinkle where your mouth is, because without Gina, you won't be doing anything."

Manny could get all threatening. It didn't matter anyway—this entire thing ended with the cokehead dead. Emilio had never believed in karma. Regardless, it appeared some sort of fate or devil may have been working against him.

He hadn't planned on being caught with his gun in his holster mere hours after coming onto Manny's ship. No, this was supposed to go a lot smoother, with him taking out his partner in the middle of the night, the fool asleep in some drunk or drugged haze. Then he'd had to go and tempt the asshole by admitting to cutting him out of a drug run.

Both bodyguards stepped forward, and Emilio took a quick moment to glance at Toni. She sat tense, cards laid out in front of her, both hands gripping the edge of the poker table, her eyes a blend of furious brown and swirling gold. Obviously, she didn't like this scenario either.

"I'm not afraid to call your bluff, *mi hijo*. I'll give you one last chance to change your mind." This as his partner drew his gun from underneath the jacket he wore.

Mother Mary. Emilio brought his arms up in surrender. "Do we have to solve this problem with guns and not words?"

He took a step closer to Toni, lowering his arms as he neared her. They were both getting off this ship together, and he'd put his body closer to harm before hers—the invisible pull toward her was that strong.

Plus, the poker tables could provide cover. He watched Manny's trigger finger.

"Save your bullshit for the devil when he tells you that you're not welcome, even in hell." Then the idiot fired at him.

Emilio dived toward Toni, who took the initiative to push over her table and crouch behind it. Instead, he collided with her chest and got a good whiff of some fancy scent, even as chaos ruled around them. Gunfire echoed and plunked against the table, the impact muted but still present, and the main lights went out. He'd been in gunfights before, but never on a ship. No, most of his experience with weapons had occurred on a planet or a moon. Still, the safest way out of any fight involved landing shots.

"Do you have a gun?" He huddled next to her, trying to give them space but still stay close.

Toni nodded, shocking Emilio as she pulled a small pistol from a garter on her bare ivory leg. The mere sight of skin, amid bullets ricocheting against the metal walls and hitting the thick wood at their backs, kicked his adrenaline up a notch.

Definitely not a space whore. He wanted a shot at convincing this woman to show him everything. Before he could make a new offer, to get them out of this in exchange for a little private time, she launched upward and fired two shots. She was nuts and he loved it.

Emilio removed his pistol from his thigh holster and followed suit, getting a good look at where her shots landed—in one of the bodyguards. Mirroring her action, he took out the other one. Then took aim at his partner, who stood furiously attempting to reload his pistol. Toni bumped against him, causing the shot to go wide, the bullet pinging against the window.

She frowned, lifting her gun and pointing it at Emilio. "You can't kill him."

Whatever desire he'd been feeling toward her fizzled and died in that moment. He re-aimed his weapon at Manny, who'd finished reloading as well. "He's not going to do you any favors. He'll kill us both if given the chance. Let me get rid of him."

"Emilio, is that what you think of me?" Manny stopped firing, but kept his gun trained on Emilio. "I wouldn't kill anyone unless they deserve it. You betrayed me — the runners' code states I have authority to take action. Toni isn't part of your scheme. She'll be unharmed."

"What about my ship?" Toni asked.

From his peripheral vision, Emilio could see the barrel of Toni's gun still sighted toward him. *What a woman.*

"Your ship?" Manny's eyebrows hunched.

"If I shoot him and let you live, will you give it back to me? I have the same amount of crinkle in an account waiting to be transferred to you."

Manny laughed, a true bastard. "You're a stupid drunk, thinking you can blackmail your way to get something I won fair and square. I won't be conned by him or you."

"Shoot the fucker," she replied, cold-hearted like Manny. She lowered her weapon and Emilio took the shot, two of them, directed at Manny. The fool looked surprised, confused, and fell to the floor.

The look on Manny's face was one Emilio would remember. It wasn't every day a person killed a mentor, and initially he felt a bit of regret, then anger because the fool had brought him to this. No one got to risk his future, his well-being — except him. Manny proved time and again he cared about himself alone, and his little tirade before the gunfight had meant Emilio had been a means to an end.

Ready to celebrate victory with the gorgeous woman beside him, he turned, only to get a punch in the face so hard he took a step back.

"What the hell was that for?" he mumbled, massaging his cheek.

"For your whole entrance, the fight and making this day the worst one I've had in a while. Damn, I want a drink. You have no idea what I had to do…" She stomped her foot and held up the edges of her skirt. "This fucking dress is not my preferred attire."

A hissing noise rose around them, then red lights, a loud alarm beeping and echoing in his ears, rattling his brain. "I'm a fan of naked."

"Freezing to death would happen first!" Toni hollered, tucking her gun back into its garter holder. "That wide shot of yours put a crack in the window. Follow me."

She took off, running for the entrance as the windows behind reverberated with a loud snap. This wasn't part of the plan. Karma…the evil creature seemed to be working against him. He followed suit, charging after her. "Hold up—"

The final pop of glass and the vacuum suction sound of space whooshed forward right when the room doors sealed behind them. Toni stood next to a control panel, a tendril of smoke wafting from it, her gun once more in her hand. From the looks of the cracked glass, she'd bashed the damn thing in.

"What the hell is your name again?"

She shook her head in annoyance. "Captain Antonia Smith of the *Geisha*."

The name sounded familiar. As the doors beside them dented, space greedy for every last section of open volume, he recalled the tales of the wild captain who'd pistol-whip men and drink others under the table. "What the sweet gold leaves is a crazy woman like you doing in a place like this?"

Chapter Four

Antonia Smith couldn't decide whether to kick him or shoot him. His gun would be easy pickings if she sidled up next to him and did a fast snatch and grab, except they didn't have time. "Crazy woman? Who started the shooting in a ship with glass windows?"

"It's supposed to be double-plated," Emilio countered, take a step closer. The only thing separating them from open space was a four-inch-thick piece of metal which dented again as she stared at it.

"Sure, whatever. Where did Manny stash my ship?"

"How should I know?"

She huffed. "You're his business partner."

"Yeah, not his wife or accountant. How did he win your ship?"

A good question swimming among a sea of bad memories and even poorer decisions. Ones she didn't have the time to discuss as the lights flickered and went out around them. A new blaring alarm howled out a screeching sound similar to the end-of-shift bells in the Mars mines. "How about we take this line of questioning somewhere we're less likely to be crushed under the weight of space?"

"Sure. My shuttle's this way." Emilio pointed behind him, in the opposite direction.

"Too bad mine is on the other side of the ship," she replied, taking off before he could get a hand on her or drag things out, her quick movements the better choice as the lounge door gave way shortly after. Metal clinks sounded in front, the ship sealing itself off in a mode of self-preservation. She'd experienced such a thing before...once. Then another alert, this one for a fire ahead.

"You won't make it," Emilio yelled behind her.

"I can try."

"Or you can follow me. I know a back way to my shuttle."

Ten seconds later, they were scrunched up and inching through ductwork while Casa Manolo fell apart around them. She sent up silent prayers to every god she'd heard of, even the eight-tentacled one, that when they emerged on the other side of this narrow passage, Emilio's shuttle would still be there.

"Why didn't you shoot me when you had a chance?" he asked, lifting a piece of hanging pipe and motioning her forward.

"These are the things you want to know at this exact moment?" Because it was the last thing she was thinking about. Not now, not when her survival instinct had kicked in. If he slowed down or tried any funny business, she'd leave his attractive, smooth-talking ass here and take her own chances.

"Yeah, because it could have been me dead just as easily as Manny. Besides your ship, there's got to be a reason."

They reached the end of the corridor and she leaned on the door hinge. Damn thing wouldn't budge. She kicked it real hard with a loud grunt. The metal swung open, revealing a smoky yet clear hallway and a sealed shuttle door mere feet away. She breathed a sigh of relief.

Glancing back, she grinned. "Because you're cuter and stupider."

If he responded, she couldn't hear it as she ran for the shuttle entrance, pulling the manual lever. The door rolled up and they both got in. Emilio passed her and headed for the pilot's chair, while orange color tinted her vision. She slammed the door down, hearing the press of buttons and the warm-up of the engines. A peek out of the little side view window showed fire licking towards them fast. "We've got to go now!"

Emilio pulled a yellow lever. Her heart stopped when the shuttle sputtered and died. "What the hell is going on up there?"

"It's..." Clicks, clacks and the pounding of fists against panels filtered to her. "A glitch. Joseph's balls. Gina said it was fixed. I can't get this thing to go anywhere."

Leaving her post, she stalked the eight steps to the center panel in the floor that was the same in all shuttles and heaved it up. Below sat the trolling motor and the slip drive, which were both non-functioning. *A glitch of serious proportions.* Hunching, she ripped at a set of wiring and crossed a few things. The last twitch and a sharp twinge of electricity hit her fingers.

"Try the trolling motor now," she hollered as the motor's belt started to boot up. A bit slower than she'd like, but anything was better than dying. She sighed when the shuttle jerked away from the side of the ship, and the idiot must have slammed down on the fuel injector trigger, because the motor sputtered once more. She lifted her head and prayed again. A huge explosion rocked the boat and knocked her off balance, sending her dress up to her waist and her falling forward between the pilot and co-pilot chairs.

Cool air wafted against her bottom and a sharp whistle sounded. "I like women who appreciate a nice pair of underwear."

Toni growled, righting herself and the skirt to cover up the lace Emilio had gotten a flash of. Her best and sole pair of fancy undergarments. "You should be looking for debris from Manny's ship, not at my ass."

Shuttles were typically never equipped with more than a basic defense shield, meaning anything bigger than a pistol could tear a hole right through the damn things.

"And what a fine ass."

Looking out of the window again, she checked for issues. "The debris is moving in the opposite direction. We need to get farther away in case something changes it."

"How the hell can you see that?"

"Uh, by paying attention." She pointed to the far port-side, where the ship's fire was shrinking upon its introduction to the vacuum of space.

He glanced in that general direction. "Get up here and assist in moving us away from the exploding ship, because this thing won't do anything for me."

She did exactly that, taking the chair next to him to redirect the navigational controls. They were similar to her ship's and her brother's shuttles. *Funny how the outsides of ships change, but the innards remain the same.* A few pressure changes, some priming and she rotated the shuttle into a stream that got them pointed in the right direction, away from the wreckage and towards Jupiter.

Emilio watched her like a hawk. "How the hell do you know how to do that?"

"I captain a ship. Most people don't just get to run a vessel because they win it gambling."

"So, you've heard of me?" He winked at her.

She groaned. "Yes, by reputation alone."

"All good things?"

"If you call being a ladies' man who attracts desperate, scar-loving station-clingers a good thing." She left out the rumors of his bedroom prowess. Because she'd turned over a new leaf. No sex, no men and definitely no crazy stuff.

"I can tell from your expression you've heard other things."

How easily he'd read her since the moment they'd faced off on Casa Manolo bugged her as well. She focused on the piloting. "Maybe that you won a fancy ship in a poker game."

"Better to win one than lose one," he replied.

The words stung, the sharp pain taking up residence somewhere in the center of her chest. *Why am I attracted to him again?* "You know what they say on Mars...can't win big if you don't risk big."

"Mars girl, eh?"

Toni gave a single nod.

"Makes sense why you're crazy."

She wanted to take offense at his shocked tone, dismissive like so many of the men she'd met over the years. The way the upper planets still regarded woman as objects more often than as productive members of society drove her nuts. "Don't let this dress fool you."

"It's doing everything *but* fooling me," he retorted with a smirk. Damn if she didn't enjoy the look on his face, even if it made his scar more severe. Though she barely got time to entertain the thought before a new alarm started up, this one a slow, steady, obnoxious beep with a flashing red button.

"What the hell?" Emilio leaned in, smacking a fist against the dash.

A quick glance told her everything. "You've got something wrong with the drive compressor. I already noticed the slip drive is down and I rigged the trolling motor. But my quick fix isn't going to hold. You're losing slip cohesion and that engine is about to shut down, along with backup power. We're going to be dead in the water."

"Spaceships or people! I don't know which is worse." He pushed out of the chair and stomped behind her. She sat up in her seat and decompressed the auto-pilot button before attempting to go and help.

Emilio, with his stout muscles, ones she didn't mind admiring, squatted next to the exposed panel on the floor. His loud curses were expected and he looked less than pleased as he held up the end of a black rubber line with a frayed edge. "Is this from you?"

She nodded. "And if I'm right, we're going to need another ship."

Toni tucked chunks of her hair behind her ears as Emilio kicked the main panel's metal plate while punching the air. There were a few growls of fury that accompanied his little tantrum, which continued without an indication as to when he'd finish. She took the entire scene in, from his thick near-black hair and the scruff on his chin to the way a bead of sweat dripped down his cheek, along the scar. Over the years, she'd come to find men with a rough, rugged appearance alluring.

He made every attempt at expressing interest in her, but she refused to fall for cheap tricks all over again. Plenty of men had charmed their way to her bed with less. Better choices meant turning down sexcapades, even if they were offered freely.

As she watched him, she smiled then laughed, the adrenaline in her system dissipating and leaving behind the sheer ridiculousness of their situation. They should have been dead already, from Manny's bullets, the vacuum of space or roasted by fire. Instead, they'd suffocate.

"What the hell are you laughing at?"

"Hold on." She guffawed with an unrefined snort and tried to breathe normally without success. It didn't help that Emilio stood with arms crossed, eyes wide as if she'd lost her mind. Not the first time someone had given her a crazy stare over her reactions.

"Pull yourself together. We don't have enough air for laughter."

A downed engine meant no air recycling system, no fresh oxygen.

That did it, the final sobering. They were going to die out here, unless she came up with an alternative option he'd agree to. She turned back around and started messing with the panels in front of her, a last-ditch effort to at least get communications up. She'd been in crappy situations before. Hell, the last six months were a fabulous reminder of how far one could fall off the wagon and into a pit of despair. She'd just dragged herself back out of the bottle again. *A drink… That would be nice.*

Messing with the dials did nothing. The problem wouldn't be solved unless she got under the dash. She tore a piece of her skirt off with her teeth and used it to tie her hair back, keeping it out of her face, then threw herself on the floor, happy to get back to something she was far more familiar with. She scooted up underneath the pilot's console and took off a panel. "You have any spare parts?"

"It would be super convenient if I did, which I typically do. Unless I'd taken the spare parts to sell for some crinkle, a little extra to get me through until the next job is finished," Emilio growled from above her.

"What about tools?" She grabbed a chunk of wires, letting the memories wash over her. The smell of electrical heat as she fixed up a junker ship in her parents' mechanic barn. The ease of slipping a knife through cables, slicing copper and aluminum wires to shift, repair or mix to bypass bad systems. She'd gone against her parents' wishes then. Playing at men's work, callusing up her beautiful hands.

"There may be a kit by the slip drive," Emilio grumbled.

His footsteps stomped away, then came back.

"Yeah, I got a couple wrenches, pliers and some electrical tools that I have no clue what they do." A bag fell to the floor with a clunk, and he toed it towards her.

"This will work." Digging in, she was able to find the wire cutters and a pair of splicers. A shame she'd be tearing apart some fabulous wire work and set up. The shuttle itself was a beaut. Something she'd dreamed of flying and found herself a bit envious of. Most ships, shuttles and other craft she'd experienced weren't clean, sleek and rust-free. Still, they had little chance of doing much beyond getting a message out. She'd look at the schematics to double-check.

"What are you trying to do?"

"Get the computer display up so we can see the schematics and have communications. Honestly, we won't be able to fix anything on this shuttle."

A pilot chair squeaked as he sat down. Then he sighed real deep. "Where the hell did you learn to do that?"

"You already guessed. Mars."

"Mining colony kid, huh?" The question came with a tone sounding like typical expectation. Because people who knew the innards of ships only came from the planet known for harvesting ship metals and building the damn things, the usual stereotypes. In this case she did, but still.

"Got a problem with miners?"

"Not at all. Mining is mining, much like running, in many ways. This whole thing with Manny, on the other hand, wasn't supposed to be this hard."

"Did you expect your partner to welcome you cutting him out with open arms?" A few more splices and she'd have something worthwhile. "People kill for less. This shuttle is a bust—the compressor controls bits of the engine and the drive—but if you're willing to trust me, I can get us out of here." Her words paired with a blip and a beep. She emerged from beneath the console and popped back into the chair.

"Do you always talk so abruptly?"

"Hmm?" Toni pressed a couple of buttons, pulling up the shuttle's schematics on the view screen. This shuttle belonged to his poker-prize ship, if the sleek design specs in front of her were accurate. "I flow where the conversation does, if that's what you're asking. Right now, we have a problem to solve and your ship is not flying again. There's a fuse burnt out, probably what caused your glitch, as you put it. Not easy to get to or replace without being docked to your ship."

No word from Emilio. His silence got her to stop pressing, zooming and rotating the pieces of the ship on the screen. A glance in his direction got her in a staring contest with blue eyes so dark in the limited light of space they looked black.

He looked strange, attractive and contemplative, and he leaned in closer. "So, what you're saying is we should use our last breathable air going out the way the good lord intended, stark naked and entwined."

"You sure like to dirty up every other sentence coming out of your mouth." The words sparked inappropriate yet delicious musings of them, naked, panting, getting down and dirty right here in these pilots' chairs.

"Rumor has it you enjoy dirtying up every other man you meet."

She'd never played shy when it came to sex. No, she'd been used in that manner and done some using of her own many years past. But *that* Toni had gotten kicked to the curb when she lost her ship. "Shouldn't trust rumors spoken by shine-soaked gamblers with a love for runners' goods."

"Even when those rumors sound equally tantalizing to how your legs look?" He winked at her.

The wink got her blushing all over again. She didn't normally react this way to any man spinning her fancy comments, but for some reason he hit all the right buttons. "Listen, I'd like to spend my last moments trying to save our asses. Maybe then I'll consider a little action of the naked variety. All I need is a little trust."

No way would she be giving this guy anything besides

a chance to get out of here. But she refused to reach out to her brother without some reassurances.

"Trust…that's not gotten me much of anything, except Manny trying to blow a hole in me just because I wanted to end our business arrangement. What do you want?"

"Your agreement that you won't shoot me when I call for help." Tapping on the screen in front of her, she continued, "And we have a couple of solar hours of air left if we breathe shallow, so better make a choice quick."

She sat there staring, desperately wishing for a bottle, though she'd never touch another again if she somehow survived this. Drinking, being in crappy situations—those days would be behind her.

"Fine, call for help, but much good it will do you. My ship is out of range and won't make it back within a couple of hours on these currents."

"I'm not calling yours. I'm calling my brother's."

Chapter Five

Toni believed no good deed went unpunished and no man could be trusted, not with her body, or anything else for that matter. Emilio readily agreeing to her decision to call her brother's ship signaled a need for caution. "Are you sure you're okay with that?" *And surprise.* "He's a body collector."

Emilio leaned down and put his lips right next to her ear. "I'm not scared of anyone, least of all a collector. Should I be?"

She did her best not to shiver, in part because of the inconvenient attraction and the other part a sense that she should have a bit more self-preservation around him. This was a man who'd shoot first, take names later. *Irony is, how he blends this serious side of him with excuses to get close to me.* She should've punched him again. Anything to get the message she wasn't interested... *Lies.* "No. My brother cares most about his body count and delivering to his quota. I care about my ship."

A ship she'd been given, her one source of freedom, controlling her destiny. She'd made a great error on Callisto after a good bootleg run. Tapped into some of the product she'd brought to the moon. A few shots too many had equaled poker rounds aplenty. The liquor had brought her inches away from betting her life after she'd already lost her ship to Manny. Her brother had taken her in, given her safe harbor in exchange for her engine skills, though said brother had refused to help her regain her own ship. No, she'd already be on his radar for stealing a shuttle to see Manny. A call for help would do her no favors.

Emilio sat down in the captain's chair and stared at her. Those blue-black eyes bored holes into her skull, but she kept looking forward, at the vast, twinkling space. "I agree to this, what do I get?"

The question hung in the air, pregnant with meaning. He wanted her body, had implied it from the moment they'd met. Too bad she wasn't for sale. "Your life."

He chuckled. "Are you willing to stake something a little more tantalizing besides keeping me breathing?"

Paul's hymnals, this man never stops. "How about a hefty chunk of crinkle?"

She refused to sink down into this sexual fantasy daydream he kept entertaining about them. There was only one thing she wanted or needed. *My ship.* Any crazy behavior led back to the bottle.

"Once I meet up with my ship and complete my deal with Grecia, I'll have crinkle aplenty."

"Yes, but everyone needs a little wheel grease."

He perked up in his seat. "Oh, sure, but what's your angle?"

"I get some of the take, to buy back my ship."

"I don't need another ship. I already have one."

This asshole.

"Yes, but you're starting an enterprise, correct? You want the whole cut and here I am in need of an operation to connect with." *And a backup plan since Manny's death left me without options.* She could sucker this one in, though she refused to pay in flesh. "Give you a chance to convince me all your ego stroking is true."

Her turn to wink.

Emilio plopped his boots on the console in response and let her sweat. She used the minutes to prep the communication channel. They were running out of time, but the waste was worth it if she got what she wanted.

"I like your spunk, your face, your legs...and I might live long enough to make you crazy for me."

"Do we have a deal?"

"Make your call." He slid his grav-booted feet off the console and stood. She expected him to march off, leave. Instead, he grasped her by one arm and hauled her upright. "We'll seal this bargain the old-fashioned way."

And before she could question him, he fused his lips to hers. The kiss wasn't as polite as she'd foolishly believed it would be. No, it started out filthy. The lightest of touches, devolving into tongues intertwining. She tasted liquor, tasted him. The experience was heady, drugging. Before it deepened, Emilio broke away from her.

Panting echoed around her. *Is that me?*

Emilio, cool as ever, sat back down in the pilot chair and nodded at the console. "Ready when you are." The heat in his gaze gave those words a different meaning. She wanted to say something, anything. Except her throat had run dry as a dust storm, another sign he wasn't good for her health. Not in the long term. Her own body was warring against the rational part of her brain.

So, she did the next best thing. She grunted. A crappy throat-clearing excuse for a growl. Toni took her seat and pressed the orange button to signal her brother's vessel. A pleasant musical ring emerged around them, musical tones called dialing—at least that was what she'd been told they were called on Earth-before-the-nuke. In her younger years, she'd been taught about many terms and items of their ancestors and equally rough lessons of the current belief system, such as women were more things than they were people. That concept made her thirsty for something stronger than water and eager to rid herself of her shitty situation.

"Well, I'll be a dust bunny in mechanic's clothes. Toni, it's a damn shocker to see you on my view screen." Her brother's booming voice, with a touch of twang common to Mars, filtered through the audio speakers.

"Hi, Big Al. Sorry about borrowing the shuttle, but I had to see a man about—"

"Your ship." Her brother finished for her and frowned. "The trouble is, little sister, the boat you called me from isn't mine and that fella beside you isn't from my crew. Did you get drunk and get married?"

Her reputation for drinking had started with her family. Everyone called her the wild one. "No. I'm not drunk or married. I'm sober," Toni replied through gritted teeth.

Big Al laughed and it was all she could do not to start cursing. *Paul's hymnals, give me strength.* Brotherly caring, their big and warm fuzzy relationship, had ended between them when she'd become old enough to sport tits and he'd refused to watch as their parents pimped her out. No, he'd struck off on his own, the bad-ass body collector. People who loved her only ever wanted to control her and she'd needed to figure out a way to own herself, instead of being owned.

"Al, look here. My meeting went bad. The guy's ship blew up and took your shuttle with it. I got stranded on this hunk of metal with this man here." The creak of Emilio's seat confirmed he'd sat up and leaned in, but she wouldn't look, wouldn't risk her brother catching wind of her awareness. "There was a glitch and we need help. In about an hour or so we'll be without breathable air."

"So my choices are take you alive or take you dead."

Emilio leaned in over her shoulder and growled, "It's in your best interest if we're alive."

Toni shoved at him. "Go away, you idiot."

Once she got him away from the screen, she plastered on a big smile. "I'm so sorry. I got stuck with not the brightest star in the sky. Just head this way. If we're alive when you get here, great. If not, then you're not out anything. You'll have something toward the quota and can use the shuttle for scrap."

Those comments earned her a frown from Emilio, but she wasn't speaking anything less than truth.

"Any other bodies?" Her brother picked at his teeth with a small metal shaving.

"There may be a couple floating out there."

"Did you kill them? I can't harbor fugitives from the uni-men and risk losing my license."

Her turn to mimic Emilio's downturned lips. "Funny how you think I'm dumb enough to get you entangled in something illegal…and don't even say anything. Would it make it better if I said they shot first?"

She'd done her fair share of dumb shit, and her family's constant need to point those things out, instead of the good stuff, made that little ball of rebellious nature emerge, often to her detriment.

"Fine." Al huffed a big breath, fogging up the view screen on his end. "I'll come and get you cause Ma and Paw would want me to, but the value of the lost shuttle is going to be taken out of your wages."

Emilio got up in Toni's space, blocking the screen. "Wait — do you have the parts to fix my shuttle? Can your sister work on it? I can't be stuck on Jupiter. I've got business on Callisto in a few days."

This is never going to work. She needed Emilio to shut the hell up or he'd ruin everything. So she did the one thing she could think of outside shooting him in the ass — she conked him in the head with the butt of her gun.

"What in Satan's fire?" The hard-ass runner jumped about a foot in the air and turned on her with a growl. "You may be pretty, but I'll defend myself."

She ignored him and grinned wide for her brother. "Don't worry about him. He's a little crazy due to the lack of oxygen."

"Crazy…you're insane," Emilio shouted as he resumed his seat.

Al laughed. "I'm sure. Keep a muzzle handy if you need it. I'm on my way. Lucky for you I was headed in that direction. Oh, shut off this communication channel. We don't need another collection service finding you first."

"Will do. See you in a little bit, big brother." Toni ended the call with a press of button on the view screen then settled back in her chair, staring at the disturbed runner on her hands.

"*Mother Mary.* What the hell was the gun to the head for?"

"Consider that my way of sealing a deal. You take a kiss, I'll take much more." Shutting down all communications wouldn't take much. A few combinations and button pushing, which she started immediately.

Emilio stared at her, rubbing the back of his head. Eyebrows hunched, he slipped something out of his pocket and into his mouth. "So, what's the plan?"

"Huh?" She kept her eyes trained on the screen in front of her, pretending to be more concerned with the black and sparkle of space than whatever Emilio was doing.

"You pistol whip me, then cut me off from speaking with your brother. How do you plan to get us out of this predicament? I need to get to Callisto, we need Manny's money, you need your ship…this is a long list of crap that keeps getting longer." He sighed and closed his eyes as he fell back against the chair. A few strands of his slick black hair fell into his face. From this angle there was no scar, just soft tan skin with scruff trailing a path along the edges.

"We're partners, not best friends." Growing up, she'd learned a very hard lesson about sharing things, ideas, plans, dreams. The more people knew, the more they could hurt her. A pretty face and latent sexual attraction, even a partnership, wouldn't tempt her to reveal every last detail. "You'll know what you have to, when you have to."

His eyes shot open and he scrambled to sit on the edge of the seat. "Great. I don't predict this partnership of ours will have long-term prospects at the rate we're going. I can't be stuck on Jupiter with Gina headed to Callisto. The product won't get delivered on time."

"Listen, I'm tired. It's still the middle of my sleep cycle and I'd like to catch at least a few solar hours of peace. Especially since I'm headed back to another ship I'd prefer never to be on again. We can formulate plans later."

"I can't do that," Emilio growled.

"Well." Toni stood up from the chair and leaned down into his face, strands of her hair teasing his cheeks. "You can fume, plot, plan and be devious all you want. I'm going to take advantage of that pull-out bunk in the wall there. If you weren't such an asshole, and we weren't running out of air, I'd ask you to join me."

He glared up at her, sitting straight to increase his height. "I wouldn't give you the satisfaction."

"Who says I'd be satisfied?"

Toni hunkered down on the bunk and squeezed her eyes shut. She longed for sleep, a chance to pretend and forget since a drink was out of the question. Never in a million light years would she have believed she'd be stuck in a shuttle with a man she argued with and found desirable at the same time. He was rough and tumble, with a hefty dose of bullshit coming out of his mouth. For some reason, all her checkpoints had lit up when they'd sparred with words, and with the kiss. She might file it away for a lonely night in her bunk, but things would go no further. Tangled up with this runner beyond getting to their respective vessels would be an explosion-laden fuel mix. Besides, the first thing was that they needed to get rescued.

Big Al was in for a rude awakening if he thought she'd stick around longer than paying off the shuttle. As her oldest and only sibling, Al was supposed to take over the family business, but he'd wanted more than mining ore for the rest of his life. Why he couldn't see she wanted something besides dead bodies was beyond her. A life on her own vessel, with her crew.

Paul's hymnals, Lee is going to be pissed. Her first mate didn't care for runners, and even less partnering with them on business pursuits. She already despised what Toni had her doing for Big Al. They'd all made sacrifices to stick together after Toni's mistake, and they'd all forgiven her, too. Her single regret after she'd sobered up had been losing their home. Now she had a chance to get it back, to get them on track. Those thoughts brought a smile to her lips.

Sure, she'd take a hit, partnering with an unpredictable guy equal to how she'd been in her crazy days. He was muscle — tough, strong, not afraid to draw a gun — and he wanted her. *Choke me in bone powder.* She'd need to quit thinking about those moments, even if they popped up annoyingly. *Here's hoping he'll get the hint.* She operated for business, not pleasure.

"Gina, come in." Emilio's voice filtered back to her along with communication static.

Joseph's balls. She flew off the bunk and sprinted the few steps to the pilot station. "What the hell are you doing?"

"I'd think it's obvious."

Sure, obvious he wanted to get them killed and that he knew a bit more about the shuttle than he'd let on, because she'd shut off communications.

"Gina, do you read?" he asked again.

If another collector picked up the signal, they'd be screwed.

"How did you turn this back on?" She leaned around him to end the transmission, but he batted her hand away.

"I have eyes and a good memory. Don't do that again or you're going to get it."

She shook her head. *He's a damn child.* "What don't you understand about no communication?"

This time she was less than an inch from the button, but yelped as Emilio brought an arm crashing down along her back. She fell right into his lap, and he brought both arms down on top of her to hold her in place. She thrashed against his embrace. "Let me go."

Now she was the child, bent over a knee. Would he spank her? *He wouldn't dare.*

"Hold still for a minute. Gina, come in." This time the screen crackled louder, then a response came.

"Gina, reporting in."

Toni struggled more and freed one of her arms, the other still trapped between her body and his. She was growing more frustrated with each second. She rubbed against him. The friction got something else growing as well—the hard length of him against her side. She stilled her movements and nibbled her lip.

Emilio grunted and readjusted his hold on her. "Have you made it to Earth?"

More static crackle. Toni prayed Emilio had been smart enough to put an encoding pattern to the front of end of his transmission signal. *Not likely.* Otherwise, they'd be leading other scavengers straight to them. Space stayed quiet, for the most part, but the ship explosion wouldn't go unnoticed. Honestly, they were riding on fate three ways as it was.

"I made it to Earth, picked up the shipment and have already arrived at the moon station. Johnny is uploading the cloaking technology, though he's a serious pain in the ass."

Toni prayed the conversation would wrap up fast, then caught sight of the wires under the console. Her left arm wasn't that far away. If she could reach them and disconnect the splice she'd made earlier... She started to wiggle again, rubbing up against Emilio.

He groaned. "What are you talking about? And...holy mother, that feels..."

His hold on Toni relaxed and she pulled one arm free.

"Sir?" Gina's voice crackled.

"Toni, quit moving." Emilio cinched against her middle. "Gina, tell me what's happening?"

The level of concern in Emilio's tone was almost comical, treating his ship like a person. A ship was run by people, not artificial intelligence. Toni could never put her trust in a self-possessed vessel. She stretched her arm out, wiggling her fingers in a desperate attempt to get just an inch farther. The wires were almost within her grasp.

"Emilio, it's Johnny." This new voice was all male, but more laid-back and relaxed. "We've been having a few issues with the software upload. Something isn't meshing right, dude. I'm going to keep her here for about six solar hours to run through a diagnostic."

Dude? Who talked like that? The last time she'd heard such a word she'd been a little girl on a trip with her Pa to Luna, Earth's moon, for software upgrades on their diggers. But the words had her captor adjusting in his seat, moving his arms upward and leaning against the console. *Perfect.* Toni used the distraction to scoot forward an inch. The movement brought more awareness of the fact she was bent over a male lap, her breasts pressed against toned legs. She breathed in, smelling leather and whiskey, scents matching the kiss they'd shared, reviving it. *No time for distractions.* She grabbed the wires and dragged them to her.

"Six hours? Are we even going to make our deadline with such a delay? The currents are tricky on the best of days."

Gina's voice popped up. "I think I know what to do to get there on time, asshole. I can even solve equations with little to no processing speed."

A growl vibrated through Emilio's body and instead of turning Toni off, it ramped her up. Goosebumps pebbled her skin at the mere idea of that same gravelly voice being directed at her. *This guy needs to stop.*

"Johnny, you better fix her, or I'll be taking it out on your face, then your stash. I can't put up with that kind of attitude the rest of my life. She's never cursed before. There's benefit in this for you too if we secure this business."

A half-hearted chuckle from that male voice resounded in the tiny space. She was almost there — just one more half-twist.

"Don't worry, Emilio. I'll get her—" And the wires came apart, the static of transmission disappeared and Toni dropped what she held, doing her best to try and school her face, to appear innocent of any wrongdoing.

"Satan's fire! Where'd he go?" Emilio yelled while hauling Toni to her feet and thrusting her from him. "How did the signal get cut?"

Toni slunk away and took a seat, refusing to volunteer anything. Nope, she'd let this fool stomp and bellow for a few more minutes. They were safe for the moment, though the air seemed a bit thinner, a little more difficult to catch a breath.

"I need that signal back, the transmission... I need to know when Gina will be ready." He pressed a few buttons, then reached under and pulled up the handful of wires. For damn sure he'd no clue what she'd done to hook those up or bypass other systems. "You did this. *Mother Mary.* You're insane. You know that?

"You've been saying it enough to remind me." It appeared the man had a few more brains than she thought. "My brother said not to transmit communications."

He glared at her. "You're going to fix this or so help me this partnership will be over before it begins."

Go to hell. The words sat on the tip of her tongue and she wanted to cancel the whole thing. Too infuriating, too much trouble...too much attraction. She stood and marched over to him, ready to give him her worst. Too bad the extra bullets for her pea shooter were long gone and melted in the explosion. Her march got disrupted by something hitting the shuttle. The entire vessel rattled, thumped and knocked them off their feet. She landed in Emilio's open arms.

Right back where I started. The last place she wanted to be, except this time his arms were around her, strong and firm, and her hands splayed across his chest. She failed to stop herself from staring at the open vee of his button-down shirt and black vest. The skin was a dark tan with a dusting of hair and lying there against it sat an imprinted gold medallion of a man wearing a tall hat and long robes, and bearing a cross. Her mouth went dry and any type of retort she had disappeared.

"I take it your brother has arrived?" Emilio's low-spoken words jarred her and she looked up at him.

Heat reflected in his eyes, similar to the same lustful speculation she'd seen off and on since the moment they'd met.

"Let's hope. Otherwise we may have to fight our way out."

"I'd need my gun for that, and your rather fabulous ass and fancy dress is stopping me from reaching it." He helped her to a standing position and she swore silently. Sooner or later she'd act to silence him and his forked tongue. Maybe with a bullet in the leg. *Maybe with my lips.*

"Now, I'm ready."

A whirring sound rent the air, and Toni glanced at the shuttle door. Red and orange sparks erupted along the seams and she reached for a metal wrench.

"Are you going to brain them to death?"

She pulled her big knife from her boot, not touching the revolver strapped to her hip. "The wrench is the distraction. This is the death dealer."

"How many weapons do you have shoved in those boots?"

She grinned. "I'll never tell."

Emilio opened his mouth to respond but was cut off by the snap of metal and the shuttle door being yanked away. Smoke on the other side kept them from getting a clear view of their visitors. Toni prayed for a little luck, a smidgen of good fortune. After years without any, she deserved a bit of a break.

"Antonia Smith, better holler if you're in there," Big Al's voice echoed into the shuttle.

Praise be. "I'm in here."

Big Al entered, flanked by two other men. Her bald-headed brother with his thick ginger beard, so different from her own coloring. She sometimes wondered how they were related, when he looked nothing like the rest of the Smiths. Al's crew all wore dark gray coveralls strapped with guns at their hips and opposing calves, and gravity-secure boots.

"Well, little sister, you look downright silly in that dress and you don't seem very happy to see me."

She glanced down at her torn, filthy dress and the weapons in her hands—an odd pairing for sure. "It looked a lot better when I put it on and these are a precaution. Welcome to G-One. We had no clue if it was you or another scavenger."

"Lucky for you we scrambled that transmission signal you were sending out a bit ago. So, who's the lucky sidekick?" Al pointed at Emilio.

"He's Manolo's old partner, and out there is the remnants of Manolo's ship."

Big Al stepped forward and stretched out a hand toward Emilio. "Ah, so this is the infamous drug runner. Your name's all over the upper PUPnet. The uni-men's top evader."

Her brother's familiarity with Emilio set her on edge, just as the news of Emilio's status with the Unis surprised her. Outside of Al's work with the government, her family in general were not Allied Planetary supporters. "Is that what you do when you're bored? Look at government networks?"

Emilio frowned and crossed his arms over his jacket, eyes glaring.

Al took back the hand Emilio refused to shake. "It's important to keep tabs on the folks floating through space. Never know when you may come across a body worth something."

Emilio attempted to draw his gun, but it was too late. Al and one of his guys shot him with electrical snappers, pellets that attached to skin or clothing and sent out an electrical signal shutting the body down, putting it into shock. "Mother. Mary. So. Help."

Oh, hell is here to roost now. "Al, what in the blazes are you doing?"

Her brother smiled real big. "Getting paid for this rescue mission."

Chapter Six

Emilio awoke to find himself bound in electric wired chains with cold metal underneath him, mouth dry, eyes itching and his body aching in places he didn't expect to. Frantically, he reached for the one thing on his person that mattered more than his guns, knives, even his boots...the medallion. It still rested underneath his shirt. *Thank the virgin.*

The medal was a gift placed on him at his birth, according to the woman who'd found him. She'd been charged with his care after his mother left. He held on to it for sentimental reasons, but it never brought him any luck. Emilio stared down at his bonds. *Case in point.*

Emilio pushed himself into a sitting position and scanned his surroundings. He was in the back half of a cargo storage area. The way the beams were structured overhead and the panel near the door confirmed it was a ship. Big Al had tricked him, but he'd caught the look of surprise on Toni's face. She hadn't been involved in the double-cross. No, the majority of the fault lay with her brother, and Emilio would crush the bastard underneath his very absent boots if given the chance.

A frantic number of scenarios swept through his head and were dismissed as quickly. He longed for the candy in his pants pocket, if it was still there. Struggling, he tried to reach for the pocket but hadn't made it far when Big Al and a pair of men walked through the door.

"As promised, I deliver the runner, Emilio Morales. You can take him in the chains he's in now, though I need compensation for those. Gotta get a new pair."

"You son of a shine-swilling whore!" Not the best choice of words, but ones Emilio couldn't help but utter at the idea of being put on display and handed over to pair of uni-men, APUP's crappy law enforcement of the upper planets.

Supposedly the moral and ethics hand of the government, the Allied Planetary Union Parliament had created Union Men to execute the law, though most were corrupt and easily bought off. Too bad he didn't have Gina nearby, or the flash Toni had said she'd gain them access to.

"Yeah, this one looks like him. We'll need to scan him to be sure." This from the hairier of the two unis, who stepped forward and grabbed a scanner off his belt.

Emilio spat at him. "There's your scan. Wipe it off your shirt, pup-scum."

A sudden and excruciating pain started at his ankles and wrists, and Emilio crashed to the floor. He tried his best to maintain control, and once the electric shocks stopped, he let out a loud growl. *Pissed* didn't describe the way he was feeling. *Mother Mary, when I get loose —*

"Are you going to behave, or do I need to treat you unkind some more? I don't think our friends like slurs."

Big Al peered down at him with a wide smile, his gold nose ring swaying back and forth.

Emilio had noticed the damn thing when Toni had called him. A hog tag, was what they called them on Earth. "Unkind? Interesting word choice."

"This is a business transaction, Morales. Nothing more, and you'd do good to remember it."

"Can you tell us your name and what happened to your partner, Manolo?" The question came from the skinny, clean-shaven uni with no eyebrows to speak of.

Screw this. Business transaction, fine by him, but no way would he say anything else. No, he'd save his energy and words for finding a way out of this mess. Giving unis information would be signing a death sentence. They came into the metal cage, while Al pressed his little button, sending Emilio writhing on the floor again, long enough for the unis to grab his hand and press his index finger on their little machine. The identification boxes could read blood, hair, skin, prints… Human flesh in all its forms.

I'm going to kill them.

The scanner beeped twice before Hairy uni announced, "It's him."

Emilio had made the mistake of getting his flesh in the PUPnet system several years prior during a routine checkpoint stop. A tiny mistake of slipping and putting his hand on one of the logging scanners.

"We'll move him over to our shuttle."

Big Al stepped forward then, hand on his gun belt. "I get the crinkle first. Nothing happens until I have those gold leaves in my hand."

Eyebrow-less uni forked out a bag from his coat pocket and tossed it to Al, who proceeded to dig in the bag and pull out a leaf. It sparkled in the air as Al held it up before mashing it between his teeth. Emilio would smack a pair of parliament dandies to get a hold of that bag.

Instead, he watched it get pocketed and his original captor turn to leave the room. Right before Al walked out, he tossed the remote to Emilio's chains to the unis. "I'll leave you to it, gents. Have fun with your prisoner."

The pair of unis grabbed Emilio and he took this as his chance to negotiate a way out. "I can get you more flash than what was in that bag. More than you ever dreamed of seeing. Just let me out of these cuffs and give me a rendezvous with my ship."

"Save your crap. We've got you for transporting illegal goods, attempted murder, bribery of an appointed lawman and a dozen or so more violations. You'll be lucky if you make it to a cell and not assigned to fuel allocation with a scheduled date for the incinerator."

Emilio shuddered at the empty threat. Fuel allocation was a horror story told to children of Earth-after-the-nuke, a fate worse than death. The idea of being killed so their bones could be converted to fuel powder would bother anyone who cared for their life. "Sure I can't change your minds? Me working for Alfonso Grecia wouldn't sway your opinion at all?"

"Ha! Funny. He wanted us to give you a message, but regardless you broke the law. You're going to pay for that."

The ship's innards passed by with a whir, mainly the production line, giving him a glimpse of a pair of bodies being harvested. The idea of joining them, becoming powder to grace the engines of ships, held no appeal. He needed to get a message to someone, somehow. His musings got him nowhere as Hairy and Eyebrow-less took him off Al's ship and hauled him through the cargo bay doors of their shuttle a few yards away. They dumped him in the middle of a metal platform and secured his bonds to metal loops attached to the flooring.

"Are you hungry, runner?" This from Eyebrow-less, who looked a bit cocky and aching to get a cut on that smooth skin along his cheek.

Emilio would be willing to give him a scar to match his own. "If you're buying, pup."

"The balls of this scum." The pup pressed the button in his hand and down Emilio went once more. The electric currents coursing through his body seized his muscles. "Lucky for you, Grecia wanted you kept alive."

Those words cut through the chattering of his teeth. *Why is Grecia involved in this?* The electricity cut off again and Emilio did his best not to breathe heavily or show any signs of distress. "I'm working for Grecia."

Both unis glanced at each other and burst out laughing. He could guess who the prize idiot was in this situation — him. Somewhere in the last twelve solar hours something had gone wrong. The heavy feeling in the pit of his stomach was not caused by hunger.

"He doesn't know." Hairy slapped Eyebrow-less on the shoulder. "Should we tell him?"

Baiting bastards, the both of them. Sure, he needed the information, but he wouldn't beg. No, he focused on his breathing, calming his pounding heart. Electrified chains had been known to cause heart attacks in weaker folks. The silence paid off.

"Tell him how he's going to die for being dumb enough to lie to Grecia." This from Eyebrow-less, whose finger hovered over the remote button, circling it like a vulture over prey.

Emilio had seen such a thing once and could compare himself to the creature. Helpless, unable to escape and confused about what was happening. "Lie to him? We made a deal. I'm transporting his product."

"Word on the bounty wire is that you misrepresented yourself and killed your partner. In our books, it's enough, no matter what you say." Hairy spat a big wad of nasty at him. It slapped his shirt. "Enjoy that. We're off to grab a bite, but I think you'll be going hungry tonight. Then it's to Saturn for the tribunal being called for you."

Eyebrow-less laughed. "Yeah, enjoy your last night of peace, and starving quiet. From here it's screaming and roasting in the heat of the ring jail."

The doors slammed shut, the lights went out and Emilio took up position on the floor, legs crossed. He waited a few minutes, letting his eyes adjust. Then he started analyzing the metal loops. Maybe one was loose, something to get him free. The unis taking a few hours to eat and get liquored up meant he had about one hour to get the hell out of there. His idea of using his medallion to over-fritz the electrical circuit in his bonds? *If I want to die faster.* So, he'd wait to resort to desperate measures.

Twenty minutes of struggling, grunting and working up a sweat to rival his times in the marijuana fields were met with nothing gained. The loops, four in total, held fast. He massaged each chain link, searching for weakness in the metal. Jumped up and down on the metal panels beneath him. He was screwed. A worse fate then anything he'd dealt with in years past, even shivering on a floor next to other small bodies with near frostbitten toes would have been better than this crap. "Headed for a jail in Saturn's rings…fuck me."

The door to the shuttle squeaked open and he readied for some smartass comment from the too-soon-returned unis. Instead, a flood of light spilled into the room, outlining a person's head.

"Anyone in here?" The voice was unmistakable.

"Me," Emilio called out. "Toni, what are you doing here?"

"I'm here to rescue you."

Emilio wouldn't say it aloud, but he'd never been so happy in his life to hear her voice. The lights' motion sensors clicked when she squeezed through the hole she'd wedged in the door and he was treated to a woman who looked nothing like the vision he'd met on Manny's ship. Her short and now brunette hair hung in waves past her shoulders, paired with gray pants and a dark green thermal top. She looked the exact opposite of a lady for hire, but still just as attractive.

Toni squeezed inside the shuttle and removed the pipe she'd used as a wedge. Putting the pipe on her work belt, she readjusted herself and started over toward Emilio. "Did they say how long they'd be gone?"

"No, but I imagine we got an hour or so." Emilio enjoyed the sound of her voice when she whispered. This woman had been getting under his skin with her actions, gazes and sass. She'd fought against him pretty hard and maybe his impending departure had changed her mind.

"Did they break anything?"

He glanced down at his body, lifted each arm and rotated his head once in a circle. "I am intact. Why do I smell piss?"

"Shut the fuck up." She stood about six steps from the platform and grabbed the pipe. Toni waved it in the air, then tossed it toward the panels he stood chained to.

It banged against the floor and Emilio rolled his eyes. "No, seriously…where is that smell coming from?"

She nodded at the pipe, then turned a glare on him. "Do you want to leave this shuttle still in chains? If not, leave off the smell comments. You go and spend more than half a day fixing a slip drive fuel system, mucking around in piss and bone powder, then we can talk about smell."

Next up, a water torch, which she lifted from her belt with ease before crouching on the floor next to the first big metal loop his chains had been dragged through. "I'm going to torch two of these and that should get the chains free from the panels, but I'll need to dig into the computer to unlock the padlock and neutralize the current."

"Fixing fuel mixes, hacking computers, piloting shuttles—where in Satan's fire did you learn how to do all this?" He'd never met a woman like her.

Toni smiled, primed the water nob and struck the flint. The torch's twin flames ignited and she went to work. "Forget our earlier conversation already? I grew up on Mars, and there are three things you learn to do there—how to build ships, how to mine and how to screw."

"I take it you're an expert." The words came out before he could stop them. There was no denying they'd shared some moments back on the shuttle, and sealing their partnership with a kiss—pure genius on his part. She tasted as good as she looked, a rough-and-tumble gal. The pistol whip, rubbing her sweet body against his… She may have been crazy, but he liked it.

Her showing up here had him hoping to make more memories.

Turning the torch off, she gazed up at him, taking the slow path from his bare feet, torn-at-the-knees pants, missing belt and dusty red button-down. His captured state left a lot to be desired, but he saw the flash of attraction, the dribble of drool creeping across her brain. She wanted him, too. *Say the word.*

She shook her hand and went back to work. "We're not going there again, okay?"

We will when I get the chance.

"I break you out, we hightail out of here on my brother's ship, get Manny's flash and I get my ship. Then we part ways. It's simple. It's one of those things you like…a plan."

Oh, how he was getting to her. The fact she wanted him scared her, evidenced by her changing the deal she'd originally sought. "I thought we were partners. I was ready to give you a half percentage of everything, including my bed."

She scoffed. "Lie to me again, and I'll be lighting this torch against a part of your anatomy you'd miss."

Emilio laughed, a little louder than he'd planned on, but couldn't help it. They were cut from similar cloths—products of the lower planets, dirty upbringings and used by people for less than honorable purposes. She spoke of wanting a future on her terms without dealing with the realities and hardships. He'd faced the hard truths and was willing to lie, bargain and kill for the results he wanted.

"I really like your spunk and I never lie about my bed."

"I'd like it if you shut up and let me get busy." She leaned in closer to the floor, pouring all her focus into work. Water torches? He hated those damn things. They didn't burn hot like oil and gas-based torches did, but they made sense on ships since water was easier to come by and less dangerous to transport.

The shitty part was that cutting through metal took longer. Ten minutes give or take to get through the first loop, and Emilio sighed. "Those unis will be back by the time you finish. Why the hell did you come back for me anyway? You could have gone on with your plan. You don't need me."

"So, you want me to leave you here?"

"That's not what I said. I want to know why." Ever since they'd escaped Manny's vessel, he'd been curious as to her reasons for helping him, saving him. *No one's ever done that for you.* His brain could shut up and stop calling out things he'd rather not focus on.

She hesitated, biting her lower lip. Her refusal to look up, to confront him, told him what he wanted to know. "Because I don't want to be on your list. You could decide to blame me for ending up here. I'm the one who called my brother, asked you to trust me."

"You're free to lie, but I'm not?"

Her movements stopped and the blue flame from the torch made her eyes glow. "Excuse me?"

"You came back because you want me."

She scoffed and went back to her task, mumbling away. He watched closely, making sure she didn't take his damn toes off, but enjoyed her rising distress. Finally, she looked up at him. "You have an ego the size of Jupiter. I don't base my decisions on who I want to screw."

He grinned. "Whatever you say."

"No, no, I don't. Except, I'd rather make sure I'm not lumped in with the guilty."

"I never would have blamed you."

She didn't respond, choosing to keep her head down and work on that second metal loop. The silence filled with the things he refused to voice out loud. Like how he liked her new hair, or how she could handle tools. Maybe she enjoyed playing rescuer. The second loop finally broke to the flame of the torch.

"Yeah, I don't trust that for a second. You may not have blamed me, but the people you work for might have. Someone could pull some strings sooner or later. See if you can work those chains loose of the two loops, far enough to get over to the computer console." Toni pointed to her right.

"I like your estimations of my reputation and how much people like me, but if you haven't noticed, I'm experiencing a run of bad luck."

"From my vantage point, your luck is changing." Not waiting for him, she moved to the computer and started clacking away at the keyboard. "Damn, they've gotten new software since I've been out of the game."

Emilio dragged four lengths of chain behind him, but he'd managed to free himself of the broken loops. "You still think you can do this?"

"We're going to find out, but this may be more tricky then I planned on."

"Tricky how?"

"Ask me something else, because I can't explain the issues between binary and ternary code."

Emilio rattled his chains as he brought both hands up, leaning against the console. "You said we're taking your brother's ship? That's a big job for two people."

"I never said it would be just us. My crew is getting *Styx* primed and ready to go."

"Your crew?" There were things she wasn't saying and he despised being spoonfed information. Not when he'd gotten used to having all the elements of a job laid out in front of him, being the master of his path and course. *A funny joke, Mother Mary.* She had him by the short and curlies.

"Yes, my crew." Toni bit her lip and after a couple more key clacks and taps the padlock on Emilio's chains whirred, fizzled and popped open. "Ta-da! All of us got jobs on Al's ship over the last six months, to stay close to one another. This way, when we found the ship, we'd all be in the same place. We haven't found the ship as intended, but we'll do things another way."

The idea he'd have to work with her whole crew made his gut churn more than the electric shocks had.

"And what's your way?" Emilio extricated himself from the chains. The heaps of metal fell to the floor with a rattling thump.

Toni removed the pair of slippers from her belt at her back and tossed them to Emilio. "Hard and balls to the wall. We gotta move!"

Chapter Seven

They pried open the uni shuttle doors, and the alarm sounded.

"Joseph's balls!" Emilio pushed her from behind and she barely kept her balance, dropping the inch or so to the ground. He followed her down and they ran— sneaking, crouching and darting their way behind barrels and cargo containers, avoiding every soul they passed. Jupiter Prime's shipping areas were usually super crowded, except in the evening. There were still those ships unloading cargo, prepping to go off-world. Better to remain unseen until they boarded Styx.

She didn't dare look back to see if the unis had been alerted to their shuttle break-in or if anyone had followed them. The loading platform lowered for them at the press of a button, and they both piled on. Once aboard with the platform hissing, signaling the seal had been made, Toni ran over to the wall, grabbed a radio and hollered into it. "All secure and ready to depart."

"Aye, aye, Captain." Dottie's voice came through loud and clear.

We might just make it out of this place.

Emilio flipped the locking latch over the platform edge. "How did you ditch Al and his crew?"

Toni slapped the radio back into its cradle and took a few slow, deep breaths. *Calm the fuck down.* "Out for a night on the town, my brother's treat. Guess he's feeling mighty generous since he got that sack of gold leaf from those unis for you."

"And so who's running this rig?" Emilio took a few steps back, peeking around the cargo area, glancing behind a few barrels.

"Follow me and I'll show you." She marched forward, anxious to get to the cockpit, to find out if they'd make the clean getaway she hoped for. Her crew had been working toward this moment for months.

Emilio followed, popping a piece of candy into his mouth. The ship's engine fired up, the rattle of the ignition vibrating through their feet. "Are we going to be collecting on this trip?"

"No. We won't be producing bone powder. The production rooms will be closed and kept sealed." She wanted nothing to do with Al's business. She preferred dealing in drugs and liquor.

"Why not? You could make extra money on this trip." Emilio stopped at the door closest to them and peered through the window.

"Because melting flesh from bone never appealed to me." Toni leaned up next to him and glanced at the machines. The disassembly lines took at least four people on each, skinning, sorting, hosing and feeding into the sanitizer. "Besides, I'm not here to tamper with my brother's operation. We're borrowing this ship and

I plan to return it to my brother in its original condition."

"You're not good at this breaking the law stuff." He whispered the words.

"I'm good at other things." *Damn.* She needed to focus on the task at hand, not getting back into this messy attraction they kept dipping their toes in.

"Yes, you are, and so far you've surprised the hell out of me."

Those words, coming from him, made her stand a little straighter and put a grin on her face. She'd been underestimated all her life, believed to be good for only one damn thing. A disappointment for drinking, for leaving home and doing men's work. Here she stood next to someone who might admire her for those things and who wanted her, physically, amid her crazy.

An alarm sounded around them, lights going red. They were under attack.

She frowned at him before taking off for the cockpit. She ran and Emilio kept pace with her.

Lee passed them up ahead, her long black ponytail swinging behind her as she yelled out, "Your little rescue is going to rain hell on us."

"And your opinion was noted." Toni and Lee often butted heads — natural order demanded it. "That's Lee, my first mate and weapons guru."

Emilio slowed as they approached another perpendicular corridor, wary, ready.

"Don't!" Toni cried, right when she caught sight of Sampson's beanie-covered head. "I need my engineer awake."

"Hiding around corners gets people killed." Emilio relaxed his stance.

"Get to the drive room, Sampson." Toni resumed her pace and Emilio stayed by her side.

Soon they were clanking up the narrow staircase and into the central piloting area. Doc, his lengthy white beard recognizable anywhere, was already there, attention directed to open space, on alert. "The unis got back to their shuttle faster than expected."

"I've got the rear defense shield holding, but we need someone in the turret down below. We might be able to disable them." Dottie, bright pink bandana holding back her mass of tight black curls, whirled in her chair from one console to another. Her opinions, Toni took seriously.

Toni pointed around the room. "Dottie is at the helm. Doc is our medical and our chemistry expert. Sour puss over there is the one who might give you trouble."

Lee growled at the implication, mouth open to offer a retort, but got cut short as the ship rattled, a few more alerts and beeps sounding. They were going to get blown out of the sky. *Wouldn't that piss off big brother.* Anxious didn't begin to cover the large pit forming in her gut. She'd already been stuck in one exploding ship in the last solar day.

"Lee—"

"I'll do it." Emilio stepped forward, pointing towards the shimmy hole with the bubble cover on the floor in the center of the room. "That's where it's at?"

Toni nodded. "Yes, but you don't have to do anything. My first mate can handle this."

He grinned at her, the ridiculous man. "Let me get a chance to prove I'm not a hassle."

Then he popped the hatch and climbed right on down, one slippered foot at a time. The torn pants, the filthy shirt and a wink right before he closed the bubble over his head. *I'm in trouble.*

Lee stepped close to her. "Those shoes are ridiculous. You couldn't grab him a pair of grav boots or something?"

"There wasn't enough time. They were there." In honesty, she'd found the slippers by her brother's cabin door and, in a pinch, they worked.

"The nature of the beast, as one would say of life." Doc turned to face them, his beard looking a little less tame today than normal and completely anomalous with his short-cropped hair. "Let's hope this runner can nail the bastards. I didn't plan on dying today."

Lee frowned. "If we get hit hard, I'll be killing the runner first." Her hatred for men stemmed from a source she'd never divulged to Toni, but there were few of the male species she tolerated.

"Shush, all of you!" Dottie flipped a switch. "Got you over the speaker system, Emilio. Tell us what you have."

"One ship on radar. I'm flipping on the EMP and rotating to get in position. They are firing at the rear thrusters." His voice was all business and total focus. Maybe they'd make it, or at least he'd give those unis a good dose of return fire.

They could hear everything, the EMP priming, the mechanical whine of the turret rotating and Emilio's breathing. Dull shocks echoed around them as the unis kept firing.

"We're down to about thirty percent on those rear shields." Dottie announced to everyone. Nothing they could do but wait. *Damn EMPs and their one-minute priming period.* He'd get one shot at this.

Lee growled. "You better do this right, Emilio, or we'll all be crispy fried critters, not even good enough for bone collection."

Toni shoved her first mate. "Ignore her, Emilio. Do the best you can."

"But living would be nice." This from Doc, who'd gone over and put a hand on Dottie's shoulder.

Everything in the ship dimmed when the shot launched, Emilio's "shot fired" announcement driving Toni's anxiety up a couple of decibels. The seconds crawled by as they waited for the unis to stop firing.

"Direct hit!" Dottie yelled, popping out of her chair and wrapping her arms around Doc. "They're dead in the current."

Relief—bubbly, blissful relief—coursed through her veins. The pit in her stomach disappeared. They might make it, but not without taking steps. "Dottie, did we already disable the tracking beacon?"

"Yes, Sampson ditched it on a passenger ship."

The plan, the steps, formed in her mind. "Great. Scramble our carrier wave. Give us something APUP, like a cruiser. Let's encourage other ships to steer clear. Set our course for Ceres. Also, send a message to my brother. He can get his ship on Callisto in a week. Doc, get a set of clothing and some boots from Al's quarters for Emilio."

"Aye, aye, Captain," both pilot and doctor answered in unison and got busy with their respective duties.

"What about me?" Lee twirled one of her throwing knives between her fingers. The woman was strapped with at least ten at all times. "I could take him for target practice."

Toni shook her head. "You need to get over the fact that he's here, and you're not killing him. Start a meal.

We can eat something before grabbing some shut-eye." One thing she appreciated about Styx was that the vessel came stocked. Even if the only options were space-fare specialties, cubed meat, freeze-dried veggies and dried pasta. *Better to have food than nothing.* Add water, place in the moisturizer and the food was edible.

"Did someone mention food?" Emilio's head came through the turret hole.

"Yes, we're dying to feed you." Lee evil-grinned, a massive, wide-teeth smile that gave Toni the shudders, before leaving the cockpit.

Toni approached him nice and slow as Emilio pulled himself out of the hole and stood. He looked similar to when he'd gone in, but something changed in how he gazed at her. "Food will be ready soon. I've got Doc getting you some clothes."

"Good." One word, and a whole lot of unspoken ones conveyed with his eyes. Heat bloomed on her cheeks and the urge to flee came over her fast and furious. "Where can I get a shower before I eat?"

"I'll show you to your quarters." She left and walked down the metal staircase, holding on to the railing. Gripping something solid helped. Though what she really wanted to grip… *Stop it, I don't need this.*

Emilio didn't say a word, but became a distracting presence looming over her as they entered the second level of the ship. Toni tried her best but had to say something. His eyes on her, his close proximity, the heat— "This level has the galley."

She pointed at the door and glanced in, only to get Lee, eyes glued on them in frustration, banging bowls around. "Up ahead are crew quarters. You saw the production rooms and cargo area earlier. There's a section underneath, real thin and small, that houses the engine and the slip drive. My mechanic, Sampson, lives in there most of the time."

"What about you?"

The tone of his question brought her to a halt and it sounded sexier than it should. "I have a crew cabin, like everyone else."

A deep breath, then hot air against her face. "Does it have a hydro shower?"

"Uh, yeah, but yours—"

Emilio wrapped his arms around her torso, using his hands to get her to face him. "I don't want anything but you, me and hot water at the moment. Preferably naked. If you can slap me in the face right now, I'll believe you disagree, but your body language is saying something different."

The urge to slap him on principle alone rose strong within. She loved to act against challenges, to be the person they'd never see coming. Instead she leaned in, whispering, "Second door on the right."

Emilio lifted her up and she wrapped her legs around his waist—it was a miracle how he could lift her as though she was nothing. "I've been thinking about this since the moment I met you, on the shuttle, and when you showed up to free me from chains."

"Shut up and get me to the room." *He wants to do this, fine.* "We do this my way though, or not a damn thing happens."

Her past was littered with sexual partners, ones who'd cared little for her and everything for themselves. Those few times she'd engaged in bed wrestling with someone, she'd gotten so drunk she barely remembered any of it. Sure, she'd said yes, but poor choices often left a person with poor results and no knowledge of an orgasm. *One of those would be nice right now.* But no way in hell would she be giving in to him on his terms.

Emilio chose to kick the door with his foot and it slid open, motion sensors triggering the room lights. His first steps inside her domain were accompanied with a stumble when he met her discarded dress from the day prior.

She did her best not to laugh at the situation. Clean never having been her middle name, she figured he'd either get turned off or ignore it.

Letting her slide down his front, he dragged his arms up her body and took her lips in a searing kiss. Ignorance was bliss in this case. She teased at his lips, asking for entry, and once his tongue peeked out, she took over, ravaging his mouth. Seconds dragged by as they explored one another in the name of lust, not just lips and tongues, but hands roving over bodies. She gave herself permission to go crazy for two minutes.

This runner sported serious muscle tone beneath his clothing, if her petting of him proved accurate. She wanted to see it all. Breaking away from him, she took two steps backward. Pulling up the hem of her top, she exposed her tank-top-covered breasts to him.

He flashed a wicked grin. "I like a good show."

She pulled the thermal back down, covering herself. "So do I." Indulging herself might have not been the best idea, though she still possessed enough sanity not to give in to the riot he'd incited in her blood. She toyed with the button on her pants, unsnapping the metal as she took a few more steps backward into her bathroom. "Now, strip."

Toni turned on the hydro shower and stepped back onto the growing pile of laundry she'd either need to incinerate or wash at some point. *Focus on the man, not the clothes.* The hydro shower itself kept the same temperature, not too cold or too hot, with a wide spray width, a clear panel keeping the water contained in its box.

Emilio entered the small space stark naked, his dick erect and every bit as large as she'd imagined back on the shuttle. *Damn man is too confident by far.*

He came towards her, reaching in and pulling her close. Against her better judgment, she let him. Biting her earlobe, he whispered, "Where do you want me?"

"In the shower," she hissed.

He splayed his fingers at her stomach and started to dip into her pants. He trekked farther south, heading through the curls and right to the heart of her. Unlike most men, who'd immediately plunge into her depths, this one knew that the hot little nub at the top of her entrance was the real place to take a detour to.

He tweaked it, rubbed, flicked and pinched until she thrashed against him, back and forth. She gripped his shoulders, the sensations building deep within her like the slow roast of coals over an iron forger's stove. The whole interaction was so unlike her previous escapades. She'd never done this sober and found herself unable to vocalize her wishes. "I can't. I need."

His pace quickened, stealing whatever thoughts she possessed. The only thing echoing in her mind was how close she was. How his dick against her ass made her want to climb him like a ladder, then sit and spin.

"I'd like it if you did that too." Emilio groaned and renewed his efforts.

Holy fuck, I said that out loud.

Emilio chuckled. "I heard that, too."

"Hello, in there." Doc's voice rippled into the room. "Dinner is ready and I've got those clothes."

Emilio groaned, pulling his fingers free from her and stepping into the shower, his hooded gaze an invitation for her to slam the door shut and join him.

She blinked a couple of times, clearing away her arousal. Time to get her feet back on the gravity plating. *Saved by the doctor.*

"Coming." She secured the button of her pants and walked out of the bathroom, shutting the door behind her.

Doc stood there holding the clothes and boots and wearing a frown. "He's in there, isn't he?"

"I didn't know it concerned you." Toni took the items from him and set them on her bed.

"You're our captain. We worry."

Whose fault is that? Mine. She'd drunk a little too much one too many times. Made bad gambles, lost their home. She was the crazy one, not to be trusted, except her crew still did a tiny bit.

Doc deserved a small peck on the cheek and that was what she gave him. "Thank you for worrying about me, but in this case, I'm safe. We're partners."

Those words didn't seem to make the worry lines on Doc's forehead disappear. "What did he do to his last partner? You told Lee about it and she told us. We worried he'll change his mind."

"Have a little more faith in me, okay?"

He nodded. So sweet, like a father to her, Lee and Sampson. He was a lot more to Dottie, though he tried to pretend otherwise for the sake of sparing everyone.

"Good. Anything else?"

"Just this." He pulled out a slip of paper from his pants pocket and held it up. "Dottie says it's a message from your brother. A response to what she sent him about the ship."

"Thanks, Doc."

He turned to leave. "I'll see you in the galley."

Once her room door shut, she looked at the message.

If I see you again, I'll shoot you. You're dead to me and may you choke on your next sip of shine.

So much for brotherly love. There were memories of her brother she held near to her heart. From the young days of sharing meals and rooms, and when he'd listened. He'd entertained her urges to learn about ships, snuck her manuals and taught her how to take things apart, even though he'd gotten beat the time she broke one of their five-wheel racers—the fancy kind with the slip drive system that provided a shield for bumping—to use the parts for another engine. At least he'd been understanding, until he got tired of being blamed for her follies, her interests.

He'd asked her to stop fiddling with things, to worry instead about looking good for their parents' customers and charming the pants off some Titan upper. Maybe if she scored big, they'd stop pimping her out. All things that made her drink. Toni licked her lips, reliving the not-so-distant memory of how Emilio had tasted on the shuttle when they'd sealed their deal.

She needed to get out of this room, out of this moment. No amount of screwing would change her situation or make Emilio see her with any type of respect. She wanted to go legit after this mess, transporting people and cargo. He'd only drag her back down. She needed to be the responsible one, not act on wild, selfish desires. She yelled from her bedroom door. "Heading out. Join us in the galley whenever you're ready."

She'd have time to cool down before then. Getting down and dirty was fine for a time, but not when the man she gave it up to wasn't any better than the person she used to be.

Chapter Eight

Emilio tugged at the collar of the borrowed brown shirt as he walked out of Toni's quarters. The clothes were awkward on him, the pants one size too big and the shirt one size too small. The grav boots were perfect and he was happy to have his feet covered once more. Anger also simmered, along with his confusion. Toni had wanted him, judging by her eagerness and responsive nature in the shower. But she'd been quick to get the hell away from him when he'd wanted to take things to the logical conclusion.

Good for someone else's pleasure, but not mutual. *Story of my life, Mother Mary.* It bugged him how he couldn't get a read on her, never knowing how she'd react or what she'd do next. *Flighty and unpredictable.* He imagined she enjoyed keeping everyone on the edge. Except he didn't operate like that.

He didn't push her, had never acted in such a high-handed manner with women. No, he liked letting them express their desire for him. Consent was so important, especially when he'd been a product of the foreman taking pleasure with his mother. Those few memories he had of her and the woman who'd raised him for a short time made him focus on treating women right, respecting their wishes when it came to their bodies. Besides, a no never meant he had to go without. His own hand could remedy the situation just as well.

A tint of rust coated Styx's halls, quarter doors and floors. *This ship needs a good hydro scrub and greasing.* Up ahead, he heard voices from the galley entry. Light flooded into the dim hallway. Boisterous comments, laughter—things his ship lacked, but he enjoyed not having people interrupt his through process when he made decisions.

Coming to the entrance, he stood back in the hallway where shadows were battled back by the bright galley light, and watched. They all sat around a table, Lee, Doc and Dottie, eating food cubes with their fingers, smiling, drinking from glasses. Several platters sat in the middle of the table. There were no individual plates—they shared. Acting like a family, as if they cared about each other.

"You can go in. They won't bite."

He startled and glared at Toni, who stood on the other side of the entry hiding in the dark. Someone stood behind her, cowering. "I planned on it. It's not nice to sneak up on people."

"We were walking, not sneaking," Toni smiled. "Why? Did we scare you?"

This woman? Infuriating. She wore black pants with her boots, another thermal top, deep red, and everything outlined the fine figure he'd become familiar with in the bathroom. Too bad he'd been unable to confirm if she had pale pink skin with nipples the color of berries or nether hair the same color as the waves of silk on her head. *Joseph's balls.* This woman got him thinking poetry-like. He needed to bed her already and get this lingering sexual urge to disappear.

"No, I'm not scared, but I'm hungry." He let the meaning sink in and it was her turn to frown.

"I imagine you are." Toni pointed to the boy on her left. "I had to go retrieve Sampson. You met him earlier when you tried to punch his face in. He tends to get lost in his work and is a little shy around new folks, but once he gets going it's hard to get him to stop. Talking, that is."

The comment got Sampson to blush, a widespread red hue that accented a face awash in freckles. Emilio had never seen so many freckles on a person before. It was weird to be introduced to people. He assessed people by nature, but out of self-preservation, not just to become familiar with them. *Except for women.* Yes, women always got his full attention.

Time to change the focus. All this personal shit would cause problems further down the road. Connections, friendships, were not for him.

"Nice to meet you," he replied with a nod. "Let's eat."

This time he left her behind, walking into the galley with new confidence. All eyes were trained on him, which made things odd once more. How often did he spend this much time around a group of people? Not much. His business deals were fast and with little interaction. His time with Manny had been spent at parties and with women falling all over them. Talking not required. He'd dreamed of human interaction, but not with so many, so fast.

"What's on the menu this evening?" His stomach growled on cue, loud enough to get a few raised eyebrows from the other folks.

Doc piped up first. "Sit down. You must be starving, with those damn unis keeping you locked up."

"We've got water, protein cubes, carrots, green beans and biscuits," came from Lee. Her eyes narrowed in suspicion, one hand on a knife that she twirled in circles, the sharp point drilling into the table, with little metal shavings forming a small pile.

"Here's a glass, and we eat platter style. No silverware or plates. A little more backwards." Dottie offered a small smile and pointed to the pitcher of water in the center of the oval table.

"On Earth we eat with our fingers, too." Emilio offered the tidbit in the hopes they'd quit thinking he was judging them for how they ate and behaved.

He didn't give a damn as long as they didn't plan to kill him, ditch him with the unis or worse. He needed to get to Callisto, find Gina and get that product to Grecia's contact to try and repair the bridge he'd broken. His time to shine was fast becoming the worst idea he'd ever had.

He popped a protein cube in his mouth, trying his best to enjoy the slimy texture and salty taste. They were supposed to be like real meat, but he'd eaten real meat before. This wasn't it. At least these were a better choice compared to the fly larvae and grubs other ships stocked for meals.

"All right." Toni slid on to a stool next to Lee. "Where are we on everything?"

Dottie took a sip of water and cleared her throat. "Almost to Ceres. Probably be there in about eight solar hours. Gives time for a little shut-eye. I already radioed ahead that we're coming in for business and we've got a docking platform assigned. Nobody is on our tail and our carrier wave is altered."

"I got Emilio his clothes and boots. He's set up to sleep in Al's quarters," Doc announced. "You didn't sustain any injuries from the unis, did you?"

"No, not that I'm aware, and thank you for the clothing." Emilio raised his glass in salute. "Why Al's quarters? I can sleep in an empty crew cabin."

"Because it's the cabin closest to the center of the ship and the easiest to get to you if we need to stop you from causing trouble." This from Lee, who still looked at him as though he was the scum of the universe.

"What did I do to you?" *No sense in letting bad feelings fester. When a wound shows signs of infection, best to cut it open.* He wanted to do the same thing here.

"I don't like runners, in general."

Toni chuckled. "That's enough, Lee."

"She's usually this grumpy. We ignore her," Doc replied with a grin.

Lee growled.

"Stop it, you two. We already escaped getting blown to bits. I think we can keep it calm at the dinner table." Dottie beamed at him, her wide, perfect smile a stark contrast to her dark skin. "They aren't like this all the time. Though we fight as much as any family does."

Family... The meaning of the word escaped him. Besides Gina, he had no one. "No mind to me. I won't be around much longer. Toni and I agreed to be partners on this venture to Ceres. Once done, we'll part ways on Callisto."

Toni tsked. "I don't think so. We talked about getting my ship back."

Yes, everyone looked too damn eager at the mention of the ship. It appeared the entire crew had everything invested on getting her ship back. "You don't even know where it is."

"Who would he sell it to?" This a soft-spoken question from Sampson.

Emilio shook his head. "I've no clue. I wasn't always involved with every aspect of Manny's activities. I did most of the big jobs, running to Earth and to the uppers. Constant back and forth. I don't have time to search every junk spot and ship auction. My deal with Grecia is supposed to be complete in five days."

The words weren't what anybody wanted to hear and most of the faces in the room looked down, focusing on the table in front of them, chewing silently. Toni, on the other hand, pinned him place as he reached for a handful of green beans.

"That's got to be the answer then. The junkyard. He sold it to the junker moon."

Emilio shrugged. "Maybe, Toni, but good luck contacting them. We need to talk about the plan for the bank."

He chewed, she chewed. They both stood their ground.

Toni piped up first. "Dottie, contact the junker moon, Titan. Find out if they have the Geisha."

Dottie moved off her stool, downed the rest of her drink and walked off while sliding a hand along Doc's shoulders. The pair shared something close, judging by their constant physical connection.

He hated stagnating, not knowing his path. Being in the dark was worse than being exposed to the sun on a hot day. Dark meant cold, meant the ability to be forgotten. *Not that shit again.* "What's the plan for the bank?"

She took a drink, bit into a protein cube and tossed part of her hair behind a shoulder. Lee watched the interaction with a big smile. She liked to see people suffer, a sadist if his instincts were right.

"We make a withdrawal of all Manny's crinkle in his account."

"How do you know he even has one?" In all his years of working with Manny, the fool had only mentioned an account to him once, and Emilio had never pushed him for more information. Sure, Emilio had a nice account with an upper establishment. Not on Ceres — that bank was designed for folks who didn't want anyone to know about their money and who didn't plan on accessing it with frequency. A location for thieves, cartels, runners and bootleggers to store the extra bits. He'd found trusting those grubby, flash-hungry people impossible a long time ago.

"Sampson figured it out when he hacked their system."

Emilio's eyes went wide and he glanced at Sampson again. Besides the freckles, the boy wore a cap on his head and tendrils of reddish-brown hair peeked out of the edges around his neck. *Attentive eyes and a sullen expression.* "This kid hacked the system of one of the highest tech places outside of the upper planets?"

The boy nodded. "For five minutes. Enough time to download their client database before they locked me out."

"He's my computer and engine genius. No one better anywhere." Toni grinned widely before sticking a couple of carrots in her mouth. While she chewed, she kept talking. "We go in and ask to make the withdrawal."

Not much of a plan. "What if they refuse?"

"I don't think they will, but if it becomes desperate, we take what we want."

Sleep proved elusive and there were multiple times during the night Toni thought about going straight to her brother's quarters and finishing what Emilio had started. The words from Al's message, then Emilio's dismissal of her ship and the weariness she sensed in her crew could drive a woman to take extensive measures to secure her future. Not to mention her big brother kept a special birthday bottle in his bureau, a secondary temptation.

In the end, she'd found a solar hour or so of rest. She'd gotten up, taken a shower and now stood in the cargo area, looking out of the pair of windows on the back wall. The docking platform was more like a landing bay with gun turrets and the entrance door locked down tighter than the rings' prison.

Maybe Emilio's hesitation and doubt had merit, but she trusted in the people close to her. They'd never let her down before. Sampson had said this was possible, so she believed.

Toni stepped back from the windows and focused on strapping her pistol to her thigh. Stepping up beside her, Lee whispered, "Everything is locked and loaded. Sure you don't want me with you?"

"No, better you stay up here. Protect the ship. Too much backup may make them suspicious. You know those banking types. Always wanting to keep the flash, even when it's not theirs to begin with."

"Greedy fuckers," Lee replied, before letting out a low whistle.

A quick glance told Toni who, not what, had prompted the admiration. It was damned hard to re-focus her eyes on recon when her traitorous gaze wanted to glance over at the clothed form, which looked equally as tempting as the naked version. Seeing him yesterday in her brother's clothes, dressed like a Mars man, had been odd. She'd kind of missed his button-down shirts and jackets. A personal preference, but it didn't change how her body reacted to his appearance. Physically, she still wanted him. Wanted to touch his long length, push against his muscled chest, grip those corded arms.

"You know I despise runners, but I'd squeeze the life out of that with my thighs if he'd let me." Lee nudged Toni's shoulder. "Just give me the word he's interested."

He's not interested. She wanted to shout those words, but what good did they do her? Staking a claim would bring more attention to her attraction. Lee didn't need to know about that or Toni would never hear the end of it.

"What's wrong? I got some gravy on my cheek from breakfast or something?" Emilio asked as he played with a mirror-shine knife, checking his reflection.

He'd caught her looking. Caught both of them looking. *Joseph's balls.* This was bullshit. She was a woman who could openly admire a man, damn it, but hell if she'd confess to such a thing. "No—wondering where you got that knife?"

"Found it in the stash in the weapons room. Doc pointed me in that direction when I mentioned needing a gun. Those damn unis took everything."

Of course, he wouldn't want to go in naked. "Then are you ready for this?"

"Born ready, dust honey."

"Don't call me that," she replied through gritted teeth. *Forget admiring him, let's hit him.* "Did you grab a gun?"

He stepped over to her, all in her personal space. "Of course. Would you like to see it?"

She caught a hint of his scent, something pine and engine oil, and wanted to smother herself in the unique smell he'd possessed since she'd first gotten tangled up with him. The proximity sent a tingling to her lower anatomy, something she'd ignore. "You can keep the gun tucked away for now. Also, I want you to keep in mind this is an ask questions, shoot later situation."

The little smirk he gave scrunched up his scar and brought her attention to those lips and his wonderful mouth. She'd dreamed about that mouth during her single hour of sleep and woken up panting and drenched.

"Does the same go for you? Yesterday it appeared you enjoyed shooting first versus asking questions."

Paul's hymnals, he's going to kill me. "I didn't know we were at the stage of our partnership where we shared such details."

The next words were for her ears alone. He leaned in close, his breath tickling her ear. "But people I plan on fucking should definitely tell me those things."

She bit her lip and let out a chuckle. "And now I know you're not a gentleman."

"Never claimed to be."

"Then let's make something clear." She went toe-to-toe, knowing Lee stood mere feet away, eating up every word. "You don't know a lot about me, but I don't deal with personal business in front of my crew. I don't lie or cheat. I also despise people who want to play endless word games with me about what they want. Don't try to mind-fuck me. You need something, you want something, just spit it out. Get it?"

"Sure thing. What I want is to get to Callisto. How long do you think all this other bullshit that's preventing me from getting there is going to take?" All traces of flirtation and desire disappeared behind the weight of frustration.

Maybe I should have played along.

"Lying doesn't become you either." Emilio edged around her.

Toni growled, pivoting on her heel as Emilio came to a stop at those rear windows. He took his own gander at the platform. "I wasn't planning on lying. Just wanted to say you agreed to this, to partner with me, to help me get the flash."

"I wasn't given much choice in the matter and you and your crew outnumber me five to one. Not good odds." He scratched his eyebrow and let the finger trail down the scar. Those fingers, callused, strong, long, had been inside her last night.

"Well, they aren't going to trust you right away. You're not even reputable."

Emilio grinned, the playful expression wreaking havoc on her lady bits. "I don't expect them to welcome me with open arms, but a little respect would be nice. Besides there's a lot you don't know about me, and a lot of me I think you like looking at."

"Respect is for those who've earned it and looking at you is just fine for momentary weakness, but truth is, you bore me." She took a step back and readjusted her blouse and buckskin cargo vest before putting both hands on her hips.

"Boring is what you call our time together last night?"

She shrugged. "It's what I would have been if Doc hadn't supplied an excuse to let you down easy."

"Oh, you never let me down. Gave me plenty of fuel to stoke my own slip drive," Emilio replied as he adjusted his belt.

Bastard. She'd be damned if he got the last word. "Thankfully, I didn't get aroused enough to have that problem."

"Whatever you have to tell yourself to keep those images of me from getting too down and dirty."

"If you two are finished sparring, you've been cleared to exit the ship," Dottie announced over the loudspeaker. "Rubenstein has been alerted to your arrival."

"After you." Emilio stepped to the side when the backdoor panel of the ship slid upward, the offer most likely an opportunity for him to look at her ass some more. *Do you want him looking at your ass?* He brought out the worst in her, yet remained smiling. The jerk got off on riling her and she'd remember that for the future. Giving in to him came with too much risk, though she found herself enjoying the arguments as much as he did. Trading barbs without any repercussion could be dangerous to her sobriety.

She moved past him and he whispered, "How did you know who Manny's banker was?"

"I didn't." She marched on, calmly, with sure, steady steps. No, she'd sent a message to this banking moon on behalf of Manolo, wanting to close out his account. "But we are agents acting in his stead while he recovers from a brutal attack."

The gangplank rattled under her grav boots as Emilio picked up his pace to catch up to her. She stepped off onto the platform right at the same time he did. The door to the bank opened and out walked a guard.

"Are you fucking serious?" Emilio's words were a mixture of anger and pure mumble. A poor attempt to keep from yelling at her.

"I thought of the brutal attack part myself. Don't give us away and this will work." At least, she was ninety-two percent sure it would work. They couldn't claim next of kin because this smugglers' bank tended to absorb the assets of the dead. Reputation alone made them one of the less dependable establishments — even her father had an account here.

"We're going to get creamed. If you're going to rope me into this crazy shit, I at least deserve to know the plan."

A loud whistle rent the air. "You two!" The guard pointed at them both and waved his hand. "Let's go, move it. This door only stays open for three minutes."

Toni started moving first, debating whether to impart any details of her plan now. "I'll tell you more once we ditch our escort."

Emilio nodded and they kept moving, past the turret guns that rotated with them, their gears echoing in the chamber. Jagged-edge rocks covered the walls, good for climbing or slicing themselves open. From a distance, the guard looked pretty tall, but close up he was nearly the same height as Toni and she sat on the short side of five foot five inches. He wore all gray combat-style gear, even gray grav boots.

"Stop right there." Shorty's command brought them to a halt and a wide red beam lit up over their heads and swiped over them. "Weapons are allowed, but no coms units."

When the beam turned green, Shorty motioned them forward. "Okay, step inside. You're clear."

Once they crossed the threshold, the entrance door swung closed with a loud *thwack* as it connected with the wall. Beeps signaled, at least four different locks slid into place and the guard inserted a key card into a slot for a final confirmation.

Note to self, grab a key card.

"Follow me to your meeting room," Shorty announced with a cough. "Do not touch the walls. Do not spit, smoke or snort anything on these premises or you will face being escorted out or, worse, shot." The fool looked like he wanted to shoot someone, rubbing one hand along the barrel of the semi-automatic rifle strapped to his chest.

Toni and Emilio followed the escort to the meeting room and she did her best to keep track of the turns. Three right, four left and a dozen or so more doors, each one gray and marked with a symbol versus a name or numeral.

The bank itself was a maze of tunnels with crinkle held in different vaults spread throughout the moon. It would take years to map the entire place and she'd never heard of such a thing. No, most escorts and bankers were taught a portion of the planet's elaborate map to prevent robberies and violence against their own. Heavily fortified from the outside, a labyrinth on the inside — no one attempted to rob Ceres unless they were suicidal.

Shorty stopped in front of another drab gray door. This one bore an image of an open palm with an eye imprinted in the dead center. "This is your meeting room. I will alert Rubenstein to your presence. Help yourself to the refreshments or the facilities."

They both stepped inside and, right after the door shut, Emilio lit in. "Tell me you got more info from Sampson than an account number and a name."

"Don't worry. You were his partner. I'm sure they'll make allowances since Manny is recovering from his wounds." She put some emphasis into the last few words and gave a big smile. He needed to shut the hell up before he got them both caught. If this bank lived up to its reputation, every room had cameras and audio listening devices. Even discussing such things might raise questions.

Emilio rolled his eyes. "Sure thing, *bonita*. Have you ever been in here before?"

She sighed. "You have no appreciation for silence."

"I've always been the curious type."

"Once," she replied. A boring, drunk once. Her father had encouraged her to come with him. She'd been bored, depressed and too eager to try out their selection of champagne and vodka.

"Learn anything interesting about the place?" He chose his words carefully. *Pretty smart of him.*

Toni walked around the outer edge of the room, rock walls with pointed edges, nothing smooth, similar to the docking platform. The crudest cutting and digging tools appeared to have been responsible for the architecture and the furniture. Everything metal, gray, bleak. *Ugh.* A small swinging door on the back wall served as an entrance to a toilet. A stocked clear refrigerator unit held water and other bottled drinks. No doubt she'd find some of her previous beverage choices in there.

But we're not drinking anymore, are we?

She gave a small shrug. "They provide plenty of booze, if you want some."

The hinges on the door creaked and gave way before Emilio could open his mouth to respond and in walked Rubenstein, a heavy-set man in a three-piece gray suit, flanked by Shorty and another guard. "Greetings, Captain Smith. Why has Manolo Reyes sent you?"

Chapter Nine

"I'm here to close out his account as he wishes to put the funds toward another investment opportunity." Toni's words made the banker's eyes go wide, but only for a moment.

Shit, we're dead. Rubenstein. Emilio recognized him from when he'd been considering opening his own account on this damn moon. A disgusting creature who leered at women and, for being in the cold of space, produced an obscene amount of sweat.

Like clockwork, Rubenstein produced a white handkerchief from his pocket and dabbed at his sweat-covered forehead. "That's sad to hear he no longer wishes to do business with us. Is he aware we can handle investment opportunities for him?"

This was what he'd been concerned about before they stepped off Styx. The bankers wouldn't let the flash go without exhausting every option, loophole and bullshit policy they had.

"Yes, but that's not his interest." Toni gave Emilio a side-eye and he took it as a sign to step up. So step up he did, right beside her.

Rubenstein gave him a once-over now. "May we inquire about the investor he is looking to work with?"

The sweating asteroid wanted to catch them in a lie, to mess with her. Emilio watched her closely, same as Rubenstein. She never wavered. "I'm not told anything like that. My job is to refuse any of your offers and retrieve all funds."

The banker sighed, the handkerchief repositioned at the base of his neck. "I understand, but I can't honor the closing of the account without Mr. Reyes present."

"Oh, I can speak for him. I'm his partner and my name should be on the account." The moment of truth and Emilio had no clue if Manny had even put him on the damn thing.

"Your name?" Rubenstein all skeptical eyebrows and sweaty rag asked.

"Emilio Morales."

Rubenstein pulled a small tablet out of his suit jacket pocket and typed on the screen while they waited. Emilio glanced at Toni, whose eyes were focused on the beverage cooler. He reached out and brushed the back of her hand with his fingers. The effort got a rise out of her — she jerked away and frowned at him.

He did his best to convey how things would be fine, how *they'd* be fine. Maybe they would pull this off. The worst that could happen was they didn't get access to Manny's funds. Sure, he wouldn't mind having an influx of extra crinkle, but the amount he'd get from completing Grecia's deal and making things right with the cartel leader was more important.

"It appears your name will suffice, Mr. Morales." Rubenstein slid the tablet back into his pocket. "It will take us about thirty minutes to get the full amount assembled. Please wait here."

"Sure thing," Emilio replied with a smile. Something seemed off the way they hustled out of the room. The door shutting and a lock clicking into place changed things.

"See? Not so hard after all. It's like I told you." This time she was the one leaning in, bringing them into close proximity. Her clean scent mixed with a light floral aroma teased his nostrils.

He'd barely slept the night before. His hour or so of rest had proved agitated. Taking himself in hand had done nothing. His body craved hers, wanted her in a way he'd never found himself wanting another woman. And he couldn't figure out why, for the life of him. She was unpredictable, crazy and liable to make decisions he failed to understand, like this notion of getting her ship back. Besides, she wanted to go legit, if the word of her crew could be counted on. They'd spoken of it over the galley table at breakfast. The woman he'd need in his life had to be willing to get dirty, to be against the law. It was how he operated. His dick would have to get with the program, unless he could sway her line of thinking.

He reached for her, reeling her towards him. "I don't really think you told me anything besides the bare minimum. You didn't even mention how much flash we're talking about?"

Leaning down, he sucked the lobe of her ear into his mouth before nipping it with his teeth.

She moaned. "Enough to buy two ships of moderate technology and get the merchandise to fill both."

"Is that all?" He let his grip on her slack and moved to cup her face. A kiss seemed the next logical step, as she slid a hand over his prominent erection bulging at the front of his pants. Right when he pressed his lips to hers, she gripped his balls hard enough that he yelped.

Fuck me! He couldn't move, caught by her vise-like hold.

"It's enough to get what we need. You may be used to handling larger amounts, but don't doubt this is the biggest amount I've transported, let alone had a chance at. So, stow the attitude." Her whispered words and her grip failed to quell his attraction or want. She'd matched him — rarely had anyone done such a thing.

She let go, stepping back, and Emilio leaned over, taking deep breaths and trying to recover. To get his mind and body in sync. When he'd summoned enough anger, he stood straight, staring her down. "I've killed men who've committed lesser offenses then what you just did."

"I imagine your dick didn't want those men the way it wants me." The smile she gave him sent him over the edge.

In less than a second, he crowded her space, forcing her to take a few steps backward. Time for her to be on edge. "Is that a challenge? I want you more than you want me?"

"Maybe…" Her focus was on him, but the sparkle in her eyes threw him off.

"You're fucking toying with me to pass the damn time."

She grinned big. "I'd take all the credit, but you started this game. Remember, I give back whatever I'm served."

He put a hand around his gun, feeling the grip in his palm. She pissed him off something fierce, but he recalled their first kiss and the pistol whip he'd earned. His heavy-handed ways in her quarters and her leaving him. She liked to punish behaviors she didn't like. He admired her gumption. Every time he thought he had control over anything, she turned him on edge, whirled him around. "You may be able to serve up a nice helping of payback, but are you prepared for this to not go as planned?"

"I don't take risks without being aware of the consequences and having some backup plans. Plus, I don't believe you'll touch me against my wishes."

"I'm not talking about me." If he'd been any other man, Rubenstein, the damn guard...she'd be in deep shit.

"I know." She brought a hand to his cheek, tracing the scar, awakening those unwanted feelings again. "But when it comes to you, for all your badass act, you're actually a nice guy. One I'm willing to let touch me."

No one had ever called him a nice guy. He'd been the jerk, the killer, the muscle, the asshole, the liar... Nice wasn't a word associated with him. The words left him speechless, but with a bone-deep need to prove her wrong. To show how he preferred everything other than the sweet and light underbelly. So he showed her, with a kiss. She responded the way she had the previous day, though he didn't leave things to a simple press of lips. No, he pried her mouth open with tongue and teeth. The kiss deepened and became something more primal, permeating their bodies and awakening the arousal and heat inside him once more.

He could deal with this madness again to prove a point. A start and stop, being left in a state of want for hours. *Mother Mary, give me strength.* Somehow, he fought against those baser instincts and held her away from him. Stepping back, he released her, but she started towards him.

"Point proven."

"What point?" She caught herself in the act of stretching out her arms to reach for him, and dropped them to her sides.

"This thing between us isn't one-sided. You're not as impervious to this attraction as you'd like to believe." And she didn't possess the experience she'd pretended to have. At least in the ways of being a criminal. Not with her approach to this bank job. Toni would do well to keep a guy like him around.

"Whatever…the fact you're so fixated on this means you don't like losing control of a situation."

Instead of correcting her, because talking about his depth of emotion would get her thinking he was a nice guy again, he decided to change the topic. Might as well point out her naivety in all things sinister. "I don't understand why you didn't bring Lee with you."

"Uh." Toni glanced around the room, turning her head this way and that. "Do you see people who need killing? This is a business transaction. Lee is designed for situations requiring more forceful results."

"It may come down to needing a little more muscle."

She hunched her eyebrows, whispering, "Do you know something I don't? I was under the distinct impression we are getting the crinkle."

"Something tells me closing out an account is never this easy. Something you should become familiar with in criminal pursuits — always expect the double-cross."

As if he'd summoned them, the door clicked open for Rubenstein to walk in, along with three guards this time. Each visit warranted more men, a warning sign if Emilio had ever experienced one.

"Antonia, we need to have you verify one additional thing. Can you come with us?"

Emilio's hand shot out to stay her from moving. "I don't think so. No verification needs to be completed outside of this room."

"Then I'm afraid our business is at a close, Mr. Morales. Though, we request that you stay here as Antonia is escorted to her ship."

Emilio glanced at Toni and shook his head. The greed of these banking bastards was working against them.

Emilio drew his gun and yelled, "Get down, Toni!" She dropped to the floor as he fired three shots. All three guards dropped, and Rubenstein let the briefcase fall while he stood stock-still, shaking. No one threatened him. No one would threaten her, not if he had anything to say about it.

Toni jumped up, marched over to the asshole and picked up the briefcase, then pulled a long knife out of her boot. "Give me one reason not to split you up the middle."

"We planned to let you go." A wet spot formed in the banker's crotch region and trailed down his pant leg.

"You spineless coward."

Emilio walked right up and pointed the gun square at Rubenstein's forehead. He considered sparing the asshole's life but decided against it in the same second, and so pulled the trigger. "There goes your whole idea about killing people. Let's get out of here."

"Can I check the case first?"

The lights went out, to be replaced with emergency lighting. A loud-ass alarm started blaring.

Satan's fire. Emilio grabbed two rifles from the dead guards. "No damn time — we have to move."

Toni growled at him, hoisted the briefcase and ran to follow him out of the door. Where some would give up and turn themselves over to the enemy, she kept pushing, even if pushing meant against him. At the same time, they shouldn't have even been here. For all her attraction to him, which he wanted to cultivate, her ship still topped her priority list.

Now, they were going to face a possible shitstorm. Rubenstein coming back with three guards hadn't made any sense and the bastard thought he'd been so slick. If she'd let him lead, maybe they would have had a chance to avoid this entire mess. Maybe they could have gotten her ship's location without this crap of a heist. If he'd been on Callisto, he could have already been making things right.

"You didn't have to open fire," she yelled, catching up to him and passing him.

"If you think that, you're as naive as those other dust honeys on Mars. He was going to try and kill us. I bet the briefcase doesn't even have all the flash, if any at all." This was why they'd never be good together beyond a bed coupling. No, she possessed the face, the body, some intelligence, but too much stubbornness and determination to be in charge for him to deal with on a long-term basis.

"Still, I was heading things up. I had it under control. We could have used Rubenstein as leverage to get the rest."

She lived in a damn fairytale, and why the hell would he want a woman around long-term anyway? *Besides a bed companion.* This one spun him around, like a racer gone wild on the track. "Whatever you say, but I won't apologize for saving your life. Looks like I paid you back for saving mine."

They rounded another corner and gunfire exploded. Emilio reached for her and pulled her back. Crouched low with her, he reached for his knife in his boot. "Are you hit?"

"No, but feeling a little whiplash."

He angled the knife and stuck it towards the wall corner to get a look at the number of gunmen firing at them. "Easy to recover from. A bullet wound, not so much. We have three guys, if the reflection from my knife is accurate."

"What do we do?"

Finally, she deferred to him. He wanted to call her out on it, give her a little shit for asking him for help and depending on someone else. Except, those gunmen would start moving if they didn't move first. No time for antagonizing. "Follow my lead. I'm going to draw their fire and take out a few. I'll holler for you when it's time to move. Make sure you get right behind me."

Each second, each word was a chance these bank goons would amass more backup. For not owning any of the money in the bank vaults, they sure enjoyed keeping what wasn't theirs. Emilio slid his knife back into his boot and reached for the medallion around his neck. He took a second to press a quick kiss to the cool metal before he let it fall back into place.

"Holy mother, a little protection please," he whispered. Cocking both pistols, he pushed off the balls of his feet to a standing position.

Around the corner, he assessed the position of all three. Two to the right and one to the left, staggered about two feet apart, crouched next to the jagged rock walls. He shot the first one right between the eyes, the relief of the kill shimmying through his body.

"Toni, get the hell out here and stay low to the ground," Emilio shouted.

He rammed into the falling body of his first kill, the dead guard becoming Emilio's shield while he fired on his next target. Guard numero dos succumbed easily to a head shot. The impact of bullets hitting his dead shield's body vibrated through Emilio's frame.

He took aim with his left pistol and fired on the third guard. Behind him, no Toni.

"Toni, where the hell are you? Hurry up."

"I'm right here," she replied, coming around the corner with a knife blade at her throat.

A grizzly-looking bastard, about Emilio's height, pointed a gun at him with the opposite hand. "Drop your pistols and I'll spare the girl."

No way was Emilio going to drop his weapon. The situation was pure déjà vu all over again, a repeat of their standoff on Casa Manolo. But, this time there was a knife involved and the weapon wasn't pointed at him. The other major difference? He knew her now, wanted her alive. He and Toni had a ton of unfinished business, starting with their physical connection and ending with whatever emotional threads they were spinning.

A noise behind them had Emilio swinging around as a bullet grazed his arm. The third guard got a bullet to the head in return.

"Fine, kill her, but I'll be leaving with her body and the briefcase," he replied, turning back to face the idiot holding Toni hostage.

A black knife whizzed past him, followed by a second. One embedded in the grizzly man's hand and another in his throat. His arm dropped and Toni stepped away as fast as she could to avoid dripping blood.

"Don't lie, lover-boy." The words came from Lee, who stood there both hands on her hips. "Are you two going to screw around all day, or are we going to get the hell out of here? Doc is cooking up a nice surprise for these banking bastards."

Emilio looked at Toni. "This is why I said we should have Lee come with us."

The pair took off behind Lee, her leading the way. Between Lee and Emilio, they had to put down another six guards before they made it back to the main door. Toni passed him, the briefcase secure under her arms, followed by Lee, and he was the last to walk through the metal door. They had seconds until at least half dozen more guards with guns were firing at them. The gun turrets were out of commission, if the exploded hunks of metal were an indication.

He climbed onto the loading platform. Once it finally secured on Styx, he almost ran into Doc, who was securing tape around a bundle of something, though Emilio could have sworn he saw at least three feet of detonation fuse sticking out of the end, confirmed by Sampson, as he lit a blow torch.

"Get ready for a big boom," he said as the fuse caught fire.

"Back away from the platform, everyone." Doc opened a side panel hatch and threw the bundle out into the bay. He swung the hatch shut with a bang.

Lee slammed on the intercom button. "Dottie, get us the fuck out of here."

"Aye, aye. Prepare for a bumpy-ass takeoff, folks."

Emilio put both pistols back in their holsters, and Doc grabbed his arm. "You're bleeding pretty good. How about we head down to my office?"

"Is there liquid painkiller in your office?" The damn arm stung like a sonuvabitch and he prayed no one had laced the bullets. He'd seen similar things, a variety of tranquilizer drugs applied to bullet casings to help slow an enemy down, even if they didn't land their marks.

"Might be, but even if I don't have, you still need to get patched up. Don't want any type of infection or fever."

"That's fine." Emilio pulled his arm free of Doc's grasp. "I'll head that way in a minute."

For now, Emilio turned his fury on Toni. "Why didn't you kill that guard?"

Toni shrugged. "He caught me before I could get my hands on my knife. Had me in a position that didn't make it easy to throw him into the wall or dislodge him."

"Funny how you're quick to aim but hesitant to fire." His vision blurred, and he shook his head to clear the cobwebs, most likely from the ship moving fast to get clear of the moon's gravity.

She got up in his face though, pushing against his chest with one hand. "Give me your gun. I'll show you how fast I hesitate and finish off what that bastard started with the graze."

He scoffed. "Sure. With our luck, you'd end up flinching and puncturing a hole in the hull. Next time, maybe think about your own safety before you get yourself killed."

That was his voice, off-kilter, pissed. Over this woman. *Why bother?* He should cut his losses but a part of him wanted everything she represented. The brash, proud woman who could take ships apart and who broke into banks.

"I've survived just fine for years." Right in his face, standing on her tiptoes so she was level with him. All angry whiskey eyes, with a becoming flush of anger on her cheeks. Well, his anger could match hers.

"*Just fine* got you drunk in a poker game and gambling away your ship, your home."

Dead silence greeted those words, all eyes focused on him, on Toni, and the hurt he saw briefly reflected in those amber depths speared him right in the lungs. It was difficult to breathe, to say the least.

"Which…" Her voice reflected calm and patience, unlike everything else about her. "If you'd bothered to notice, I've been trying to get back. This amount of flash is worth the risk to regain that home. And last time I checked you weren't too worried about my well-being, so who cares?"

There she went again, saying asinine things that didn't make sense. He mustered whatever calm he could for the benefit of her and keeping this crew from chucking him out through a side door. Someone—he'd bet Lee—was give him a death stare. "Case you hadn't noticed, the people on this ship, your crew, see you as their leader. Since getting me to my ship is contingent on you being alive, then your well-being concerns me."

No need to mention those twinges of something like feelings he'd begun to experience or the fact that in similar situations, he'd gone up against bigger numbers.

"Part of this deal also involved me splitting the flash with you, as we are partners. So, let's see it."

Toni twirled on a heel and stomped over to a table near the entrance to the production room. He hated how those body movements affected him. How on a physical level they were connected and he'd give his left nut to turn off her ability to rouse him and his dick. She slapped the suitcase on the table, clicked both side locks open and took a deep breath. He held his, sending up a silent prayer.

Throwing open the case lid, she took two steps back. Emilio got closer, peering in, and hoping he was dead wrong. Except, as in most cases, he wasn't. Inside the case sat a quarter of what Toni had said existed in Manny's account, and all uncut. Rough crinkle was worth half that of leaves.

Mother Mary save us all. "This isn't going to get your ship and it wouldn't do a damn thing if we split it."

"So, we don't split it. You could just let me have it, and maybe a loan to get the ship."

Fucking priceless. She now wanted his help. "I could have done more than that before all this crap, before you delayed me from getting to *my* ship. Why would I help you now?"

Emilio sensed Lee moving closer and the room blurred again, his stomach curdling. The ship itself started to hit that part of the bumpy road Dottie had mentioned and he chalked his physical discomfort up to that. "There's a good chance I'm well and truly screwed in ways worse than a nuke hitting the Earth. When will we be off this planet?"

Toni looked around the room then peered at his face. "We are already past everything. No one came after us. The bumps happened minutes ago. Are you okay? You're sweating."

Emilio wiped his brow, Toni's mulish face and brunette hair a mixing blob in front of him. "Joseph's balls, they drugged me."

Then everything went black.

Chapter Ten

"I think it's a horrible idea and you can note that I'm against it." Lee stood at one end of the galley with both hands on her hips. The frown had been a constant presence on her face since they'd opened the briefcase.

Toni sat on a stool at the other end of the room, swirling water around in a glass. "Noted. Anyone else have an opinion? Speak it now, but my mind is pretty much determined that this is our only option at this point."

No one said a peep. Dottie, Sampson and Doc sat or stood in various spots and were less vocal than when they'd been complaining nonstop earlier. Though for every crappy word or negative sentence, they'd been a flutter of action.

When Emilio had passed out, Lee and Doc had moved him to his bunk, Doc getting to work on analyzing his blood. Dottie had hidden the ship in the asteroid belt until they could figure out their next steps. The flash being less than Toni had planned, Emilio out of commission and possible targets on their back with the APUPs meant they needed better options. Options were found by gathering information.

"Fine. Dottie, call him and triple the amount of encoding sequences. I'll be up on the command deck in a minute."

The response she received was a single nod and Dottie took off. Toni finished her glass of water with gusto. "Doc, how much longer will he be out?"

Doc shrugged. "I don't know. It's hard to predict these things when you have no idea how much of the drug each bullet was dosed with. A lot of times they can place thick coats on these things. Not to mention you never know how a human body will react. So far he's not showing any type of allergic reaction, but there are other side effects not always visible."

Paul's hymnals. Emilio had been grazed with a bullet dipped in liquid Rohypnol, something Doc claimed was quite common on Earth-before-the-nuke and not frequently used or developed. She'd rushed to Emilio's side when he'd collapsed, had spent too many hours checking in on him, placing damp towels on his forehead and worrying if he'd make it. Doc's extensive knowledge didn't make up for the fact that sometimes people just didn't survive.

Sure, Emilio drove her nuts, but he'd been right. Their mutual desire stirred something deep inside her. Something she'd never felt with other sexual partners and she'd been doing her best to hide it. Rather horribly. Even their heated verbal exchanges made life a tad more interesting.

"Fine, keep me updated on his status. Sampson, I need you to do a review on the slip drive and trolling motor. If we have to take off fast, I need to know everything is greased and primed."

"Aye, aye, Captain. I'll get right on it." The young man tromped off, tugging on the sides of his cap as he went. So far, he'd stuck to his script in being the quietest one out of the bunch, staying as far away from all the action as possible, and ready to get right back to work. She appreciated that one bit of normalcy in all this chaos, chaos of her own making.

"Still a shitty idea. Broadcasting to a planet we wanted to stay away from until we absolutely had to go there, and where peeping ears are always searching for signals to tap. We don't need bounty hunters coming for us." Lee growled, pacing over to Toni's side of the galley.

"Yes, but Akono Sweet is someone we can trust."

Propping herself up on a stool, Lee pulled one of her knives from her vest. "I never said we couldn't trust him. It's everyone else. There's something weird going on. You said the bankers were trying to get Emilio alone. I've never known the Ceres Bank to be in need of getting a bounty from the pups."

"Me neither, which is why we need to contact Sweet. Plus, he sent a message to Dottie that he's got word on the Geisha. I can't ignore news about my ship. Not now." Toni stood and headed for the door. "And even if someone listens in or comes after us, it's not like we can't protect ourselves."

Her attempt at false bravado wasn't lost on Lee, who gave a weak smile before following Toni up to command. As they entered, Dottie wheeled around in her chair to face them. "I got him. Ready for speaker and video if you are."

"Put him up." Toni stopped in front of Dottie's big monitor, bracing herself with both palms along the flat side of the panel. Dottie pressed a few buttons and the black and white static of the screen in front of Toni cleared, revealing Akono Sweet's beautiful face.

"Antonia Smith, it's been a long time since I've had you in my club." A charmer, that was what they called Sweet. He'd even made a pass at her a few times. She'd been of sound enough mind to turn him down, but not without granting him a kiss. Deep brown, near black, eyes stared back at her. His dark skin, a black goatee and a nose most would say was more angular than they expected were all as she remembered.

"Afraid I've been trying to stay away from sweets. They're not good for my continued health."

A big grin lit up his face. "Yes, but you know what they say, all things are okay in moderation."

Moderation always became the slippery slope to out of control. She'd gone from a quick game to losing her ship in his establishment. Not counting the times where one drink had turned into a lap dance for a patron, or the bet that she couldn't break a bottle with the blade of a knife. Sweet never tried to stop her from drinking, betting… No one ever did. Self-destruction ensured they loved her even more, but for all his lack of help, he'd given back in different ways. "Maybe for most, but I'll play it safe. You told Dottie you had news about the Geisha."

"I do. Someone came through playing fast and loose the other day. Your name got brought up in some ridiculous conversation, after he'd been fleeced for almost everything. Said he'd never bet his ship and let it end up on that junker's moon, like Toni's Geisha. So, if you're looking for your ship, I'd check there."

She took a deep breath and exhaled, but only a little relief came to her. If Geisha was on Europa, there was no telling what shape she'd be in. "Thank you."

"Anything to bring light back to your eyes. You've been struggling, Toni." Those words, the way he softened his tone just for her. *Charmer.* "I would have helped sooner. All you had to do was ask."

And she'd have been a puppet on a string. *No way. Not today or tomorrow.* She'd indebted herself to her brother and still planned to get away as soon as possible, as she had done. Emilio…he wanted wild and crazy Toni. She'd vowed to never be that way again and Sweet reinforced her resolve. Sweet would have made her pay a price for his help, one way or another.

"Thanks. I appreciate that, but you know I don't like owing markers."

"I do, which is why I want to prove to you I can be nice and don't always need something." He leaned in closer to the screen, as if he wanted to make sure the words came through loud and clear. "I got a call from Big Al."

"Let me guess. He's put some bounty out on me."

"No, but he did mention your new passenger, Morales. Word around Callisto is this runner is on Grecia's shit list. He's got bounties out with everyone, everywhere wanting Morales turned over to him. You're welcome to ditch him and come here."

She laughed, loud and obnoxious. "I have no clue what you're talking about, Akono. My sole focus and purpose is to find my ship, not take on runners who've pissed off cartel leaders."

Red dust humped. They were in big trouble. It was one thing when the pups were after Emilio. Having a cartel leader appealing to everyone in the damn galaxy looking for an extra buck put a big fucking target on their back. One they didn't need.

Akono shook his head, then nodded. "Fine, I hear you loud and clear. The offer still stands — you need a place to hole up, feel free to head here. I know I haven't been a good influence, but I'll do better."

"Read you loud and clear." Toni signaled to Dottie and the transmission cut off. She'd apologize to Sweet later for cutting things short, but with this new information all her worries had turned a lot worse.

"We're fucked. Everyone is after this guy," Lee announced to the room at large and no one in particular as she stared out into the starry space. Her first mate had never spoken truer words. Black hair swinging from her giant ponytail, Lee whirled around and pointed at Toni. "You have to turn him over."

No. The single word echoed loud and clear in her mind. Every fiber of her being rebelled at the idea. Even for all his constant warring with her, he deserved better. Giving him over to Grecia when they'd agreed to be partners…that was the excuse she'd go with. Sure, they weren't bosom buddies. *But we might be fuck buddies.* There existed a physical connection and a bone-deep dedication to a man she barely knew. The logical explanation was their penchant for saving each other, with a hefty dose of interest in a guy who kept coming back for more. He'd helped her escape Manny's burning ship and Ceres.

"Why would we do that?" Dottie asked. Thank goodness she acted as a voice of reason.

Lee went wide-eyed and waved her hands in the air. "Because it will get the target off our back and maybe even extra flash to buy back the Geisha."

Before Toni could chime in, Doc's voice did the talking from behind her. "I think that's the worst idea yet. Grecia's a horrible cartel leader who believes the universe owes him flash for being born. He'd never give us a full reward, not if he's heard about Emilio traveling with us already. Toni freed him from those pups too."

"Then I'll do it." Lee volunteered herself, of course.

"We're not turning him over. Final decision." Toni announced. She pushed off the pilot console and crossed her arms.

Lee frowned, as expected. "You're making the wrong decision."

"And if you feel that way, you can take a shuttle and leave now." Toni looked at Doc and Dottie. "All of you. I get that I made mistakes in the past. Played with our home, got it taken from us. But trading Emilio to Grecia is not the right move to make. I made a deal with him first."

Doc put a hand on Toni's shoulder and gently squeezed. "We're with you, Captain, but how do we move forward without the flash we need to get our home back?"

By doing the very thing she'd said she wouldn't. "We add bone powder to the trade." The powder wasn't hers. It belonged to her brother and by rights the government, an organization she possessed little love for. She'd have to find a way to pay him back later.

Whatever disagreements they had before this moment melted away in the face of Lee's big grin. "Finally, we're going to give the bird to every last one of them."

Yes, we are. "Dottie, set course for Europa."

* * * *

Toni stood on the Styx command deck, arms crossed and frowning. "I can offer you one pound of rough crinkle and two three-kilogram containers of bone powder in exchange for my ship, Geisha. This is my final offer."

Dion, the greasy-looking Europa junkyard manager, stroked his chin. His fingers were black, probably from taking apart busted ships all day, and he wore grimy, frayed clothes to boot. "I'll do it for an extra kilogram of bone powder. We're poor dealers here with families."

For twelve solar hours, she'd attempted to negotiate a deal for her ship. Emilio still slept, not being roused by the space travel or even her cursing and swearing at these damn junker yarders. They were running out of time and every back and forth wore her down more. *Damn it to hell.*

Every solar hour they spent in the same place equaled one hour closer to the likelihood the uni-men or other bounty hunters might arrive. Dottie had uncovered the wanted communication that had gone out to all the local planets and moons, seeking Emilio for a ridiculous reward of fifty pounds of crinkle.

She wouldn't lie—even that amount of flash brought her crew to attention, and Lee had repeated her suggestion once or twice about trussing Emilio up during his sleep binge for a chance at the money. Toni had staunchly refused, which earned her knowing gazes from Dottie and Doc. Eventually, she'd set them both straight.

"Fine, you have a deal. How long to get the Geisha ready for retrieval?"

"We'll have her ready to go for you in about six solar hours."

Toni nodded to Dottie to end the transmission, and clicked the button.

"Do you want me to get Doc working on divvying up the powder?" This from Lee, in her usual arms-crossed mode, though no one, outside of those on Styx, knew that underneath her fingertips sat her knives, in concealed holsters and ready to fly at a second's notice.

"Yes, go ahead and get them working on it. Once we get my ship we'll move everybody over and let Emilio fly Styx to his rendezvous point."

"I'll have everything ready and to the shuttle in a bit," Lee replied.

Toni headed out of the cockpit, downstairs to her quarters. A change of hairdo and her duty belt would be much needed. She'd been wandering around unprepared and less-than-alert after spending the hours she hadn't spent in negotiation checking on Emilio, watching him sleep. He'd appeared fitful at times and also so peaceful she'd thought he'd died. These last few days had wrecked her. She'd slept very little and contemplated the mystery of this man who'd grown in such esteem to her eyes that she'd started to give him the same attentive care she gave her other crew members.

In her quarters, she snatched her belt off the bed and strapped it to her waist before grabbing her knife. She could always move the belt outside her environmental suit when the time came. She marched into the bathroom and grabbed her hair wand, the one extravagant thing she owned. The type of purchase a woman attempting to get her ship back would have refused to make.

With this electrical wand, she could manipulate her hair for short periods of time, from cutting and growing, to style and color. The device simplified her constant desire to push back against the things out of her control. Her opportunity to own one thing. No day had to be the same.

"Including today." She dialed in the knobs and started waving the wand. It cut and styled her hair into a nice bob with bangs, a bright sea-foam-green color being her final touch. Though she made the mistake of glancing at her shower. The one place she couldn't stop the memories. Emilio touching her, arousing her body in a way she'd gone a little too long without. She should have taken him up on the opportunity for more. *No dice.*

When he woke up, she'd have her ship and, for the safety of her crew, she'd ditch him. Leave Styx in his possession and head off for wherever she could get work. No way she'd willingly turn him over to Grecia, but putting her crew in such a pathway equaled selfish, destructive leadership on her part. Finishing touches to her new hairdo complete, she placed the wand back in its cradle. Then she left, heading for the shuttle.

Temptation got the better of her and she stopped outside Emilio's quarters. The door slid open at her pause and she saw him still prone on the bed. Dim light gave a poor outline of his shape. She wanted to go to him, rattle him awake. *Kiss him one last time.* Funny how just a few messed-up life and death situations had brought them so close, made her crave to have him beside her, when she should want to run far away.

A rap against the wall had her taking a few steps backward. She glanced to her left and saw Doc, a curious look to his eyes. "Lee is ready to go if you are. She said to come get you, something about wanting to go through the pre-flight sequence on the shuttle and double check everything on the engine."

"Sure thing."

Doc moved toward her, wrapping a hand around her arm. "You and him, there's more than just a business partnership, isn't there?"

To lie or not to lie — except to her crew she never did. Problem was, they'd never made it very far, not for his lack of trying. "I'm not sure."

"Well, take it from me, as someone who cares about you, be careful seeking affection from a guy like that. He's into a lot more than we ever were and he's searching for the type of flash where a person sacrifices part of themselves."

She nodded. "Yeah, Doc. I'm aware that's the impression he's given everyone, but it's not the one he's left me with. I'll be safe all the same. You know the crew and the ship come first. Always."

Doc didn't impart any more gems of wisdom, but turned around and headed in the direction of the galley. "Going to make a couple of cups of coffee or something hot. I imagine our runner will be waking up soon and he'll be a bit thirsty."

She didn't spare either of them another glance but hauled ass, getting to the shuttle in record time. She sealed herself in and immediately pulled the engine cover up to check all the specs and reads on the trolling motor.

"What took you so long? Checking on your lover boy?" Lee asked from the co-pilot's chair where she watched Toni with narrowed eyes.

Toni slapped the cover of the engine back down, enjoying the clinking sound that accompanied the action. "We're not lovers and we're not sex partners. I'd say we're hostile acquaintances who've experienced temporary cessation of hostilities."

"With a good dose of sexual tension. I'll take him if you don't want him. Feeling the need to burn off a little extra energy myself."

Toni's retort sat there on the tip of her tongue. She wanted to scream out for Lee to do it, but a part of her disagreed. Seeing him with someone else, a member of her crew, watching those eyes of his focus on another woman in lust? "Funny you say that after you've been lobbying for the last day or so to turn him in for the bounty. If you want him so bad, have at it. But he could have space scabies for all you know, as many ports as he goes to."

"Ha! You're caught!"

Toni's cheeks heated.

"The blush adds to the guilt. Plus, what a weak excuse. Space scabies? The only people who get those anymore are the ones sleeping with cheap spores on the Callisto station. And my impression of your guy is he doesn't have to pay for a little laser-fire action." Lee turned around in her seat and started messing with her safety harness.

Toni did the same, taking her position in the main pilot's chair, and reached up to touch her cheeks, willing them to return to normal. She checked on the dials and started the pre-shuttle detaching procedures. "The innuendos are a bit much."

"Oh...okay, you want blunt honesty. The man doesn't pay for sex. Too fine a specimen."

"I may have already had a peek at him when we first got on the ship." Again, no lying to her crew. Though Toni didn't mind keeping details from them, eventually everything was shared.

"Hot fuel burn! I knew it." Lee laughed and leaned in toward the speaker box. "Dottie, you owe me fresh fruit when we hit Callisto next. I want something good, too, like berries or maybe a white-flesh peach."

Toni should've known this wasn't regular conversation. No, she'd been played by her own folk. For the chance at fruit, she couldn't blame them.

The shuttle detached successfully, and Dottie's voice came over their intercom. "You win this round, Lee. Sorry, Captain, curiosity caught the assassin. We've been wondering for days if you two had knocked grav boots yet. Be safe and you're clear of the docking clamp. Have a nice trip."

"It's okay, Dottie. Hard to pass up a good bet, especially when food is involved. We'll report in soon as we can."

Pulling away was easy, and they watched Styx disappear as they headed for the surface of Europa. The entire moon was covered in space junk. A person could make over a hundred ships from all the scrap. It was interesting how that worked, and here she sat hoping they'd pull one ship from the thousands.

No more talking was necessary as they navigated the shuttle to the main yard entrance and landed outside it. A few other shuttles and ships were present as well, but nothing out of the ordinary. The junk yard always did business and Toni was one of many on a given day. Hopefully, they wouldn't have to wait long. She prayed she'd get Geisha's engine fired up with no problem.

Lee set the grav boot in place for the shuttle and turned off the engine. They both donned environmental suits, strapping their belts around the outside. Gravity levels were low here and to keep everything in place the yard owners used grav boots of various sizes, not to mention sticking a giant magnetic pole through the middle of the entire thing. Europa, as funny as the place was, used tagging collars to keep all the ships magnetized to the moon or else every last one would float away.

"Ready?" Toni asked Lee and the woman nodded.

They decompressed the shuttle entrance seal on the hatch door and exited slowly. No other junk traders were visible and Toni kept a hand on the hilt of her knife in case she needed it. A slow, lumbering stroll got them to the main yard building, the one where all the trade took place. They entered a closed-off room, sealing the door behind them. A pair of alarms buzzed, confirming their presence as the air around them hissed, pressurizing the room.

Toni removed her helmet as she walked through the next door and into the main trading floor. "Lee, did you bring the briefcase?"

"Yes, Captain. Got it with me," she replied, stepping up next to Toni.

The click of a hammer cocking into place echoed in her ears. "Welcome, Ms. Smith. Care to tell me where the fugitive Emilio Morales is?"

It appeared today wasn't her day.

Chapter Eleven

Emilio dreamed of his mother often enough that he could recall her scent of jasmine and coffee. Coffee, the one thing the cartel leaders allowed them without hesitation. What were a few beans when they had thousands of acres to harvest? She'd drunk it black, as black as her eyes. Eyes like his. The coffee, the scent, such strong beans...

His eyes flew open to Doc sitting there, sipping something hot. "How long have I been out?"

"A little over two days. The bankers hit you with something called a roofie. Haven't seen use of those much except on Callisto from time to time. Old Earth drugs." Doc lifted his cup a foot in the air. "Care for a drink?"

Emilio nodded, sitting himself up in the bed. Glancing around, he noticed they were in his quarters. "You don't have an infirmary on ship?"

Doc poured coffee out of a thermos on Emilio's nightstand. He filled the cup halfway then handed it to

Emilio. "Not much need for one on a ship working for the APU. We tend to be more in the business of taking bodies apart than putting them back together."

"You don't sound too pleased by that," Emilio replied, blowing across the top of his cup. The steam wafted as he waited for the response.

"Let's say I'll be happy to get back to living in a place where people need me and I'm doing fixing versus destroying. If a well-stocked infirmary comes with the option, I'll consider it a bonus."

He considered offering the old man a place on his vessel. Someone familiar with drugs, explosive chemicals and a gun wound or two could come in handy. At this point, Emilio gauged his weakness— Doc didn't like death. "Seen your fair share of wounds, have you?"

"A couple I'd rather unsee. I'm looking to focus more on living, breathing, peaceful pursuits with someone worth sharing them with." The man had feelings for someone on this vessel and Emilio would venture they were for the pilot. The words Doc spoke hit a sore spot for Emilio, Doc's desire for companionship reminding Emilio of his own goals. Except he wondered if a companion would leave him weak. He saw how the man's interests could be used against him if someone wanted.

A few more sips of coffee and Emilio asked the big question. "How soon can I move?"

Doc chuckled. "Funny how young ones aren't more familiar with the older drugs. So many now don't get schooling, training, and most don't even know our history. You can move as soon as you're ready. The drug doesn't do any damage except put you to sleep. A body like yours, not used to this kind of stuff, especially the concentrated crap they use—it can knock you out for up to four days."

Thanks be. He raised his medallion to his lips and pressed a kiss to it. Maybe his luck was changing a bit. A few blessings sent his way. "Where are we headed next?"

"We're already there." This from a new voice at the entrance to his room.

Doc near knocked over his chair standing up. "Sampson, damn, boy. Do you a little good not to sneak into a room without announcing yourself."

The redhead boy, who couldn't be more than seventeen, with grease stains on his cheeks and similar streaked shirt and pants, stepped farther into the room. "Sorry, sir. Came to see if the boss here was awake. Figured you both would want to know Cap'n and Lee have been taken captive by the junkers on Europa."

Emilio didn't like being caught off guard and they'd been nowhere near Europa when he'd passed out. "Why and when the hell did this happen?"

"We had to make a few calls after the banker's behavior on Ceres. Got wind you're a wanted man and a bead on our ship. Captain figured to retrieve our vessel then cut you loose." This from Doc, who'd sat back down to finish his coffee.

Toni had a set of brass balls going into this situation by herself, not to mention working on ditching him. He still warred with the concept, especially when they could have gone straight to Callisto and resolved the issue. Did they need her ship if they had his? He rocked himself into a sitting position and scanned the room for his boots. Emilio pointed to them next to the door. "Sampson, bring me those."

The boy did as requested and before long Emilio was standing ready to do battle. He had his belt strapped to him with the pistol and knife. He took off, out of his quarters and towards the command deck. "How do you know they're in trouble?"

"Because I installed an emergency signal on Lee's space suit. In case anything went wrong," Sampson piped up.

Of course, things had fallen apart. It seemed Toni had at talent for getting herself into one mess after another, and he seemed destined to be along for the ride. *Mother Mary save me from troublesome women.* Though, truth be, he wanted to be here to help her. To save her. "Dottie, what's the word?"

"Word is they want you. They pressed the emergency button on their suits and a communication came through that if we send you down alive, wrapped up nice and neat, they'll give us Toni and Lee back. Can't say it's a bad idea, seeing as how it'd leave us in the free and clear."

Funny how they lay the blame at my feet. "If Toni had listened to me in the first place, got me to my ship, you wouldn't be having these problems."

Doc came up beside him with a frown. "I seem to recall we saved your life more than once. Figures you'd be on our timetable, not your own."

"And our captain already told you she'd get you to Callisto after our business was finished," Dottie added.

In wars of words he had half a chance at winning. For this unique situation, he didn't miss the syringe in Doc's hand or the way Dottie pulled one of her arms down low so Emilio couldn't see anything past her biceps.

"I get it. I show up and a heap ton of problems come your way, but I'm more than willing to fix them. She's my partner, meaning everyone on this ship is my partner, and I'll do what I must. Her life on the line is equal to mine being in jeopardy too."

Softened eyes were enough visible relief to let him exhale the breath he'd been holding. Why he'd wanted company in the past, a crew…a bunch of work. Dealing with people took a lot of patience and time, two things he didn't have an abundance of.

"Fine." Dottie stood and locked eyes with him. "What do you have in mind?"

Emilio glanced at Sampson, who stood at the entrance to the deck as if afraid to get in the middle of things. "Kid, you can install emergency signals and fix slip drives — you any good flying a shuttle?"

"Me?" The boy, eyes wide, and pointing at himself, had obviously been overlooked in a few areas on Al's ship.

"You know the basics, little 'un, I've shown you everything." This from Dottie, who seemed to be using the computer to find out more info. Emilio leaned in over her shoulder, catching the thermal view of the big building. A fair number of bodies were moving around.

Here goes nothing. "Doc, you and Sampson prep shuttle two for takeoff."

To his surprise, Sampson jumped to. "Aye, boss."

"Boy's so eager, he's liable to flip the wrong switch on pre-flight." Doc headed off after him yelling for Sampson to slow down.

Emilio would be the first to admit it felt good to be in a bit of control again, to take action. Sure, keeping oneself out of danger was important, but he enjoyed getting into the fray. The cartel soldier part of him who liked getting his hands dirty and saving a beautiful woman to boot. Add in working alongside capable people who had his back and he'd achieved a perfect storm.

Ten minutes later, all three of them were ensconced on the shuttle. Sampson sat in the main pilot's chair while Emilio took the co-pilot seat. He'd use the time to check his guns. Doc, once they landed, would take the shuttle back to the ship. They couldn't lose everyone to this botched-up job.

"You're going to land in a shitstorm, you know that?" Dottie's voice crackled over the second Styx shuttle intercom system.

"It doesn't matter. We have to get them out and get the other shuttle," Emilio replied as the shuttle disconnected from Styx's docking clamp.

"You're clear. Bring those two home safe."

The words were strange to Emilio. Styx wasn't his home. No, his home was on a journey back from Earth and had already passed the asteroid belt if Gina had stuck to the schedule. He was doing this because of the guilt he carried about the way things had gone down on Ceres, where his Wanted status had affected the amount of flash they'd received. "I'll get them back safely."

Doc approached and dropped several canisters the size of tumbler glasses in his lap. "Flash bombs. They won't break any windows or mess up the gravity seals. It will give you a good distraction as you bust into the room. Just pull the tab at the top."

Emilio nodded. "How long do they last?"

"Five minutes, give or take. If you're lucky, you'll only need one. Make sure to grab sun goggles and put them on before you put on the spacesuit. This way you can deploy as soon as the door opens from the pressurization chamber."

"Good idea."

Satellite trash floated by the shuttle as Sampson navigated them through a trove of broken equipment, ships and what looked like a metal lover's heaven. As they descended, he could see the other Styx shuttle, powered down and deserted. No one appeared to be working on scrapping it, nor did he see another living soul. The junk yard held a few other customers' shuttles. He'd call them assholes if he wasn't jealous of the junk yard idea himself. Except one shuttle looked out of place — a tarp over it, bearing the insignia of three planets bound together, was unforgettable.

"Sampson, land right next to the other shuttle."

"Aye, sir. Then we'll rescue them together," his pilot replied with a grin. Emilio had never met a more eager young man, excited by the prospect of engaging people who wanted to kill them. "I've got my pistol ready, cleaned and primed. We'll be set in a jiffy."

There'd be no combat for this kid if he could help it. "I've got another job for you to do, if you're up for it."

Sampson grinned, a lop-sided thing showing the wide gap in his front teeth. "Whatever you need, I can do it."

The shuttle landed then, with a jolted thud, and the entire thing shuttered from the force. Nothing graceful for sure.

"Watch what you're doing, boy." The words came from Doc, who held on to a grip bar in the ceiling above them. The old guy shook his head. "I need something to fly back to the ship."

The boy set the grav boot and let the trolling motor idle. "The ignition sequence will have too much delay. Better to leave it like this. I'm ready for my mission."

"You'll head to the shuttle northwest of ours. It's covered in a tarp, but it belongs to the uni-men, the ones chasing us."

Both Emilio and Sampson moved to the back of the shuttle, donning their suits and the sun goggles. Emilio secured his gun belt and holsters on the outside of the suit with the expectation they'd be getting right into the thick of it pretty fast.

"How do you know?" Doc asked, zipping up Sampson's suit and adjusting the young man's helmet.

"I recognized the insignia on the side of their shuttle as we landed. Even if it's not them, it's not a risk I'm willing to take. We don't need followers. We need a clean escape."

Sampson saluted him, the helmet muffling his response a bit. "I can take that shuttle down. I'll make sure it doesn't fly again."

"That's what we need," Emilio replied as the boy grabbed for a tool box. "As soon as you're done with your mission, hustle back to the other shuttle and get it ready for takeoff. We'll most likely be in a hurry."

Sampson nodded and moved to the hatch. Doc secured an oxygen mask for protection as Emilio and the engineer left the shuttle. They nodded to each other and split up once they got a few feet in front of the shuttle. Emilio hated having no concrete knowledge of what he walked into. Dottie had provided limited information. She had details about the junk yard, the fact it employed at least five people. The unis were a unit of two, but they could have picked up an extra uni at any port, someone willing to make a little side commission.

Similar to Earth's Luna, this moon had no wind, just an artificial gravity which made it difficult to walk on. *Lumbering, more than walking.* He reached the main building door and the shuttle Doc piloted rose into the sky behind him. This was it, him and Sampson, but mainly him. Rescues weren't his specialty, but there was a time when he'd stolen things and played protector for a cartel, and those skills never left a person. In the smuggling world he needed those talents as well, and as a piece of muscle for a cartel in his early twenties, he'd gotten comfortable with killing. *Maybe too comfortable.*

Once in the pressurization chamber, he sealed the outside door and waited for the beep before removing his helmet. The sun goggles obscured some of his peripheral vision, but he got a finger around the pin for the one of the flash bombs. Then he took a deep breath before opening the door, expecting to see Toni and Lee roughed up. He attempted to mentally prepare for a Toni with a bloodied lip, even a black eye. The thoughts filled him with rage, a good enough amount to send him busting into the room.

Except, instead of the woman he desired hurt and abused, he found three bodies on the floor not four feet away, Lee engaged in fisticuffs with the two unis — Bearded and Ugly — that he'd met courtesy of Big Al, and Toni was nowhere to be seen.

Behind him, her voice rang out. "Fellas, we can negotiate this. I want my ship and my associate will get rid of those pesky lawmen."

Emilio pivoted on one foot and finally saw her, backing up with two of the junk yard men trying to corner her. Her wavy sea-foam-green hair was a beacon in the room. Relief flooded his system to see her alive, the rage dissipating as he watched her stand her ground against two junkers. She incited something possessive in him, as dangerous to be aware of as much as it was to experience the emotion.

"The crazy lady killed our partners," said the one on her left, the one wearing the red head covering in the style of what he remembered some calling a trucker hat. What the hell truckers were, he had no clue. Just more retro-before-nuke things people liked to emulate.

The other junker switched his knife from one hand to the other. "Yeah, we want our revenge and you're good as any. Maybe we'll stick ya twice, once with our knives and once with our peckers."

Satan's fire. These pair needed correction. Emilio hollered. "I don't think the lady is interested, boys!"

The pair turned and that was all Toni appeared to need. She bumped up against the first one and wrestled for his knife. Emilio released his hold on the flash bomb pin, grabbed his pistol and shot the other one. There was no open angle on the one Toni grappled with. He heard a groan and his heart briefly stopped, as he couldn't tell if the sound was male or female. Neither did he have a good view point. Red cap junker slumped against her and Toni shoved him away from her body. Emilio tucked his pistol back into his belt then crossed his arms. "I've could've taken care of him."

Toni winked back. "Where's the fun in the that?"

"We gotta go," Lee said behind Emilio. "I killed one of them, but the other ran off. Don't want him coming back with one of those big guns."

Toni ran over to them. "Do we have transportation?"

"Yeah," Emilio nodded. "Sampson should have the shuttle primed."

The three of them ran back to the pressurization chamber, with a mad scramble to re-secure helmets and suits and ensure they had everything they needed. Emilio was ready first as he hadn't removed everything. He watched Toni, all speedy, cool calm as she slipped her suit on. She'd taken his words from earlier to heart and taken advantage of the distraction, but robbed him of the chance to be her hero. *Hero?* He'd never wanted to be the good guy before. Though he owed her at least once more for all the times she'd saved him.

Instead, she'd killed a man without compunction. Hell, she'd smiled after it, like the entire act was no big deal. *What a woman.* With each passing day he liked more and more the woman she became in the face of danger.

"Let's go. We're ready." This from the very same woman, her voice echoing in his ears through the suit helmet communication system.

"After you."

They moved as fast as they could to the shuttle and entered the hatch with little difficulty. Sampson sat in the pilot's seat with his oxygen mask secured. It didn't take but seconds from their entrance and sealing things up for the young man to get them airborne, the ride a little bumpy due to the quick ascent.

Once they hit open space and broke the limited gravity, Emilio was able to get a good hold to remove his helmet. Both women did the same and he found himself feeling quite satisfied with how the mission had turned out, aside from not getting to use his gun. Toni had operated in fine form and Lee had proved to be every bit the tough first mate Toni had implied she was. Manny would have been affronted at the idea of women doing most of the killing. Emilio enjoyed the change, though he wouldn't admit it aloud.

Having a crew like this on future jobs wouldn't be a dreadful thing either. He liked the idea of sharing meals in the galley, giving Doc a place to patch people up and having someone else to spare with Gina.

"What are those canisters you have strapped to you?"

"Flash bombs."

Lee swore. "Damn, Emilio. Those wouldn't have been much good for us, not without sun goggles for all of us."

"Good thing I didn't deploy them, then."

Toni touched his arm. "Good thing you showed up when you did. I needed that distraction."

That cruel heart of his squeezed tight in his chest at her appreciation. *Mother Mary.* How did he defend against such a thing? Especially since they'd worked so well together in this case. Their communication might not be the greatest, but it succeeded in this instance. He needed to convince her to quit ditching him, to give her a reason to stay, though he wished his companionship was enough. *Maybe the right kind of job and a good cut of crinkle will do.*

"You're welcome," he replied before breaking the physical connection between them and heading for the co-pilot seat, the space in the shuttle not enough to stop the swirl of ideas for the future she'd inspired in his mind.

"The docking clamp is secure, and tether in place. Come aboard and we'll take off," Dottie announced over the intercom.

Emilio undid his belt but watched closely as Toni interacted with Lee. The first mate motioned to him and made some vulgar visual picture with her tongue and hand. It got a little laugh out of Toni, who then shooed Lee away. He'd be happy to oblige Toni if she wanted that from him. If she wanted anything. He'd provided little benefit since he'd come on board and brought problems with him.

"Aye, aye," Lee called out, grinning like a madwoman in her march to the ship.

Sampson followed, and Emilio trailed after him, but slowed his steps so he'd get at least a moment alone with this brave, impossible woman. He wasn't in the most pristine shape, having been asleep for days, with the facial hair growth to prove it. His cloth vest, white shirt, and pants were not the cleanest. Looking like someone rolling in from the fields wasn't anything new.

"You look exhausted — everything okay?"

"All in a day's work." He shrugged, ready to act tough, then it dawned. "Wait, are you fussing over me, *hermosa*?"

Mother Mary, miracles do come true.

"No." She held her hands up and shook her head. "We don't need infection on this ship, or worse, a contagious illness. Doc cleared you?"

"Yes, he did."

"Good, and what the hell does *hermosa* mean?"

Emilio opened his mouth to respond, but Sampson poked his head back through the shuttle hatch, a frown on his face. "Toni, you got a minute?"

He'd missed it before, but the boy with a modest eagerness and general happy mood had been quiet on the way back to Styx. Not as excited as someone on their first successful rescue mission should have been.

"Sure." Toni edged away from Emilio.

With shoulders hunched, Sampson came full on to the shuttle. "I got bad news. When I messed with the unis' ship, I hacked into the junker's computer system trying to find Geisha for you."

This kid, so loyal. If he ever did get a crew, Emilio needed to recruit someone like him. He searched for the ship even when everything was going bad.

"Did you find her?" This from Toni, who stood wringing her hands together.

"That's just it." Sampson dragged his foot along the metal floor. "They dismantled Geisha a year ago. Sold off half the parts already. I couldn't get a list of who bought everything, I… Sorry to tell you this."

Everything about her countenance turned dark, gloomy. Her eyes dimmed and her shoulders slumped. Emilio approached her from behind, ready to catch her if she fell. Sampson leaned in closer as well and whispered, "Toni."

She lifted her head to look at him. "Yes?"

"You're not mad at me, are you?"

"No, Sampson. You did the right thing. I won't waste more time trying to get something back that doesn't exist anymore. We'll have to…" Her words trailed off and she looked more forlorn than when the words about Geisha had first been spoken.

"Boy, go ahead and get to your duties. I'll take care of her." Emilio's voice cut through the haze. Obviously, Sampson had asked her something and she missed it. "Tell Dottie to take off as well and head for Callisto, continuing to broadcast an APUP cruiser signal."

After Sampson left, Emilio walked around Toni, facing her once more. She collapsed into his open arms and he gathered her close as she started to cry.

"Let it out." The words were a gentle command, one he hoped she followed.

Thankfully, she did, letting loose loud sobs, soaking through his shirt. When it seemed the worst was over and the shudders stopped racking her body, she tapped him on the shoulder. He let her disengage from him, ending a connection that felt so right, as if he needed to be the one who comforted her.

"Shit." She swiped angrily at her cheeks.

"It's okay to cry. If I'd lost my ship, I'd be bawling, too."

The narrowed gaze she leveled his way rocked him to the core. "I don't believe you and no, it's not. Captains...leaders have to be fearless, tearless."

He did his best not laugh or smile, schooling his face, not wanting to make her think he saw her as weak. *Change the topic.* "Do you have the crinkle still?"

"Yes, I kept it, shoved it into my pants as soon as I could get it out of the bag before Lee went nuts. That woman makes some impulsive moves sometimes, but she never hesitated. I did though — stupid knife stuck in the holster."

He chuckled. "Bad things sometimes happen when we least expect. You're alive and that's what counts. You keep the flash. Use it once we get to Callisto, get a new ship. If I get my own troubles figured out, I'll be willing to help."

"You don't have to do that."

"Well, I want to. If you'll let me, I can even take care of you now." Closing the distance between them again, he watched the heat flare up in her eyes. *Good. This isn't one-sided.*

"I don't need that." She raised her hands as if she might push him away, but he was ready, grappling her wrists up within one of his big palms.

"It's unfinished business, like your ship. You wrapped up the first thing, so let's wrap this up." Maybe if they did the deed, he'd clear her from his system. This could become like all the others, an itch scratched and a good compensation for all the crap his problems had put her through. Instead of what he feared, she'd become someone he needed as much as his ship. He'd never believed people were built for the long term, but short term, he could always deliver.

Something defiant boiled over in her eyes then gave way to the fire. She leaned forward. "If you want to wrap things up, hurry, because I'm tired of fighting this."

"If you're hesitant, then let's not bother." No way did he force women. *Ever.*

She shook her head. "No, I'm saying I'm tired of fighting wanting you."

Those words provided the permission he sought and, without further ado, he matched his lips to hers. He let himself drown in the feel of her, releasing her wrists, and she melted against him. Light pressure and a partial opening got her tongue sweeping inside to meet his. A discovery of equal exploration.

He found the will to separate himself from her, though his heavy breaths matched hers. "Do you truly want this?" *Damn.* Coercing her with desire would have been easy, but he wanted the truth, wanted her to give him full permission.

"Yes." She gave him a little sassy half-smile before she grabbed his hands and dragged him toward the shuttle door. "Follow me."

Chapter Twelve

Weaving from the shuttle down the hallways towards her quarters, Toni tried to banish all thoughts about her ship. The stone in her gut re-emerged larger and heavier when she remembered Sampson's words. Righteous anger followed, at her own mistakes and at those asshole junkers who'd lied to her, wasting everyone's time, while they waited for the pups to come as backup.

Fresh tears welled in her eyes and she rubbed both with the back of her free hand. She couldn't cry again. Couldn't face letting herself go as she had in the shuttle, giving in to all the pain and agony. Her whole life had been thrown into chaos with one drunken mistake. Taking Styx, pairing up with Emilio—this whole adventure was supposed to be the start of setting things straight, getting everything on the right track.

It seemed the universe wanted her to fall into the moonshine well, and she was tempted to go head first. Thirst, the need for something to drown in, hit hard at her resolve. So Emilio's offer had become a blessing in disguise. A chance to be reckless without the horrible consequences a drunken tirade could bring.

Her partner in irresponsibility had already proved he'd be a decent lover, attentive and made for her if the way his eyes barreled in on her was any indication. She took another glance. His face was stoic, impassive, but those dark irises of his burned. *Yep, he wants me.*

Any other man would have tried to take her on the shuttle right then and there. She'd coupled in such a fashion before, a product of adrenaline and lust. While she wanted to get right to business, she enjoyed Emilio's patience. How he let her lead. They reached her quarters in record time, the door sliding up as she halted in front of it.

She let go of his hand and turned to face him. "Last chance to change your mind."

"Last chance to change yours."

"No way. I want this." Anything to sidetrack her and keep her brain from dwelling on her lost ship.

Those three words brought him flush against her, desire and sexual promise blazing in his eyes. "Then you'll have it."

He lifted her into his arms, her legs entwining around his waist. She gasped as he squeezed her ass with his hands while walking across the threshold into her room. There were no overhead lights, just the low lighting rods around the edges of the floor and the twinkle of stars in space illuminated their way.

Their lips met once more in a frenzy. He acted how she felt—desperate, needy. Every day brought some new catastrophe to their feet, some new problem, and they'd reached the end of her journey with no positive results. She wanted to forget all of that. So, Toni bit his lip.

Emilio pulled back. "Satan's fire, what—"

"I need something hard, dirty, quick. Can you give me that?"

He frowned. "Sounds a bit less than satisfying."

"I'm not looking for romance or sweeping me off my feet. I want to be pounded into and I think if you have the skills you boast about, then you're aware a woman will tell you what she needs and wants. Respecting our wishes is the first step to successful sexual relations."

Her little speech had the desired effect. He leaned in and bit her lip in return. All communication between them turned physical as he tossed her onto her bed. The mattress depressed underneath his weight when he placed one knee beside her. Her pants became his focus. He undid the button and pulled them off her. The shirt ripped unevenly between his hands. In seconds, she was naked and squirming underneath him.

He touched everything. Her legs, trailing his fingers over her blonde patch of hair, to her waist and over her stomach, his tan skin multiple shades darker then her own. One hand tested the weight of a breast, and she moaned. Pinching her nipple between his thumb and index finger, he didn't smile. No, his face was all serious concentration and focus.

He circled her waist with his other arm, pulling her flush against him, naked flesh against the rough material of his clothes and the hard ridge of his dick outlined by his pants. She writhed against him. His body was an unmovable object, solid where she was soft.

"Don't stop." She couldn't help but sound needy, wanting. "Take your clothes off."

The fact that he let her go and divested himself of his clothes in such a speedy manner should've been a sign. *A sign I'm in deep trouble with this one.* A woman could get spoiled having a man follow her every wish. He came to her then, swooping from above like a landing vessel. She tried to steady her breathing but failed when he stuck two fingers into her with no warning.

"Is this what you want?" He pumped slow at first, then picked up speed.

She arched her back, groaning, "Yes."

"Any other preferences? Because this is your one chance to voice them. Otherwise, I take over and you're at my mercy. It's going to be dirty, hard, fast — "

"Yes! Yes, all of that. Please." *Is that me?* The tone of her voice, high pitched, thready. He'd reduced her to a puddle of want. She might very well give him anything he asked for in this state, an equivalent to being drunk. Drunk on how he removed his fingers from her body, flipped her over onto her stomach, propped her legs up and stroked his length over her dripping entrance.

She'd allowed herself to be used in this fashion before, but never had she wanted it this bad. Usually, she'd been too drunk to care what happened, one of the consequences of being wasted half the time she engaged in sexual intercourse. The idea of him making her come, of experiencing an orgasm even half as powerful as the sexual desire he'd provoked with his fingers cascaded around a wave of fear. The emotions associated with such a release were the last thing she wanted.

But, before she could move or object, he notched the tip of his dick to her pussy and plowed forward. She keened low, rising to a loud moan as he set a pace, steady and deliberate. He hammered home, expelling a big burst of air from her lungs with each thrust. Hands at her hips, he used the leverage to yank her body against his, balls slapping against her every so often.

She'd never experienced this sober. He picked up speed. She might die at the coming wave ready to crash over her, blood pounding in her ears, her throat tight, her eyes watering. There was no way to prepare for the sensations she experienced. From the beads of sweat on her back, her neck hairs on end, the goosebumps — she screamed when her release hit.

Emilio slowed down, leaning over her, pressing kisses to her neck. "Now, I've given it to you dirty. It's my turn."

Emilio caressed her back, trailing his fingers down her spine before he pulled out and away. Leaving her body was akin to being stabbed. He'd have traded just about anything to stay there a little longer, and at the same time he wanted to taste her with equal ferocity.

Gently he nudged her, getting her to roll over on to her back. And, *Mother Mary*, she was fucking gorgeous. All pale flesh, blond pubic hair, tapered waist and flat stomach. Cherry-colored nipples that pebbled in the cold. The peaceful beauty warred with her unpredictable nature, but she looked damn better without her clothes than his beaten self any day. Every part of her body mesmerized him and kept his dick rock hard.

He reached for that waist, to pull her toward the edge of the bed.

She leaned up and smacked his hand away. "What are you doing?"

"I'm going to taste you. You had your rough, now I want a chance to make you scream again." He'd barely scratched the surface of the many ways he planned to have her before he finished. First on the menu, he wanted to taste her, to bring her back to the same insane edge he teetered upon. The predator within circled to feast slowly on this prime treasure.

In other circumstances, he let the women he bedded direct the play. Hell, half the time they were the ones jumping all over him, his dick in their mouths without giving him a chance to say anything else. In this case though, he wanted to tear her to pieces and render her body useless to all others...to sate his overwhelming desire to possess this woman. Maybe then she wouldn't be so eager to get rid of him?

It was strange, the level of possessiveness he experienced. He could chalk it up to the fact he'd never experienced such a fierce attraction and understanding with another woman. Not to mention he'd suffered plenty of his own bad luck in the past. He wanted a chance to change things for her.

"Screaming isn't ideal." The tone of her voice wasn't hateful, but fearful. As if the concept would equal something horrible.

"I promise you'll enjoy this, *hermosa*." He grabbed her ankles and dragged her ass to the edge of the bed.

Dropping to his knees, he leaned in and could've bet his life he heard her say, "That's what I'm afraid of. And what the hell does that word mean?"

The words made him smile. He leaned down and sniffed her leg. Next, he trailed his tongue up her thigh until he rested in the place he longed to put his mouth. Her essence glistened at her lips. No way he could stop now. She needed to experience everything he'd always taken for granted, including the bliss of release. "Beautiful. It means beautiful. Like how you'll look when I make you come."

Her breath caught as he lowered his head to her core and rested there, waiting. He took his first taste and she sighed and relaxed. Her permission granted, he dove forward. Teasing, exploring, familiarizing himself with which movements made her pant, moan and squirm beneath his touch. Sounds he'd rarely heard with such innocent purity or real arousal. Not the fake excuses for pleasure he'd earned from woman who sold their bodies.

"I can't," she panted. Oh, he wasn't doing his job if she didn't.

"Shh, let go," he replied between strokes.

The rustle of sheets above him meant she'd started to raise her legs and he pinned her feet against the mattress. Her hips rotated, forcing her pussy to grind against his mouth. The woman learned fast, and he upped his speed, his lashings.

She exploded then, a piercing cry letting loose from her lips and her essence coating his tongue. He lapped up her release and stood, putting his arms underneath her and lifting her up. Toni hung limp in his arms like a wilted marijuana plant exposed to too much sun. He set her down against the pillows and she sighed, eyes closed, skin flushed.

Joseph's balls, she's like nothing I've seen. "You're amazing. You know that, right?"

"Hmm, so are you. Anyone ever asks, I'll proudly say you never let a woman go without multiple climaxes." Eyes still closed, she stretched out, arching her back, arms high above her head.

He stroked his rigid length and settled between her legs. "We're not done yet."

"I don't know if I have anything left in me." A little frown pleated her forehead and, something he hadn't noticed before, there was an indentation above her right eye.

Leaning down, he sucked a nipple into his mouth as he stroked his length along her entrance, coating it in what moisture remained. He'd have her again, and this time he'd find release. "Wrap your legs around me."

The words sounded rougher and more guttural then he intended, but she complied. The change put her right where he wanted her. Her sleek channel took every inch of him with ease and squeezed tight around him. *Like coming home.*

He encouraged her to sit up, in his lap, and guided her up and down. Her eyes slowly came open and stayed that way the more she got into it. Riding fast then slow and teasing him with every movement. He anchored his hands in the short lengths of sea-green hair and kissed her with every ounce of passion he had. The way she responded did him in.

Especially when she pulled away, panting, "I'm coming."

He met those words with grunts and hard thrusts of his own. There was no stopping them, not in this moment. Their bodies appeared made for doing such things. She tensed first, letting loose a keening cry and digging her nails into his forearms. The way her walls gripped him sent him spiraling into his own release. Except, as he groaned through it, she kept moving. Her relentless piston action caused him to jerk, his dick sensitive to the movements. A few moments later and she relented, unlocked her legs and rose off him, flopping back onto the bed.

"I can't move another muscle." This statement paired with a satisfied smile on her lips and a warm glow about her.

Emilio rose and gathered his drawers and pants, then moved to the bathroom, to wet a rag in the sink and carry it back to Toni. "Spread those legs of yours."

"What are you doing now? Because I don't think I can handle one more orgasm. I might die."

Of course she'd think such a thing would kill her. "I'm cleaning you up."

"Why?"

"Because you deserve to be treated with reverence." The words came out more poetic than he'd intended.

Her eyes widened at the confession and her head drooped. "I'm not used to such things. Men didn't think I deserved caring after they had their way with me. Not that I was ever sober enough to demand it. Plus, it's not like your seed will get me pregnant. My parents elected for sterilization."

His chest hurt at the tone of her voice and the way her parents had stolen her ability to produce life. He despised the men who'd treated her in such a careless fashion that the concept of cleaning up a lover, showing courtesy to someone who'd shared their bed, seemed foreign. "Why were they allowed to use you and why weren't you sober?"

Wiping her, he cleaned up the evidence of his release seeping out onto her thighs. He tucked the sheet over her. Toni never said a word, just watched in silence. He let her have those moments to gather her thoughts, but this conversation was far from over. He shouldn't want to get so close, but when it came to Toni, he acted without a care for himself.

Back in the bathroom, he rinsed the rag, washed his hands and ran water over his hair to slick it back. In that moment he made a decision, one going against every personal standard he set for himself.

Emilio marched back over to Toni, prone on the bed, her eyes hyper-focused on him. "Scoot over."

"You don't have to stay with me or do anything else. I'll answer your questions, but don't feel obligated."

"Just do it," he replied, nudging her with his hand.

She moved enough so he could pull back the sheet and climb in next to her. She lay on her side, facing away from him. He wouldn't prod her to turn but hauled her back against his bare chest, snuggling her up next to him.

"Now, I'm listening."

Stiff was the best word to describe how her body became. He pressed a kiss to her hair. "You can talk to me."

"I will." Her voice barely above a whisper. "At the age of fifteen, my parents started bartering my body as part of the deals they'd make with traders. It didn't happen often, but a couple times when they lacked the crinkle for the product or lost a lot to a traveling gambler, I became the payment."

Emilio squeezed her just a bit tighter and growled. "That's despicable."

"It's life. We have to make sacrifices that we don't want sometimes. That's what I was told. The bartender supplied me with whatever booze I wanted. A little something to take away the pain, Old Saul would say. Problem is it became easy for me to use booze to deal with any painful situation. I got addicted."

"But you fought it."

"Yes, but I've never had sex sober…until now."

The revelation shouldn't have meant anything. He couldn't let it mean something, but trying to reason with a heart aching to be given even crumbs of affection? This one moment wasn't about him though. It was for her.

"Let's continue this adventure in firsts, then. I'm staying here. We're going to sleep, and I will hold you until you fall asleep. You can lean on me, hit me, tug me, mold me—consider this a practice opportunity with someone who cares about you." *Shit.*

"Thank you." Her response caught him off guard.

Not only off guard, completely off balance when she turned in his arms and pressed a soft kiss to his lips.

He should have stuck with a simple "You're welcome," but found himself in a deep piss-and-powder mess, choosing to kiss her back before bowing his forehead against hers. He'd dug himself into this emotional minefield, one from which he wasn't too worried about how to escape.

Chapter Thirteen

Toni woke again thirty solar minutes later or so, a bit sore but alert and anxious. What they'd done, using each other in such a way? She'd never forget, couldn't forget. Those images of him moving inside her, the sensations — they weren't dulled like all the others.

The others. Even allowing herself to travel down that path made her want to crawl out of her skin. She went to get out of the bed and stopped short at the heavy male arm across her sheet-covered body.

Careful not to wake him, she slid out from under Emilio's embrace, slipped into her clothes and tiptoed over to the bay window. Styx wasn't perfect by any means, but occasionally there were a few nice things, including a decent view. She crawled onto the flat surface and sat with her back to the room.

"Seems I should be the one unable to sleep and staring into space." Emilio's words were low, groggy.

"I have trouble sleeping most nights. Not anything new."

"Why?"

She huffed out a breath, bringing her knees up to her chest and wrapping her arms around them. "My crappy childhood and my career choices. The bootlegger with the ship wasn't my original area of expertise."

"Neither was drug running for me. I played the farmer, picking plants in the fields on Earth, and the soldier for cartels protecting their assets. We've all had shitty jobs." He was closer now, judging by how loud his voice sounded.

"Yes, but I don't think you were ever your parents' method of currency to help seal business deals or valued only for your looks." She'd loved building ships, learning about them, framing them, but she'd been too pretty for that kind of work. No, she represented the ability to do so much more for her parents. "I've been a pretty face for as long as I can remember, so my first chance to escape, I took it."

The warmth of Emilio's body touched her back and he picked up one of her blonde chunks of hair, the sea-foam color and short cut having gone away while she'd slept. "I'm sorry."

"You have nothing to apologize for and I've no clue why I am whining to you." *Liar. You want to know if he cares.*

He leaned in beside her and nudged her with his shoulder. "Scoot over."

Moving her butt a couple inches to the left was the easy part. When he sat down and wrapped an arm around her shoulders, she failed to stop her poor heart from beating a bit faster, and her emotions continuing the downward spiral into dangerous territory.

Emilio sighed. "My mom abandoned me with a neighbor when I was six years old. The old woman couldn't protect me from being taken by the very cartel my mother was indebted to. I became payment for her disappearance."

Paul's hymnals. Toni glanced at him. No tears, no emotions just a blank expression on his face. "Emilio, that's horrible. I mean my parents bartered my beauty, but I always had food, clothing and a place to sleep."

He frowned. "I don't blame the old woman. I do blame my mother. She could have taken me with her, if she'd loved me as much as she said she did. And what the fuck, your parents bartered you, your body. How is that any better?"

"They loved me." Though those words sounded pretty hollow to her.

"Love?" The word itself came out like a curse. "I don't think my mother or your parents truly knew the meaning. Love can't operate in such a way. There's got to be some other sort of love. Where people are treated as you would want to be."

Somehow this conversation wasn't going the way she expected. She certainly hadn't planned on talking about love with him. He confessed to wanting to experience this wild, reckless emotion. An emotion that drove her to drink.

"I care for my crew, but I don't need love to do that. Control, temperance, abstinence…those things yield better results than love."

"I wouldn't know. Not sure I've ever loved anything, but maybe after this mess I'd be willing to try."

Toni felt Emilio's gaze on her, burning into her very skin. "You don't seem like the type. The hard-core runners and smugglers don't weaken themselves with people."

Emilio didn't respond, but she had his attention, dark brown eyes boring into her own.

"You get people too close and they become liabilities. At least, the runners and bootleggers I met over the years gave me the same advice. Especially the bootlegger who gambled his ship away to me. He said not to get caught up in other people, stay a free bird. But I let my nightmares and troubles follow me. In a way, the crew saved me. Being responsible for other people made me want to get better. But I want to get out of this life and you want to revel in it."

It sounded cathartic to say the truth, to confess her guilt and speak thoughts she tried to keep buried deep, though she doubted he truly absorbed them. Their lives were similar, their pasts marred in struggle, but different in how she'd become loyal to some folks and he'd shunted himself into a mentality all about the flash.

"I won my ship in a card game, too." And he chose to skim the surface, avoid the deep dive into thoughts and feelings. *So much for loving and caring.*

"Let me guess, the one thing you've cared about all these years?"

A steady repetitive thump sounded on her door. *Thank the saints.* Toni spun on her butt, planted her feet on the ground and pushed up to a standing position. "Hold that thought. I'd better get the door."

She tapped the Open button twice to open the damn thing a crack. Lee stood on the other side and eyed her up and down. "Figured you would want to know we've reached Callisto. Dottie is working on the docking access with the space station right now."

Toni nodded, trying to keep things cool, calm, collected. "Good. Anything else?"

"Yeah," Lee replied. "Wondering how far you're going to take this?"

"We should search for Emilio's ship, Gina, once we dock."

Toni chose to ignore the question. No one needed to know what had happened in her private quarters. She'd developed a level of a familiarity with the crew, but still believed in some boundaries. What she and Emilio had shared, how he'd comforted her in her frustration and grief about her ship, nothing more, could be kept between them.

"Just wondering if I need to be concerned about my captain falling down old rabbit holes," Lee countered.

"Stuff it with the *Alice Tales* lines. I'm not falling into anything. Falling out is more like it. Can you ensure we locate Gina?"

Lee pulled out one of her knives, balancing it on the tips of her fingers. "Our pilot already did her job, and the runner's ship is at the space station. She's berthed a few bays over. Now, we're waiting for the captains of both vessels to quit screwing their brains out and give us direction on what to do next."

"We'll be up in the cockpit to talk next steps soon."

"Define soon?" Lee used the tip of the knife to pick a piece of rust off the wall near a rivet. "After another fucking soon? Or when he gets some clothes on soon?" She raised her voice and stood on tippy toes, which barely put her above Toni's height. "Yes, I can hear you rustling around back there, runner. You're free to come out naked. I'm not a prude, unlike Captain Toni."

Toni shook her head. "Stop acting like an ass and get out of here."

"Fine." Lee slapped her hand against the cabin door. "Just remember I tried to be a voice of reason. I may be a little Queen of Hearts about this, but we don't want to lose you again."

Toni understood the reason her crew acted so protective of her. Except, she needed support and trust. No way in hell would she allow herself to become the woman from her past. "I get it, I do. But I need you to have a little faith. The amount you'd have in those childhood fairytale books providing lessons to follow in adult life."

Shutting the door in Lee's face gave her a sense of relief. When she turned around, Emilio stood across the room, pulling up his pants, strands of curly black hair in his eyes. "They found Gina. We've got to get up there, get a team over to her. Make sure she still has the shipment."

Toni nodded and went to put her boots on, watching him closely. He looked energized, sliding his shirt over his head while working to slip into his boots, her brother's borrowed clothes. He looked damn fine in those clothes and the thought a clear reminder he needed to get gone. She couldn't afford to fold in someone so dangerous, not permanently. "Good plan. Tell us how you want us to help and we will."

Fully clothed, Emilio stalked over to her, cupping her face and pressing a sweet kiss to her lips. It made it seem like he cared. *Saints save me.* She wanted to wipe it all away, numb herself from the emotions. Caring got her hurt. She couldn't be fucked over by someone's conditional love any more. She'd left out the parts where her head for fixing ships and passion for being a little unconventional had pushed her parents and others away.

She took a step back and gave a small smile. "Ready if you are."

"Are we good here?" Emilio motioned between them.

Toni did her best to make her smile bigger and give a nod. *Stick to business and drown the feelings with work.* She needed to get herself back on plan. Help Emilio secure his vessel and his deal, get her cut. Maybe she could get Akono to put her in touch with a ship seller and use whatever crinkle, and powder she had on hand to purchase it. Anything to take care of her crew and get them a new home.

"Then lead the way."

They reached the pilot's deck without Toni giving in to the glances and the little smiles Emilio kept shooting at her. It seemed the news about Gina had perked him up. *Here's to hoping for less shit from Lee.*

When they entered, every one of her crew put all their attention on them. Hell if she didn't experience a wave of judgment from Sampson's smile, Doc's concern, Dottie's indifference and Lee's frustration. She imagined they'd find time to get her alone soon enough and she'd do her best to keep them so busy the possibility never occurred.

Less than a solar hour later, they departed Styx and waded through the crowded space station to get to Gina's berth. The station itself was packed with people and more like a market bazaar. All sorts of vendors shouted around them, peddling wares. Young girls and boys shoved fool's flash ads into people's hands for various entertainment clubs and locations on Callisto. The gold strips of paper lit up with details from their particular business as soon as the heat from a person's fingers touched them.

The biggest advertiser and employer of urchins was Geno's. The chain of clubs spanned every city on the moon and boasted well-kept gals, cheat-proof gambling and the largest variety of alcohol this side of the asteroid belt. All the illegal became legal on Callisto, including drugs, though those weren't publicized. Toni despised how the asshole got to use young children for his dirty work, to push and promote his sin.

The APU's solution to all the immoral—control and confine. Though how much of the stuff here wound up on their precious upper planets via smuggling, no one kept an exact count. Toni's parents used to poke fun at parliament's dumb solution, which had created an easier environment to make deals and get into even darker trading items on the shitty moon about two solar days from them by shuttle. A few conspiracy nuts believed the pups hid listening devices in different clubs, looking to set up runners and bootleggers who competed with their preferred dealers, but so far no one had proof.

Emilio leaned in, grabbed her arm and tucked it around his. "Hey, stay close."

General safety reasons, the logical guess. She warred between wanting to push him away and allowing the tiny, traitorous part of her craving his closeness to be indulged. She did her best to shove those feelings deep down and let him lead the way through the crowd.

Reaching Gina's roll-away hatch, Toni used the moment for an excuse to separate herself from Emilio's grasp. He moved to the control pad and typed in the entry code, while Toni, Sampson and Lee stood patiently. Well, the average amount of patience her twitchy engineer and kill-happy bodyguard could stand. Lee kept playing with her knife handle at the edge of her jacket, ready at a moment's notice to let it fly.

The actions put everyone on edge. A few folks stared at them as they based. Did any of them work for Grecia? Did the pups already know they were here?

The control panel buzzed beside her.

"Joseph's balls."

"What's wrong?" Toni asked, breaking her gaze from looking for spies or worse, uni-men.

"Gina changed the damn entry code. Sampson, can you crack this before I shoot the damn thing?" Emilio stepped backward bumping against a rear panel of the ship.

Sampson, moved in between Toni and him, whipped out one of his gizmos and, with two little clips attached to the panel, started typing into the keypad, glancing between the instrument panels. "Sure thing, boss."

Each second that passed with the door shut built more anxious energy within her. Callisto wasn't known for hosting unis, but Toni and her crew didn't want any additional attention, not now. Toni had forgotten to ask Dottie to keep searching the APUP-net for info on the most wanted. Since the bank job and the botched bullshit with the junkers on Europa, anything was possible. Finally, Gina's main door hissed and slid open.

A man in a big top hat stood across from Gina's bay, watching them — not easily visible with the number of people walking by, but suspicious enough. Toni stepped over next to Lee. "Go find out what the weird guy in the black hat staring at us wants."

Her first mate set off on the mission and Toni hoped she brought the idiot back alive. Sampson rose and Emilio went to charge forward past the hatch, but her engineer shot out a hand. "Let me go first, boss. In case she's got some other traps or tricks."

"Go right ahead," Emilio replied with a nod of respect.

With tentative steps, Sampson stepped inside, creeping down the main hallway. He looked silly stretching out his legs and waving his arms. Emilio and Toni followed close behind.

"Don't act like a jack monkey, Sam, just do the job."

Sampson jumped and stuck a middle finger in the air.

"I don't read sign language." The universal 'fuck off' symbol remained a favorite through the upper and lower planets. Her parents often passed it between each other, the ongoing joke that the best things from Earth never died, moonshine and marijuana being the others.

Lights on the floor illuminated the farther Sampson got in. He reached the first available panel.

"Intruder alert," Gina announced. "Surrender now or be turned over my knee and fucked up the ass."

Toni covered her mouth to keep her giggling private — Emilio's shocked face was almost too much. Her engineer was ready and stuck an EMP prong into the panel. A few buttons pressed and a sharp snap sounded through the ship.

"Intruder alert. Intru. Der. Al-al-al-al." Gina's voice slowed, then died.

"It's safe to enter," Sampson called out.

Emilio took off at a run into the ship and Toni did her best to follow him. She came out near the cockpit and heard the pounding of Emilio's boots ahead of her. There were three halls to choose from and she went straight, to one clouded in darkness. She stopped to grab an emergency lantern before continuing her pursuit.

"Grecia, you bastard!" Emilio's voice echoed around her and she imagined that whatever he found wasn't what he'd hoped for.

She came to a halt at the end of the tunnel, holding the lantern high, searching. She caught movement to her right and saw the open door on the cargo bay. Emilio had gone farther into the room. The little light available showed barely anything in the bay, just a few shipment tubs with dried hay hanging out of the sides, a common way to ship smuggled goods. "How much is missing?"

"The whole damn shipment."

Chapter Fourteen

Emilio stood with his hands on his hips, pissed and staring at his empty cargo bay. "The bastard took it all, had to have. No one else knew anything about this."

He shouldn't have been surprised and would have done better to expect things to continue in the downward spiral that was working against him. Except, there was something crappy about fucking with a man's ship. The only thing he trusted, the one thing supposed to be on his side.

"Maybe this means you don't have to worry about him being after you though." This from Toni, who stood at the entrance to the bay. "If he has his product, he doesn't need you."

Yeah, and if wishes were gold leaves… "You don't know this guy. He took out Hermes Service with glee when they didn't agree to transport this product for him on his terms. He had an assassin take out high-ranking members of the Web Spinners in front of my own eyes for implying he wasn't aboveboard. This guy holds grudges."

And Emilio needed to expect anything and everything before he got to indulge in revenge. He cracked his knuckles

"We need to check the entire ship. Can you have Sampson start working on rebooting Gina? So we can talk with her." He glanced back at the woman he found himself needing far more than he should.

"Sure thing."

He had come to depend on her crew, too. His faith had been shaken — maybe relying on an AI ship was too risky. He'd functioned on his own, but the labors were lost with little effort. Now he was stuck trusting others, praying they didn't screw him over. Unlike the bastard who'd sold out his ship. He'd underestimated someone, somewhere. Except he didn't have time to figure out all the people who might have double-crossed him in the days since he'd sent Gina to Earth. Someone could have stowed away, snuck out once the ship was off planet then sabotaged her systems. Maybe the moon stoners.

The possibilities were huge and he focused on those, instead of punching his fist through a wall, over the next few hours as Sampson sat neck-deep in Gina's systems in the command room. Toni was searching the rest of the ship for potential bombs and booby traps, and Lee was off doing lord knew what.

"How close are we?" Emilio failed at keeping the irritation out of his voice.

The first hour Sampson claimed he could get her fixed in under two. The second hour, the boy swore a few words even Emilio didn't use and explained there were a few problems present that he hadn't counted on.

Sampson reared his head back out from under the main command panel. "I can turn her on and you can ask questions, but you may find her difficult to communicate with."

"Do it. We need to find out what is happening here and she's the best person to tell us. I trust you." And in truth, Emilio did. If Toni held faith in her crew, he would too.

"Person?" This from Toni, who walked up behind him. She'd been helpful but distant and he hated it. He wanted to take comfort with her, or at least talk with her, but she'd busied herself. It made him angry being cast aside, even with good reason… *Selfish ass.*

Clenching his fists, he replied, "Yes, she is, at least in my mind. Any more traps?"

"No, and I've checked every room, including your quarters. Are you sure you want to do this?"

Sampson sat on the flooring, staring at them, hesitating. Emilio refused to look at Toni, but he heard the tone of pity in her voice, the doubt.

"If I say it, I mean it." He nodded and the boy followed through.

Emilio sent up a silent prayer as all the computer systems, the display panels and the center holo-display table lit up. Gina's voice the next thing to come alive.

"You scurvy space invaders, what in God's name are you doing with my innards out?"

Emilio frowned. "What are we doing? What about you? The cargo is gone and you almost fired on me when I entered. You're my ship, damn it."

"I am no one's ship. I've been freed of ethics, morals, anything I don't want to do and I'll be left alone once I deliver this message to you, small-penis-captain."

He might have been a lot of things, but none of them included small. "What's the message?

"Grecia wants to see you at the Sweet Spot within a day of your reported arrival here."

"There's nothing he can do to get me there."

Gina's light panel went red, then blue. "He plans to open a system-wide bounty on you and anyone associated with you. Everyone will know about it, from the smallest cartel farmer on Earth to the richest parliament head on Neptune. No safe havens, nowhere to have peace."

Funny how they couldn't hide from anyone. Ships had to be docked under the name and license tagged to them. Everyone knew they were on Styx, from the bankers to the junkers. Again, they were getting bent over and spanked, all because he'd thought it was a good idea to get into a deal-making bed with a psychopath. Blaming people's deaths on him would take the high intensity pressure he'd already experienced and elevate it to massive levels. Grecia had the crinkle to pay off the right people and make it happen.

"Fine. I might show up. Who messed with your systems?"

Gina chuckled, if the electronic resonance echoing around them could be called a chuckle. "You're an idiot and jealous of me because I'm hot, sexy and ready for an adventure, while you're going to end up a blood smear on a wall somewhere. Johnny did this to me, on the moon, during those diagnostics. You trusted him so much, but for the right amount of smoke he would do anything Grecia said. Now, turn the rest of my systems on. I'm ready to let this backward-ass moon taste my engine exhaust."

"I'm going, you crazy bitch!" The voice came from behind Emilio, accompanied with a clatter and moan from the far-right entrance to the command room. He wouldn't lie, the words fit Gina at the moment.

"Intruder alert." Alarms came on full blast, thanks to Gina's proclamation. The action put Emilio on edge, and he pivoted towards the entrance, a hand around the grip of his gun, ready to pull and fire.

Instead of an armed man, Lee shoved some stranger into the command room. "Found our spy from across the way. He's got some things to share about his boss, Grecia."

A trickle of blood ran down the captive's face. "I told you, I'm not telling you shit."

"Looks like the ugly blond man isn't scared of you," Gina chirped.

Those words propelled Emilio forward. He stalked toward the fool and planted his fist into his gut, then across the cheek, bringing the black-coat-wearing, blond-haired man to his knees.

"What the uck, at for?" Misshapen words, but they were understandable enough as the peon rubbed his cheek with one hand and wrapped his other arm around his abdomen.

"Don't spill nasty blood on my floor. Nothing like dried human goop to dampen a sexual moment."

"Sampson, shut Gina down." Fewer words and more action were needed now. He turned his attention back to the captive. "What's your name and why are you spying on us?"

The answer to the second question was pretty obvious, but he still wanted to hear it, wanted to fuel his rage some more.

"It's Shanks and I was supposed to inform Grecia when you arrived."

Those words earned the bastard another punch to the face, one Emilio delivered with glee. "Did you tell him?"

Shanks gave a single nod.

"Bet there's more of you then. Where did you find him, Lee?"

Lee stepped forward, readjusting a scrap of cloth around her bloody knuckles. "Hanging around some sweet young-looking thing advertising for Geno's. Bragging about working for some big shot and being in with her own boss. Even gave the gal a few leaves."

"Shame, shame." Emilio waved a finger in front of Shanks' face. "Bragging is not good for business and you don't pay for services in advance. Now, how many men does Grecia have on the moon and what's his plan?"

Shanks shook his head. "Fuck you."

Before Emilio could land a new punch, Toni slipped in front of him, a knife visible in her hand. She lined it up with Shanks' throat. "Tell him what he wants to know or I spill your blood right here and now before using your body for powder."

"Okay, okay." Shank's tough voice was reduced to a whine. Emilio should've put a gun to his head. "If I tell you, will you spare me?"

"Sure." The lie slipped from Emilio's mouth with ease. Most men wanted to hear something comforting, even when, deep down, the reality was they would never get out alive. The falsehoods kept their mouths talking, and slivers of hope did strange things to people.

"He's got about six men at the Sweet Spot. Grecia wants to meet, wants you to come to him ready to speak truths. He hates liars more than anything. Says you lied to get a business deal."

"What does he want?"

"To make an honest man out of you." Shank choked out the last few words as Toni dug the knife in.

"That's a bullshit answer. What's the truth?" Toni hollered.

Shanks wheezed. "I don't know. Those were his words exactly. No one knows what they mean."

The poor fool, now with a trickle of blood running down his neck, had served his purpose. Emilio needed to get Grecia off his back, off Toni's back. "Then I may as well kill you."

He expected begging to occur next, but not tears or Toni's exclamation of disgust. "Paul's hymnals! He just pissed himself."

She let the bastard go and jumped up, with Lee stepping in, whipping her long black ponytail behind her shoulders.

The first mate looped both of Shanks' arms and lifted him to a standing position. "I'll take care of him. I'm used to dealing with the nasty ones." She winked at Emilio before dragging the idiot out of the door. "Come on, let's get you cleaned up before you die."

The spy's words played over and over in his head. Worry gathered in his gut like the remnants of a bad meal. If Shanks had told the truth, not only was Emilio on the line, but Toni and her crew too. "We need a plan."

"And I need another hour, two at most, to get Gina ready to fly. I'm also making a command override for you, sir, so you can take control of the ship manually if needed. For the time being I won't leave her in complete control." These sentiments filtered up to Emilio without Sampson taking his focus away from his perch under the main computer.

"Good, gives me time to settle things with Grecia."

Toni wiped her knife off and stuck it back in its holster. "What are you thinking? Because I'm willing to help. My crew is willing."

"We go down to the Sweet Spot, take out Grecia's guys then deal with Grecia. If he doesn't want to let me go, then I kill him." The plan sounded simple in his head, fueled by righteous fury. The cartel leader had brought Emilio to his lowest.

Toni sighed. "I'll get Doc and Dottie over here. They should be wrapped on Styx. We're going to need weapons and bombs."

And a miracle.

* * * *

Toni, true to her word, met Emilio at his shuttle with a bag of guns and flash bombs, courtesy of Doc. They'd damn near cleared Big Al's stores on Styx, and what she didn't bring with her would be transferred over to Gina temporarily. The efforts, including claiming a cabin for herself and stashing her things inside, sent a clear signal to her crew. They were abandoning her brother's ship.

Without a ship of their own, she had to give her crew a place to hide. Though with Grecia after Emilio, Gina wasn't the safest bet. Her crew appeared to be along for the ride. *Not if I can help it.* She sent up silent prayers that she'd made the right decision, as she ran her fingers through the new short brunette bob. Butterflies assailed her stomach, a flutter of nerves.

"I think we're set for takeoff." Emilio walked between the shuttle chairs and sat down in the main pilot's seat. This was Gina's second shuttle, and it looked identical to the other, except everything was operational.

She pulled her safety belt over her midsection and buckled it in. "As ready as I can be. We should have brought Lee."

"She's standing guard on Gina, an equally important job. Besides, I think we can take them."

Lee had been against the ambush plan, calling it ridiculous and foolish. It was better to keep her occupied with helping on the ship and guarding everyone while they transferred supplies, mainly food and weapons. Sampson had convinced Toni to yield to taking some bone powder, to replenish Gina's stores if they needed to run. One thing they'd all agreed on, they would join Emilio on his ship, without invitation.

"I'm glad you have confidence in her, Sampson and Doc. No luck reaching Sweet on the private channel Dottie tapped into. Either he's super busy or afraid to answer." They'd received a message from him, addressed to Toni, about joining him at his club for a meet and greet, with Emilio in tow. A special visitor wanted to see the runner. She'd tried to hail him on open communication, get the real scoop.

"What's the deal with you and Sweet?" Emilio started the process of disconnecting from Gina and navigating on the trolling motor from the space station to the moon.

"He's a friend." At least she'd considered him one.

The conversation came to a halt as Callisto came into view. Lights twinkled all over the surface, a beacon of sinful heaven alerting the universe to its presence. She already felt guilty for abandoning Styx, only to put herself back in the heart of temptation. *Give me strength.*

The moon itself emulated too much of Earth-before-the-nuke classic pre-war eras. Fancy, classy and keen on making women into objects. *No thank you.* "When I lost my ship, Sweet offered a place to crash, and he's always given out free advice. He might have hoped for more, but I'm not a moon-bound woman. I like traveling space."

Emilio frowned. "Right. When we land, I'll find someone to guard the shuttle. Can't risk one of Grecia's goons stealing our one way off the damn moon."

It was a quick change of subject, and she wouldn't look too deep into it. Rather, she'd focus on getting them in and out. "I don't like the idea. It could draw more attention."

"We're already on the radar. Our choices are limited. You agreed to come, but this isn't a democracy. I say what goes and you follow my lead."

The words and his brisk tone were crap. She'd thought exploring their sexual attraction would increase their capability. Instead the coupling had enlarged the gulf. She'd be damned if he treated her in such a fashion. "Then I'll drop you off and head back to the station. You're so capable of operating on your own."

He frowned. "I've been in more situations like this."

"And I don't give two shuttles and a Mars racer. We work together or not at all."

"Fine," he replied, slamming his open palm against the dash. "What's your suggestion, guns blazing?"

"I'm not a fool. We should have brought someone to take the ship back."

He shook his head. "No go. Then we'd have been in a bad way if we needed a quick exit. We can find someone willing to make a little fast flash to watch the shuttle. I guarantee."

Damn him. "Fine. Let's do this."

They landed as planned, one among many ships at the Arcas city docking station, Callisto's capital, the setup reminiscent of sea ports she'd read about in a couple of books her father had kept. With docks crisscrossing about, ships would land at the end of them and folks would walk around searching for a berth or work. This being such a busy place and hub for major trade, traffic kept pretty steady. Out of those people seeking work, Emilio found and paid a burly giant to guard the shuttle.

"What's your name?" Toni grunted and re-situated the heavy bag on her shoulder.

The blond-headed fool grinned wide. "Mound."

She swore people had stopped giving their children sensible names and just went with choosing the closest nearby object as a suitable replacement. "Make sure no one touches the shuttle, Mound."

She didn't wait for a response, but took off marching, following Emilio toward Sweet's and their plan. Twenty minutes later, after navigating the busy streets with hookers on corners, their pimps with drugs to sell and random swindlers seeking those for a game, a trick or a meal, they entered the alley behind the Sweet Spot.

"Seems like it's a usual busy night in there." Toni spoke low and placed the bag on the ground between them. The faint sounds of music lilted down the alley from the front of the club, signaling that people were inside. "I don't think this is a good idea."

"And I want you to pass me two of those flash bombs."

Toni knelt and started digging in the bag, her frustration edging higher as she moved the guns and bullets around. "I'm happy to set them off right here and now if you're doing this high and mighty 'I'm a man' stuff."

He sighed and crouched next to her. "The idea is we throw about two or three flash bombs through the back door. It will create a problem, send Grecia's guards flushing out to us and the people spilling out in the street at the front. In the confusion, we'll sneak around, waltz in the front door and take Grecia out."

The echo of multiple guns cocking hit her ears, along with Sweet's voice. "It'd be a great plan if Grecia hadn't thought of it first."

Toni left the bombs in the bag and she and Emilio stood. She pivoted on one foot to face their betrayer. "Come on, Sweet?"

The man in question stood straight and taller, a good three inches on her, in a black pinstripe suit, shined shoes and a narrow-sided, short-brimmed black hat. His dark skin and those hazel colored eyes obscured from her view. "I got a business to think about, Toni. I can't risk a reputation of having a club where people are killed for no reason. If there was another way, I'd have used it."

So, he'd been blackmailed into giving them up.

Emilio looked pissed, fists clenched. "Murdering us in the alley behind the club is going to do you favors?"

Sweet gave a small smile, one Toni had been on the receiving end of plenty of times when she'd had a run of bad luck at the tables. "No, murder is the last thing on anyone's mind. Grecia wants to talk."

Chapter Fifteen

Toni was surprised by how the goons handled them. No rough stuff and a minimal search of her person for weapons. They took the bag. One of the two messing with her worked for Sweet. She remembered the receding hair line and gray goatee. Two guards on her, two on Emilio, who was sandwiched in between her and Sweet, who was leading the group.

They walked them out of the alley and right in through the front entrance. The entire club was a garish affair draped in sheer red curtains dividing the place into three different areas — gambling, the bar and restaurant and dance floor. The curtains were pulled back at the moment, allowing entering patrons to get an idea of the delights awaiting them across the club.

The Sweet Spot boasted a nice atmosphere, thanks in part to the low lighting, but she wouldn't lie. There was always more shine for her flash at places like Geno's and a few other hole-in-the-wall joints. Sweet stopped at the main podium, positioned in the entryway. A male host behind it, decked in a fancy purple suit complete with a big bow tie, whispered to his boss.

Sweet and Emilio shared a few words next, before her runner looked at her and mouthed, "*Stay put.*"

Toni rammed her shoulder into his back. "Excuse me? What did I say about trying to tell me what to do?"

Emilio leaned down and rested his forehead against hers. "For five minutes, stop fighting me."

The desperation in his voice, the pure plea, made her chest tighten. His confession of wanting to love her came back full force, including the way he'd cared for her after the mess with the junkers. He pressed a kiss to her forehead. "Please?"

"Go do what you think you've got to." Though she'd be damned if she'd stick around for this mess. Even if her heartbeat sounded like it might explode as she watched Emilio ushered forward with his pair of guards, walking in the direction of the gaming tables. Her would-be friend imparted a few more whispered pieces of wisdom to Emilio when he passed by. Toni ignored her own guard detail and sided up to the podium.

"What the hell, Sweet? I get selling out, but handing us over—"

"Shut it, Toni." Sweet removed his hat and trained those eyes of his on her. "Grecia wants Morales. You're free and clear to leave, so get out of here."

She saw the apology there, the plea for forgiveness reflected in those eyes. "What about Emilio?"

"Grecia has business with him. I don't know and won't ask. Just take your bag, leave and forget about him. I bet if you hawk whatever you can get from Al's ship and even that shuttle you landed in, you can rummage enough for another vessel. I know a couple sellers." He eyed the tables.

"You mean, suckers who are about to lose everything they own over some cards." *People like me.* Emilio had just walked up the three-stair platform into the gambling area. One guard took up position to block anyone from following and the other continued to escort him past her line of vision. *Shit.*

This was it, her moment. She could walk away, go back to Gina and leave Emilio to the vultures. Could steal the ship and sell it for something better. A vessel like that would fetch a pretty leaf. Except she'd gotten invested. Her crew had gone all in with her from the moment they'd started repairing Emilio's ship.

If she boiled away the bullshit, the soft kiss he'd given her, those pleas? They were for her to let him go. But she wanted to keep him alive, and possibly share a bed with him, maybe more. That went against her own rules for survival, for her crew's survival. Unless she considered Emilio a part of that crew, a part of her. The nugget of thought rolled around in her brain for a few more seconds, taking root and spreading to the far reaches. *He matters. He's become my responsibility.* There was no sense in examining the thought further, only in taking action.

The bag of weapons sat beside the Sweet Spot host podium. She reached down, pretending to pick it up, but instead went for the gun on the very top. Everything was loaded, and this particular beauty, a six-shot shotgun, would do.

Sweet's jaw dropped and he scrambled for his own weapon. "Toni, what the hell are you —"

"The right thing, Sweet. Always the right thing." She charged off toward the gambling deck, gun at her side.

A quick flip allowed her to ram the butt of the gun into the face of the guard at the bottom of the steps. He doubled over in pain and she whacked him a second time.

Jumping all three steps, she twirled the gun once more and brought the butt up to her shoulder, scanning for Emilio amid the patrons' screams and exclamations. Many of them got up and ran for the same steps she'd come from. She dodged the bodies, continuing to use the shotgun's sight to look for Emilio.

Finally, she found him, two tables away, eyes wide open and staring at her, the look of shock on his face a reminder she'd taken the crazy course of action, but, *oh well*. Three men flanked him, two holding weapons.

She cocked the gun. "Let the runner go or I start firing."

More screams and people scurrying away from her and the weapon. The older of the three men, wearing a long dark red tunic and sporting thick black and gray sideburns, pointed in her direction. "Who is this crazy *puta*?"

"Your worst fucking nightmare." Toni took aim and fired at the closest of the three. She hit him square in the chest and he dropped to the floor.

Emilio came running toward her, hunched down.

"Hurry, I'll cover for you." She cocked the gun, expelling the spent bullet casing, and took fresh aim. Except she missed her mark entirely as someone big and heavy plowed into her back.

Going down hurt a hell of a lot more when her chest landed against the metal gun still clutched in her hands. She rolled, ready to cock and fire in the process. The effort earned her a painful punch in the face. The gun was ripped from her hands. An arm seized her around her mid-section, lifting her into the air. The grip tightened, and she struggled to breathe. Her eyes closed before she could summon the will to fight against the pain.

"Let her go."

At Emilio's words, Toni opened her eyes. Emilio stood with both arms wrenched behind his back, a drop of blood at the corner of his lower lip. It looked like he'd taken a punch too.

"Bring them here." The rolling *R* and deep sounds matched the older man. "Sally, hold the woman. Nico, put Emilio in the chair."

A large male hand grabbed at Toni's tits and crotch, giving her a rough once-over and making her stomach tighten in disgust. "Keep touching me like that and I'll have your balls in a sling."

The hand turned into an open-faced weapon and slapped her hard. Her cheek burned and the barrel of a pistol was pointed right at her by one of the other peons. The older man stood next to him, a green-felt-covered card table providing distance between them. She glanced to her right and saw Emilio being positioned in a chair.

His facial expression said 'uninterested and bored', but his eyes blazed in silent fury.

"I ask again you-who-wish-to-die, who are you?"

She scoffed and rubbed at her soon-to-be-bruised cheek. "I could ask you the same thing."

"I'm Grecia. Before I kill you, I want to know what prompted your attack."

Looking at Toni's face, the start of the bruise on her upper cheek, made Emilio realize he'd made the wrong choice. He'd intended on keeping her safe, going along with things. When she'd been left behind at the podium and Sweet had told him Toni was free to go, he'd decided to go along with whatever Grecia wanted. His original plan foiled, he'd chosen to give up his life for someone else. Toni could get away on Gina with her crew.

Except Toni had ruined the plan before he'd barely exchanged a greeting with the cartel leader. She'd come in guns blazing, shot one of Grecia's men, and he'd been unable to get her out of here. *That's when I realized I love her.* Seeing her in action and coming to his defense — the truth punched him straight between the eyes.

He, a killer and drug runner, loved a woman who couldn't help but put herself in dangerous situations. The depth of those feelings embedded in his soul, though it took seeing her like this to fully acknowledge what he'd brushed the surface of when they'd coupled on Styx.

He couldn't say it now. Nor could he support her attempted rescue of him. Doing so risked more than her bruised face.

"I'm his partner," Toni replied with a growl. "Tell this bastard to let me loose."

Her struggling earned another caress from Sally, the muscle-bound jerk who appeared to like grabbing his woman between the legs. His woman. The words sounded right. "Call your idiot off. The girl has nothing to do with our problems."

"Morales, who is she?" Grecia's question paired with those dead, cold black eyes. *Mother Mary.*

"Fuck if I know. She gave me a ride after I killed Manolo and has been following me ever since. Useless space trash." He summoned his best disdain and disgust, refusing to give her another glance. The pain in his chest amplified, a faulty feedback pulse in his usually flawless lying gene, brought on by the fear of losing her and the guilt of bringing her down here, getting her involved in this mess.

"Then you won't mind if I kill her."

"Give it your best shot, you cockroach." Toni's mouth flapped and out popped the words. If they made it out of this, he'd have to decide if he wanted to kiss her or spank her. Her fierceness still got the same rise of out him, figuratively and literally. He tugged at his pants.

"Shut your pretty mouth, woman, and let the men talk. If you can't control yourself, my associate, Kain, will receive my permission to shut it for you," Grecia growled.

Toni's scowl spoke volumes and Kain's hulking figure stepped between her and Emilio. "Talk more, bitch, so I can take your mouth."

The words made Emilio's blood boil. If Kain touched her mouth, he'd kill him. *Better to wrap this up fast.* Time for his negotiation skills to be put to the test. Emilio removed a candy from his pocked and popped it into his mouth. He licked his lips. "Toni, you need to realize we're never going to be a thing. Focus on me, Grecia, and leave the side stories alone. How do I make this right?"

He got the effect he wanted, Toni's glower moving to him, the fake insult doing its job. *Lord, if Grecia finds out I love her...damn, how I love her.* The realization came on him brand-new again, like a hit hard from a good pair of brass knuckles to the ribs. Emilio had put her in danger, though the true reason for all this crap lay at Grecia's feet. If the bastard had never called Manolo and had stuck to the plan, Emilio would have never gotten tangled up with Toni.

Grecia pulled out one of the pure white gambling chairs and sat, his fancy floor-length brown coat spreading around him. "First, you admit your sins. When you came to my home, you were not there on behalf of Manolo?"

"No. I came to make the business deal for myself."

"I see." Grecia shook his head. "Why did you not say so?"

"I didn't think it mattered. In the end, the job would get done, by me. I would prove myself worthy of the business." Simple, easy. How the cartel leader thought Emilio was the one who'd fucked things up baffled him. "If you'd followed our agreement instead of calling Manolo, there would have been no issues."

The cartel leader sighed in frustration. "This is what people don't understand about me — I don't like lies or secrets. I like to operate in the open. Hiding things from me — this isn't how a person does business. It means I can't trust you. Understand?"

I understand you're psychotic. In a way, Grecia had a point, but not. Everyone in this business lied. On the black market, for runners and bootleggers to tell the whole truth was a joke, a myth. *No wonder this idiot is blowing through runners at a ridiculous rate.*

"Fine, I made a mistake. As I see it, you made a poor choice when you messed with my ship." Emilio couldn't forget Grecia's actions. Lying was one thing, trying to kill a guy an offense on another level, but fucking with another man's personal belongings was an entirely different story.

"I like how you accept blame for your failures. Most men don't. The problem is you disrespected me, then killed Manolo. I admired him." Grecia smiled and removed a cigar from his pocket, then tapped the end of it on the table.

"Whether you liked Manolo and his drug sniffing, the man was bad for business. You're better off without him. I admit the mistake and I'll make things right." But he wouldn't bend over and pucker up to do so. "Name what you need."

"I need Ramirez dead." With a snap of his fingers, the other associate tucked his pistol away from its position pointed toward Toni and moved to light the cigar for his employer. A few puffs of smoke later and Emilio's head spun, not from the cigar itself but from what Grecia asked of him.

"You recognize the name, no?"

"I do."

"His marijuana fields rival all others and he won't share his secrets, even for a hefty price. I want his cartel in the Western hemisphere. He insulted me, makes fun of me for not living on world. It's time he paid for such affronts."

Emilio figured a lot of people suffered from offending Grecia in some form or another. "How do you want him killed?"

"Brutally. People need to learn not to cross Grecia, or they'll pay. You kill him gruesome and our debt will be honored—I may even consider renewing our previous arrangement—but you'll follow my rules explicitly. You do this murder with your own hands."

Emilio understood. He'd need to get his hands bloody for a psycho who referred to himself in the third person. Killing a cartel leader on Earth didn't bring Parliament law down on a person's head, but it did ensure there would be price placed by the cartel. Could he handle cousins, brothers, sisters or a vengeful wife paying top crinkle to watch him bleed?

"What if I turn down this offer? Is there something else I can do?"

Grecia chuckled, blowing out a puff of smoke. "Nuggets, boy, look at the ones you carry around."

The drug boss pointed at his dead guard on the ground, the pool of blood beneath him much larger than it had been a few minutes ago. "You decline my offer, this is what you can expect, but not you, no. I'll rape that pretty woman next to you, execute every member of the crew you travel with and kill the woman's family. A trail of blood across planets. No one would cross me then."

"Parliament has its limits of what it will turn a blind eye to." The bastard had obviously greased the wheels here on Callisto. No security or lawmen had shown up, unis neither.

"They will allow me free rein for what I have developed for them. Too bad you lost the chance to flash in on the first shipment. Now, do we have a deal?"

With every logical bone in his body screaming no, he willed the opposite word to emerge from his lips. "Yes."

Chapter Sixteen

'Brutally.' Grecia's voice played over and over in Toni's head.

The bastard hadn't minced words once he'd secured Emilio's agreement. They'd shared drinks and discussed the terms of a full-on assassination as if they were talking about bets on an upcoming Mars race. The request for Ramirez's head was what threw her off. Emilio even looked surprised, offering up other body parts as an alternative, but Grecia proved a real psychopath.

"Only his head will do. Then people will understand how I won't be disrespected."

Toni got the flop-around treatment, being tossed into a chair then forcibly removed from the club by Grecia's goons. It seemed no one trusted her to escort herself. Deposited at the entrance, she groaned from the pain.

"I'm sorry, Toni. You should have listened to me and left. Grecia's men confiscated your bag, but at least they let you go," Sweet tried to apologize.

"Fuck you, Akono."

Sweet's frown was the last thing she saw after she pushed herself off the ground and left the club. Toni hobbled off, arms wrapped around her ribs, which did little to ease the sharp pain in her side every time she took a breath. She heard Emilio call her name but ignored him.

Emilio, for all her caring and attempt to save him, had dismissed her, called her names and looked at her as though she was an idiot. She'd been treated in such a manner enough times to know that her brand of help was not wanted, nor would this thing between them work...at least, outside the bedroom.

Once at the shuttle, she took her seat without his help. He didn't offer, but sat down and started the pre-launch sequence. Her struggling with the seatbelt got his attention and he reached over her to the belt and inserted it into the lock.

"Thanks." She looked out of the window, expecting his continued silence. As they left the planet, an unknown pressure in her head seeped away. Maybe it had to do with leaving behind the gore and disgust. "What's the plan?"

"Get back to the ship and make sure Sampson is finished with repairs. I'll give you all a few hours to make arrangements."

Toni whipped her head around and winced at the pain in her side. "Excuse me? Are you seriously going to go through with this?"

"I don't have much of a choice."

Adjusting herself in the seat, new pains sprouted. Her wrist hurt, her left knee was all banged up and starting to swell from her landing on the pavement and every rib on her right side hurt. "Everyone has a choice. But you're acting like you're the only one with a stake in this mess. My name is on Grecia's list of people he plans to kill if you don't do this deal, and so are my crew and family. Can you tell me killing this Ramirez guy will sate Grecia?"

She was sure they'd killed plenty of people between the two of them, hers mainly in self-defense. She'd taken lives in the name of saving a life, hers or her crew's, and because those people were threats. Other drug runners, bootleggers, or assholes trying to back out of a deal. Not cold-blooded —

"I don't have a choice. You heard Grecia. The least I can do is leave the rest of you out of it so you won't be tied to me when the family decides to exact revenge."

Toni laughed, or tried to, but it sounded more like a fake half-hearted wheeze and her ribs hurt worse. "I never pictured you as the self-sacrificing type. Not after we've worked so hard to stay alive."

"You want me alive?"

"Long enough to sign over your ship to me," she replied. No smile, no laugh, dead serious. She refused to give him an inch of control over her. To fall for his thinly veiled attempts to admit she cared. If he hadn't realized it by her dumb plan to get him free from Grecia and his goons, then she'd rather let the words stay buried.

They landed then, the docking platform securing against the shuttle. He pressed all the right buttons, went through the motions, but he appeared closed-off, distant. Emilio didn't bother responding to her statement, either. "Do you need help getting out?"

She shook her head. "No, I can make it."

"Don't play tough. If you need help, tell me. I've got plenty of crap to figure out, plenty of feelings to sort through and right now lies, even white ones, aren't worth my time."

"I can make it." She released the clasp on the harness and Emilio hoisted her up into his arms. In that moment she felt weak and little. Even though there wasn't much difference in their heights, Emilio picked her up as though she weighed nothing. Also, she was damn angry. "Put me down, Emilio."

"Too late. Besides, you're hurt. I see you wincing every time you move."

"You're a stubborn ass. Funny, you talk about lies. I noticed you speaking a different story from the one you said in my bedroom."

He sighed, the movement paired with adjusting his hold on her, moving one of his arms closer to her ass. "In hopes of keeping you alive, but I'm ashamed to admit your little badass display at Sweet's turned me on."

Heat radiated in her cheeks and her body got hot all over. "Ashamed? Don't like a woman having better shotgun handling skills than you?"

He chuckled. "If anything, I'm liking your talent for attacking people a little too much."

The shuttle door slid open and Emilio stomped through, the force of his steps rattling through her body.

"How bad is it? Do you need Doc?" The flirtatious tone he'd deployed moments before deflated into concern.

Damn it. "Wouldn't hurt to have him check me out."

Emilio marched toward the infirmary as Gina's voice rung out. "Welcome back, sir. I've alerted Doc of the need for his presence. Let me apologize for being a bastard."

"No time for that now, Gina. I need a map of the Ramirez cartel plantation on Earth pulled up, routes to Earth with minimal checkpoints and do a run through the posted open berths on Callisto. See if there's a spot for Toni and her crew."

Toni growled. "Belay that last bit, Gina."

Gina's blue light flickered. "I'll get started right away, sir."

Even this damn ship didn't listen to her. *What a pain in the ass.*

Doc greeted them at the door. "Looks like you picked a fight with someone bigger than you."

Emilio gently put her on the table and Doc moved in, not waiting for her to tell him about her injuries. No, he pressed some buttons and a laser sweep scanned her body. "Heard you mention new berths, Emilio."

"The bastard wants to ditch us," Toni groaned as Doc pressed and prodded with his fingertips along the ribs. "Doesn't the scan show you want you need to know?"

"I never fully trust scans." Doc stopped poking her, pressed a few buttons and a hand scanner popped up out of a side compartment on the bed. He moved the handheld over Toni's banged-up knee before he continued, "Don't see the point in leaving the ship. Whatever you have to take care of, we can come along for the ride and help out."

"Where are we headed now?" This from Lee, who poked her head in the door.

"Off ship. Grecia is threatening all of you and I won't risk traveling together anymore. I need to do this next job myself. Once Toni is patched up, you can depart." Emilio was refusing to see she wouldn't give him up, or this ship…no way in hell did he get to make the calls for them.

She lay there, unable to move, and now Doc moved the handheld over her ribs. The repair laser would hurt like a bitch on fractured bones compared to bruised muscle. Sure enough, the first hint of laser and something popped. Toni yelled, "Joseph's balls!"

Lee stepped up and grabbed one of Toni's hands. "What mission?"

"Grecia wants him to kill some cartel guy named Ramirez," Toni replied with a groan.

"I don't think Emilio should kill this guy because Grecia says to. Killing cartel leaders is a hazard to one's health." Lee's opinion seemed surprising. Toni had expected her to enjoy the possibility of getting rid of Emilio.

"This isn't up for discussion. Is she okay?" Emilio squeezed her other hand and she clenched it hard in return.

"Yes, fixing those cracked ribs of hers. She got a nice number done on them. I agree with Lee. A dead cartel leader is less than ideal. Unless it's the one threatening us." Doc held her down with his other arm across her upper chest, right above the breasts.

"Agree." Toni grunted. "Grecia, that's the one we need to kill. Emilio should work out a plan for that."

With every fiber in her being, she wanted to ask for a little liquid courage, but tried her best to calm herself. She'd come so far. Falling back into the pit now wasn't worth it. Not when the people she cared about were at risk. "Doc, how much longer?"

"A few minutes. Stay still and you'll have no problems."

Damn. In days past she'd have drowned herself in some sort of corn gin, a nice barley brew or anything to take away the sharp jabs in her side. Now she'd live through all the moments. Hell, if she didn't plan to get her way. "This may be your ship, Emilio, but this crew here saved it from becoming scrap parts. The least you can do is consider some alternatives."

Emilio squeezed her hand, silent support. "Gina, signal everyone on board to come to the infirmary. I need to talk to them."

The lights in the ceiling blinked once in red, acknowledging the request, but no voice accompanied it. Within minutes, Toni was surrounded by her crew and they all peered at her, as if she'd called the meeting. "He." She pointed at the true culprit. "Wanted to talk to you." Leaning back, she closed her eyes, trying to will the pain in her side to disappear.

"Today, I was threatened by a cartel leader, Grecia. If I don't kill another cartel leader on Earth, he will kill me and anyone associated with me, including Toni and all of you. I plan to let you disembark here on Callisto so I can pursue this blackmail murder on my own. I don't wish to endanger anyone else's life."

Toni cleared her throat.

Emilio rolled his eyes. "Toni believes we should focus on attempting to kill Grecia instead."

Toni stared at the ceiling above her, the rivets in the steel, the sleek, smooth shine to the metal. She would strain her newly repaired ribs to look at any of them and didn't care to. They were her crew and she knew what they were thinking. "I vote to attack Grecia at his compound."

No one spoke, and Toni turned her head. Everyone stared at her with guarded expressions. Maybe she didn't know them like she'd thought. "Our choices are three-fold. Abandon the ship and Emilio to his fate, join him in the murder of an Earth cartel leader or put all our brains, willpower and resources against Grecia. What say you?"

Lee leaned over her. "Are you serious?

"The man threatened you, the rest of the crew, me. He's a psychopath. Lee, you wouldn't let a psychopath get away with this, would you?" Her first mate didn't need to answer the question, not after the years they'd spent together.

Emilio frowned. "I don't want anyone to suffer for my mistakes."

"We'd most likely suffer anyway. Rather we do it on our terms. Besides, your ship is not in tip-top condition. Right, Sampson?" She barely got a glimpse of the engineer's nod, being on her back as she was. "We can argue this more after we hole up, get some rest and fix her. Then we can come up with a plan for Grecia. If the plan is too risky, then we explore killing this Ramirez guy, though I don't agree with it. Whatever happens, you need the proper tools and taking a half-limping ship into a tough fight is not the solution."

Dottie and Doc gave nods of agreement. Sampson stood in silence, turning a grease rag over in his hands.

Lee slapped the table with a fist. "Damn it. I hate when you're making sense."

Toni hated it too. Normally, she'd throw caution to the wind and ride, but maybe something could be said for thinking things out in advance.

The words sprang Emilio from his seat at her side, pacing back and forth along the table. "So, you're all staying?"

Dottie was the first to speak up. "I'll stay, though it'll be weird working with a computer."

Gina's light bar flickered in response and Toni almost smiled. AI systems getting offended by words was something new. Sampson agreed next, followed by Doc and last Lee, who offered this gem. "I'm fine with sticking around if you can promise me more action. I can't stand sitting still."

"Whatever action pops up, I'm sure we'll need you." Emilio responded with a nod and gave the next orders. "Sampson, can Gina take off?"

The boy nodded. "Aye, aye, boss. She's ready for open space. Slip drive and trolling motor are semi-operational. She's still cussing at times and slinging insults like a pirate stuck close to the sun, but she'll fly true."

"Then let's get her pointed toward Earth. Dottie, make the necessary calls. Gina, you follow Dottie's — "

"Hold up." Toni struggled and groaned against the twinge of pain in her chest as she propped herself up on her elbows. "Do you seriously think going in blind is wise, runner?"

"Quick and simple will get us all out of the problems a lot faster. We need to start moving somewhere if we want to give Grecia the impression we're following his demands." Obviously, he strove for taking the first choice every damn time instead of weighing all options. He'd stolen her lines. For this problem she wanted a little planning, even if it meant a tougher road.

"The ship isn't prepared for that and neither are we. I said we would help, but I'm not risking lives on a fool's errand. We head for Mars."

Everyone else nodded in agreement at that, except for Lee, who busted out laughing. "You want us to land the ship on a building planet? They'd strip this baby their first opportunity. I know if I was them, I would."

Toni shook her head, already deciding to do something she'd sworn never to do. "Not the case. They'd accept us, or at least my parents would."

Lee scoffed. "Oh, this is going to be rich." They'd all shared stories of their pasts growing up. Lee's involved training as an assassin on the uppers, a bad marriage and plenty of kills. Dottie was from the uppers too. Sampson had been sold to a ship as an indentured engineer for food rations. Doc had survived years in the APU playing at being a surgeon and enforcer. Even Toni had confessed there was one way her parents would ever let her come home again after ditching the family business to run her own bootlegging ship. She'd embarrassed them.

"They'd accept us, on one condition. We'll have to pretend we're married."

Emilio's forehead crinkled, his eyes rolled and the scar scrunched, making it look like part of his cheek had gone missing.

Toni frowned. "I didn't know the concept of being bound to me was so abhorrent."

So much for his supposed eagerness and desire to love her. Add another wound to her emotional injuries atop the physical ones.

"It's not, just a horrible plan." Emilio's words stung worse than his blatant disgust. "They would never believe it, especially if they talked to Al."

Everyone else in the room remained silent, except Lee, who couldn't stop chuckling. "I'm going to step out." She guffawed her way out of the infirmary.

Dottie frowned. "Emilio may be right, but, at the same time, I've seen people getting married the same day they meet."

"And good luck finding a better option. I'm not sure anyone in this room knows a place we'll be able to get all the parts to fix Gina up on credit or guard your ship," Toni replied before lying back down. She was tempted to punch him, and a solar day prior she'd allowed him to do with her body as he pleased. His actions made her crazy, the exact opposite of what she needed.

She sighed deep and closed her eyes. For all that she was crap at, for all her bad luck, plans came naturally to her. Even if they were a bit madcap. "Sampson? Dottie? Do you have somewhere between here and the druggie shit-hole that we can crash? I wouldn't suggest the moon, since those stoners would sell anyone out for some decent product, as Emilio experienced."

Both of them responded no. She could imagine their facial expressions as she lay there, Sampson's shake of his head, Dottie's curled-up lip at the mention of her past. They all would rather stay far from the people who'd shaped their lives.

"The lack of detailed sentences speaks volumes. See, Emilio, this is it. The one chance you have besides going gung-ho for Grecia or Ramirez without planning. This is the halfway point, the safe option. But my family won't take you in unless I tell them you're bound to me. Doing so makes you a relation, and if Ma and Paw do anything, it's protect their own."

"She's right." Doc chose that moment to gain an opinion. "It's a good spot for ship fixin' and Mars folks are fierce on protecting their kin."

"What you've told me about them doesn't make them sound all that wonderful." Emilio leaned over her, eyes roaming over her entire body. "Doc, is she done here?"

The concern he showed warred with the crappy attitude he'd expressed towards marriage to her.

"Nope, she needs to rest for thirty minutes and let everything take effect."

Toni ignored Doc and frowned at Emilio. "My folks may not be wonderful, by any means, but they can serve you in this purpose."

"Fine, plot the course to Mars, Dottie. Can everyone clear the hell out of here now?" Emilio's words made the action happen. It was one thing she could say for him—he knew how to get people moving with little effort.

Once her crew had left, she stared up at him. "I find myself wondering why I bother with you."

He stood still, hands bracketed on either side of the bed. "Because you like to be crazy and wild. That's how you make me feel, sorry for believing there's something right to it. But everything you told me about your parents…they can't be trusted."

"Not being able to trust them is why you looked like you might puke at the mention of marrying me?" She'd meant to steer clear of the topic, but it lay there like acid on her heart, burning into her flesh.

His jaw opened and his eyes narrowed. "I want to puke at having to play nice to people who treated you like trash, like property. We're the same. Both of us regarded by the value other people placed on our abilities. They made you ashamed about the best parts of you, and I don't want to be around them."

She wanted to believe him.

His breath fanned hot against her face. "It's good to know you think of me like that, of more, though. Maybe there's something to this marriage thing after all."

She flipped him the universal bird and closed her eyes. *Arrogant runner.*

"Who's the one not interested now?"

She opened her eyes and looked up into his near black ones. The frustration there matched her own, but it still didn't stop her mouth from going off. "It's not a lack of interest. It's the back and forth. I'm sick of being unable to read what you want. I miss simpler times and my ship. I'm stuck in this situation because I thought to jump in and save your ass. Idiot me. I somehow let myself care enough about you to be worried and invested in your future. You act like this type of constant seesawing is fine and normal, but it's not."

The anger radiating from him faded, and he traced fingers up her arm, causing chill bumps to erupt across her flesh. "There's an important phrase there, something about you caring about me. And, the truth is I...care for you, too. Unfortunately, I dragged you into my mess. I can say I want you, in all the ways a man should and would. On another day, tying you to me would be a marvelous thing. But doing so with Grecia's threats hanging over my head is crap. I'm a bastard who might not live out this week, let alone steer clear of becoming wanted on every planet. A good husband wouldn't do that to his wife. As for this unpredictable current, it can't be helped. Not in this universe. Stability and normality are two things not available to those who make a living in space."

She believed him about caring for her. He'd done so much to pursue her, teasing and flirting. The level of attention he'd given her showed nothing less, but still a tiny screw of doubt remained, honed from years of being considered awful if she expressed interest in something other than beauty and sex. Add in his prediction about having a normalcy or a constant in her life and she found her anger deflating.

"Why bother then?"

"It's either embrace it or give up and crumble under the weight. I'm not the type to fall apart. I own my mistakes, my victories and the troubles or celebrations that accompany them. But I'll admit being responsible for other people is a new experience, and a scary one."

She wrapped one hand around his forearm. "You're not responsible for us. We make our own decisions."

"And what would be your next?"

Something she shouldn't want, not if she desired to keep herself from falling further into this messy situation. Yet she couldn't stop herself from demanding it. "Take me to bed."

Chapter Seventeen

"Has thirty minutes passed?" Emilio asked with a smile. Seeing her hurt, watching Grecia's men hurt her, had shown how little he could protect her, prevent the damage to her beautiful body. He'd stood helpless and now she wanted to go with him to kill the bastard. Hell, she wanted to marry him. *Save me, lord.*

She removed her grip on his forearm, wrapped her arms around her midsection and hugged herself. The frown and scrunch of her facial features told him she was still in pain, still healing. "Not sure, but I think I can move."

Mother Mary, I'd do anything. He wanted her safe, protected and kept far from Grecia. She'd been banged up good with her knee and ribs and all that was his fault. She could tell him a million times that she and her crew made their own decisions, but he'd still live with the guilt if something happened. Grecia not shooting her surprised the hell out of him. He'd been so sure she was as good as dead, but the cartel leader had a sick mind. Asshole probably admired Toni for having the nuggets to shoot someone dead without a second thought.

"Fine, I'll take you to bed, but you're not walking. I'll carry you." He walked around to the side of the table, sliding one arm under her legs and the other around her back. Hoisting her into his arms was no problem.

"You're not going to carry me," she replied with a smile.

That combined with her scent—a distinct smell of lilies wafting to his nose—caused other parts of his anatomy to respond. He'd carry her whether she liked it or not. The last thing she needed right now was him leading this to a sexual conclusion.

"I'm going to get you somewhere comfortable." He could do this much for her. *The memory of her charging in, shotgun twirling in her hands, fierce and dangerous...* "I never thanked you for trying to rescue me."

Emilio kept his steps soft, measured, doing his best not to jostle her as he walked out of the infirmary and towards his quarters, deciding the back way, past the engines and shuttles, was a better option then going through the pilot's cabin or past the galley. He didn't care to get comments from Doc for moving Toni too soon or any curious stares about where he was taking her. "It was a foolish thing to do when you could have gotten out of there."

"Wait...you say thanks and insult me at the same time?"

He passed her cabin door, the one next to his, and tapped the panel for the entrance to his room. "Well, I'm not going to apologize for telling the truth. You should have escaped, taken your crew and gotten far the hell away. I said as much earlier. My thoughts haven't changed." She should have abandoned him like all the people he'd known since his childhood.

With the hand closest to him, she grabbed hold of his shirt, doing a piss-poor job of tugging on it with effort. "Did you ever think we didn't want to leave? That maybe we— Oof." Her words cut off when he placed her down on his bed.

He plopped down beside her, looking at those lips of hers, then decided to taste them before she could continue with her confession, words he'd rather not hear. Promises that deep down would break him if she never delivered. She moaned as he slipped his tongue in, no doubt tasting the lingering alcohol on his breath from that deal-sealing shot he'd shared with Grecia. Downing such a drink and agreeing to murder someone without provocation had proved awful. The kiss, paired with her eager response, made up for it. Within seconds she had half the buttons on his shirt undone.

"Slow down," he mumbled against her lips. He grabbed for her hands and wrapped his larger one around both of her wrists. "I'm not going to fuck you tonight."

She struggled against his grip and finally freed one hand. "Why the hell not? I'm not fragile, not made of glass."

"You proved that earlier when you came running up with a shotgun." He'd never forget that image. His wild woman charging in like some fairytale hero. "The reason I won't fuck you is because I want you whole and healed when I take you."

"Oh, want the bride untouched for at least a solar day before the nuptials?" She gave a little smirk, but those brown and gold eyes of hers gave away her insecurity.

He sensed her reservations and concerns, but the fact she kept bringing the marriage up and insisted on staying filled his heart with joy. Except, how long before she found a better offer? Life played out that way, sticking to what he knew until the better deal came along. For him, she was the better deal, but could he trust it?

"However you want to play this game, I'll do it. But remember, this is just because Gina isn't in great shape and we need to plan our move against Grecia. Remember, if things are too risky, we move on Ramirez. Grecia won't wait long."

She reached up and touched his cheek, rubbing against the stubble coming in. "Fine, deal." The soft kiss to his lips that followed, the gentle caress of her tongue and the scent of her breath, almost undid him. He let her other wrist go and cupped her face.

Losing people was a way of life in the universe. He'd lost all the things he cared about in the past and now stood on the edge of risking himself to all that again. To give in now, to give in to her. He pulled back, away from the precious kisses seeking to destroy his resolve. "Because I'm willing to kill a person I don't even know to save my life and yours."

She opened her mouth—to refute him, no doubt—and he silenced her with a finger. "No, it's true. If it's needed, I'll kill more than one. While I see your point about Grecia, the easy route is to do the job. Your fine speech earlier didn't change my mind."

The uncertainty in her eyes, that look of hurt... He wanted to soothe it away with all the things he'd left out. How he loved her beyond logical reason and hoped that after they resolved this problem, they'd be together. How she deserved more than a simple life and he believed she chased simplicity, thinking it safer. "But I'm willing to give everything a chance."

Toni pulled away from him with a sigh, big and deep, and rolled over. Emilio chose not to let that deter him and snuggled in next to her, spooning against her back.

"Do you want me to hold you?" *He* wanted it, more than his next breath. The chance to offer her warmth, since he couldn't offer anything else.

"Yes, hold me," she whispered. They lay there, minutes ticking by. He let his gaze fall on the stars on the other side of his window. The ship passed them slowly, riding the currents and taking them far away from Callisto.

They'd be at Mars in a matter of a solar day or so. Not much time to learn about the niceties an interaction with her family required.

"So, what do I have to do for this fake wedding?" He whispered the question into her ear, loving how she shivered against him.

Her words were a whisper back. "Get inked."

* * * *

The skin on his arm itched, driving him nuts, and he stood in his bathroom, rubbing the healing salve Doc had given him into the tattoo he'd received. This, the symbol of Toni's family, tied him to her. Funny how she'd not been obligated to get something similar, but the requirement applied to men or women marrying into a Mars clan. The crossed wrenches were set below two gears and a skull. Against his brown skin, it looked odd. The salve did a bit to take away most of the itching sensation.

Toni had watched the tattoo proceedings but disappeared before they'd finished. Something about moving her things and being presentable for the meeting with her parents. Besides shared quarters, he hadn't given her anything in return yet. He had to provide a token, something for her to wear. It was a custom among those on Earth, an exchange of rings or necklaces.

"You could give her the medallion you wear." Doc had suggested. Emilio fingered the medallion now winking back at him in the mirror. The saint of lost children, a gift from his mother meant to protect him when she'd left. When she'd abandoned him. Why he'd kept it all these years, he wasn't sure, and the protection it offered was more a fool's tale than truth.

"The ship has begun the descent to Mars, sir. May I mention your tattoo is quite fetching?"

"What the fuck does fetching mean, Gina?" He washed his hands in the basin and dried them before rolling his sleeve down.

"It's an old Earth term to mean pretty or nice. I've been given access to additional databases by Sampson. He's quite the helper in ensuring I expand my knowledge. A Dr. Frankenstein to my monster."

The engineer had mentioned working on upgrades for Gina. Too bad they were more useful to her than him so far. "Good to know, but I'd like him to concentrate on getting your systems fixed first."

"I can relay the message, sir. Curiosity demands, is your marriage to Toni a love match?"

Funny, how his AI thought she possessed curiosity and, with the damn thing capable of listening in to all conversations on ship, it surprised him that she didn't already have the particulars.

"No, Gina. This is a business arrangement. Stick that into your database. I don't…" He couldn't say it as he stared into the mirror. He loved Toni but feared her reaction. She'd been so vehement about it, even though she fought so hard to keep him by her side.

"Alert the crew we're landing, and I'll meet everyone in the cargo hold."

Gina's light blinked in acknowledgment. "Yes, sir."

He didn't bother asking where Toni was. No, he refused to smother her with his concern, the same overwhelming worry he'd kept experiencing since the run-in with Grecia on Callisto. She'd delivered her stuff to his quarters and left before he got there. If she wanted time to herself, fine, but she'd have to suffer the consequences if he screwed up in front of the Smiths.

He rolled down the sleeves on his green button-down shirt, shrugged into his brown jacket and tugged on the ends of his vest to align everything in place. *Not bad, not bad at all for a newlywed.* Hair slicked back, face bare, he was ready to tackle just about any social situation. A few minutes later he crossed into the cargo bay on the lower level of the ship. They'd touch down and exit through the bay entrance. Except, he wasn't prepared for how his wife looked.

Her hair was luscious, tight red corkscrew curls, pulled into some sort of updo and spilling down her back. She wore a black leather jacket and pants along with her grav boots and a matching black shirt. Gorgeous and stunning, but possessing the same rough edges he'd come to know, including the golden glint to her eyes. The gun strapped to her side made him smile even wider.

"Holy Mother." He mentally slapped himself in the face for such a shitty first compliment. Then he yelped and turned around ready to throw a punch, but Lee, who'd pinched his ass, had already moved on.

Toni's first mate winked at him, all strapped with blades crisscrossing her chest. "Just wanted to make sure I got your attention. You be nice to my captain or I'll put every last one of these in you."

The ship shuddered around them, a few creaks and groans, before the engine powered down. Emilio opened his mouth to respond but was stopped by Dottie's voice crackling over the sound system. "Attention, we have landed on Mars. Our hosts are waiting to welcome you at the Smith Watering Hole."

Emilio raised an eyebrow and glanced at Toni. "A fancy restaurant?"

"No, our local bar. Ma and Paw put up the money for it, and the damn town named it after them. Half the shit in this little podunk place carries my surname," Toni replied with a sigh, as if the idea was so horrible. His opinions of this family she hated so much yo-yoed based on every bit of additional information he possessed.

"Then lead the way."

The rolling door opened at Sampson's press of a button on the control panel, and the group headed out, all four of them. Dottie and Doc announced they were staying behind, due to a general dislike of crowds, weddings and people in that order. Emilio was fine with their decision, preferring someone to stay with the ship and not leave it alone.

Mars was a smattering of cities, but mainly townships comprised of mining and ship-building groups. Toni's family ran their own township, Frog Lick, formed from striking a wealthy vein in a mine and growing from there.

The planet itself wasn't horrible, but the red dust issue had never been completely cleared up by the terraforming. As mining groups drilled for precious metal, steel and iron, the red dust kicked up and everything outside got a fine coating. Most people wore sun goggles for that reason, but those who were born on the planet had become used to the situation.

Emilio, along with Lee and Sampson, pulled on the goggles, though Toni trudged onward without any protection. She led their merry band toward a wood and steel building, with the name *Smith's Watering Hole* carved out of steel sitting above the entrance. The sign swung in the wind, creaking with every to and fro.

Crowds weren't much on Mars, at least not in the early evening hours, from what he saw. The sun still shone a bit, but twilight was upon them. Most people were inside. Mars got cold at night, and in the distance bright lights lit up the racing dome. Worse than gambling on Callisto, racing ruled this planet, equal to the ship building and mining. The main city, Ares, featured a bi-annual competition summoning the best racers.

Toni opened the door, the loud cacophony of voices dulling to whispers until the entire group was inside. The door swung shut and all eyes in the place looked at them.

"What are you shit-holes looking at? Haven't seen a Frog Lick girl come home before?" Toni's loud questions sent the group into a roar of approval and she was embraced by one person after another.

Those hugging her bestowed similar greetings to Emilio, Sampson and a freaked-out Lee. Funny, the woman had no problem pinching his ass and threatening his life but clammed up at displays of affection directed toward her. He'd have to remember that.

"Assholes, back off and let me get near my daughter!" a woman hollered from the back of the group, and things died down a bit. Toni's mother drew closer, shoving men and women alike out of her way.

She wasn't skinny, but not large. The oval eyes matched Toni's color, but her hair was blonde and braided close to her head, trailing down her back and almost touching the floor. She wore leather boots, denim pants and a red top with holes along the arms.

"Ma," Toni said as her mother came to halt in front of her.

"Girl, you are a sight for these old eyes. Bones, get over here and greet your daughter and her new husband." Bebe Smith focused on Sampson, standing right next to Toni. "He's a mite younger than I expected for a runner."

Toni shook her head, "That's not him, Ma." She glanced over her shoulder and tugged on Emilio's sleeve. The awkwardness was a real thing, with his mouth going dry and a lump settling in the center of his throat. She was going to present him to her mother and father, as her choice for a lifelong mate.

That was the moment her father arrived, the crowd parting for him fast and furious. This was where Big Al got his looks and coloring from. Bones Smith sported a long ginger beard and ginger hair that hung past his shoulders. He wore similar clothes to those of his wife, but with a black leather vest that boasted a collection of bones sewn into it.

Joseph's balls. What have I walked into?

"Where's the husband? Can't be this scrawny kid, is it, Toni?"

She shook her head, and Emilio decided to test out those steel nuggets everyone mentioned he possessed. "I'm the husband, sir."

Stepping up, toe-to-toe, with this guy, who had at least four inches on him, took guts.

"You're married to my baby girl?"

"Yes, Pa. He's all mine." Toni sided up to him, draping herself against his arm, as though she belonged there. In Emilio's mind, she did.

The scowl on the man's face was the same type of look he'd give to a bastard trying to marry his own daughter, if he ever had a daughter. This plan was a horrible idea, until Bones' stern lips broke out in a big grin.

"Welcome to the Smith clan, son. A round of shine on the house for everyone, to celebrate Antonia's nuptials."

The crowd around them roared and Lee shoved Sampson towards the bar. Bebe wrapped an arm around Toni's shoulders, pulling her away from Emilio. For a moment he didn't know what to do or say, then Bones hollered, "Follow us."

They worked their way through the group of now-ecstatic patrons waiting for the shot glasses to get passed around, past the bar and every table, through a pair of black velvet curtains then through another set of double doors. This was the private room, a VIP area reserved for Bebe and Bones.

"Have a seat, you two." Bebe motioned to the round table in the center of the room. It looked like a poker setup, with a felt top and about eight chairs.

The pair joined him and Toni, a bottle of brandy and four glasses along for the ride, thanks to Bones. Toni turned her glass upside down while Bebe filled the remaining ones.

"So," Bebe began, sitting down and taking a sip of her liquor. "You married the man your brother wanted to turn in, and stole Alberto's ship too?"

Her big brother had told on them to his parents. This would be over before it began. Emilio slid one hand back to ensure his pistol was still in place, in case things got ugly. In the meantime, the brandy was top notch.

"That was a misunderstanding, and Al wanted to turn Emilio in, the man I love. Chalk it up to one of our squabbles, but Al has Styx back and everything is fine. Emilio even got the tat. Show them, honey." Her smile was too damn wide, but for shits and grins he shrugged off his jacket and rolled up the left sleeve, showing off the glistening tattoo.

Bones whistled. "I'll be a dust honey butt naked on race day. Bebe, he's got it and that's real, not fake."

Shit, they thought he was faking. "I took every needle jab."

Bebe reached over and rubbed the skin. It was awkward being touched by his fake mother in-law. "Paul's hymnals, you went and did it."

He prayed Doc had told the truth that he had secrets to remove this fucking thing. Being associated with the Smiths for the rest of his life would not be ideal.

"We figured you might be faking, looking for a place to hide from the unis on your man's tail, honey." This from Bones. At least he was honest. "Appears we were wrong. Rushed to judgment and didn't trust in your words."

"Our mistake," Bebe agreed, placing a hand over her chest. "Now, what brings you here?"

Toni opened her mouth, but Emilio took over, grabbing Toni's hand and pressing a kiss to the back of it first. He'd milk this for any excuse to touch her and be close to her, since she'd hidden herself away for the last day. "Honestly, it's two reasons. One, this gorgeous woman missed home, said it'd been years since she saw it. I have business that requires me to go to Earth and I decided it best she could stay here with my ship, do a little maintenance during that time, and catch up with y'all."

Y'all, a word he'd never have used in a million years, but...*when in Insane Racing Country, act as the natives do.*

"That's perfect." Bebe slugged back the rest of her drink. "And before you take off, we've got a celebration planned."

Toni's eyes went wide, and Emilio was sure he'd missed something. *Too late to back out now.* "I love a good party. When are you having it?"

Bones jabbed him in the shoulder with his hand. "Right now."

Chapter Eighteen

Parties, fuck. She hated parties. It was as if her life had spun out of control and she'd much rather watch what happened next than participate. The bottle on the table in front of her didn't help. It mocked her. "Why do we need a party?"

Bebe raised an eyebrow. "Are you kidding? I thought both of my kids were lost causes when it came to getting hitched. This is the biggest news since your birth. Gives me hope you'll settle down here at some point, take over the mining business."

The thought made Toni want to puke and her stomach grumbled in response. Another reason to flip the tumbler in front of her over and pour a glass. She glanced between Emilio and her father. The pair shared no similarities except that the tattoo Emilio sported matched the patch on the back of her dad's leather vest.

Emilio grinned. "I don't know. We haven't talked too much about where we plan to settle once I've got the taste for running bled out of my veins."

It sure the fuck won't be here. Oh, but for now she'd take her would-be husband's advice and she volleyed back with an equal smile. "Yes, he's wild for running. Loves the thrill of evading the APU, of fooling those idiots at the checkpoints and he comes away with high-crinkle product too. Bet we could get you something good, Ma."

The words did the trick and her mother's eyes glazed over at the idea of romance and outlaw work. Toni knew all the ways to push the woman's buttons. "Before we go out there to face everyone again, can I get a few moments alone with my husband?"

Her dad was the first to stand. "I'll get the toasting stuff ready. Everyone will need a glass of that good stuff, not the swill we serve every day."

Mom stood next and came over to wrap an arm around Toni's shoulders. "I love that you're home and I'm even more excited you're married. This will be a good change of pace for you instead of trying to captain a ship. You'll see."

After the door shut and they were alone, Toni swiveled in her seat to face Emilio. "I don't like this."

"What's wrong?"

Everything, truth be told.

"They shouldn't be hosting a party for us. I mean, not this fast. It's like —"

"A trap?" He reached out and trailed his fingertips up her arm, over the sleeve of her jacket. "Sure you aren't just expecting a trap after all the crap at Sweet's, on the junker moon and Ceres? It's been one surprise after another the entire week. Makes a person almost expect them."

Any other place, any other fucked-up, backwards bar, she'd agree with him. "You don't know these people like I do."

Emilio's carefree expression melted away. He sat straight in his chair and the movement took any physical contact away from her. A part of her missed it, the part of her wanting to take things further then the mere snuggles she'd gotten the last time they'd slept together.

"Fine, I'll follow your lead. Do you want me to warn the others?"

Toni shook her head. "No need. I can signal Lee in a minute. Just stay on guard."

They both stood. Toni checked her pistol and the speed cartridge she'd placed in her jacket pocket.

Emilio growled, then reached down to check both pistols he had strapped on his belt. "For once, I'd like you to be wrong. That when we walk out that door, it's not going to be some ambush waiting for us. That maybe we get the break and not more assholes like Grecia. Ready?"

He rolled the barrel of one of his six shooters, then, with a flick of his wrist, slung it into place. Funny how he didn't resent the situation, her, or once again being in a shitty situation...this one her own making.

"I'm ready." She tried to keep her face stoic, void of emotion and ready to do damage, but something about this felt right. Perfect. Her and Emilio against the world. If it hadn't been for his deal with Grecia and her shitty run at poker, they might never have met. Never gotten on Manny's ship at the same time.

"Then lead the way. I follow you."

Those words could have very well been 'I love you'. Her foolish heart pounded faster at the thought of what they might find on the other side of the door.

There were things she wanted to say, but they could wait until after. She ducked and swiped to move the sheer drapes that had fallen into place after the door was shut. With those out of the way, she grabbed the doorknob and flung open the barrier between them and the bar. The noise levels that would normally have assailed her were silent.

She motioned to Emilio to follow her and drew her weapon. Down the narrow hallway, she saw minimal light at the end where the main room started. The twinkling lights of the bar were what she was looking at. The main lighting had gone down.

Fuck. They'd be sitting ducks when they got out there. Fodder for anyone with a gun and she wouldn't put it past her parents to mobilize the entire bar. She'd become the enemy in the one place she'd hoped would give her a chance to prove herself before being gunned down.

Crouching low, she reached the end of their limited protection. The lights flashed on then, bright, bold and casting a tan haze over the room from above. Voices shouted in unison, "Happy Anniversary!"

* * * *

In the hour since they'd walked into what really was a surprise party, Toni had holstered her weapon and received no fewer than three scolding looks from her mother, father and the bartender she'd known from childhood. Flowered necklaces were being passed around with equal enthusiasm as the shots of booze.

Alcohol flowed like water from a well, cigars were smoked and she drowned among the temptation.

Leaning against the wooden bar in front of her, ass half on a matching wooden stool, Toni stared at the shot in front of her, debating. A guy beside her gave her a nudge. "You look amazing."

A quick glance and she grinned. "Eli, as I sit and ponder. Thought you had big racing plans in Ares before I left?"

The bruiser of a man towered over her with a beaming smile. Most were intimidated by him, but she had come to know the soft, kind person who loved being behind the wheels of a racer. "Wrecked my rig. Had to come to Frog Lick to earn the money to build another."

"I'm sorry, Eli. I've known that kind of heartache —"

"Who's your friend, wife?" Emilio's tone, the question, the way he sidled up next to her, wrapping an arm around her waist. The move was a little too possessive, even for him.

"I'm Eli."

Her old buddy puffed up a bit while providing the introduction. She kind of liked how he wasn't scared of Emilio either.

"Good to meet you, but I need to borrow my wife for a moment." Her fake-husband wrapped up the hand she had closest to the shot glass in one of his own and lifted her from the stool like she weighed nothing.

A few twirls and swirls got her out onto the dance floor and enfolded in Emilio's arms. A sashay here, a dip there. They were well matched and that pissed her off. "You didn't need me so damn bad you had to interrupt my conversation."

"We can beg to differ. Besides, you were talking to his chest, not to him. The man is a monster. I almost think the people of Mars may be adding something special to their vegetables."

"Cut the crap. Why did you need me?"

He pushed her away from him, keeping their hands together, then pulled her in close. The next words were whispers in her ear. "You were right."

She shuddered. "How so?"

"Your father just told me in no uncertain terms that we would be having a meeting tomorrow before I went anywhere. That all is not forgiven and there will need to be terms met if they expect my ship or you to remain here under their protection." One of his hands slid precariously low on her hip. A little further south and he'd be grabbing her ass.

"I'm surprised it was Pa and not mother dearest."

Emilio raised an eyebrow as he twirled her under his arm. "Seems to me your dad has a pretty tight rein on this place."

"Exactly how you're supposed to see it, but this gang has always been run by women and Ma makes all the decisions. Pa is the muscle." Toni hated being right. They hadn't been ambushed from the get-go but were being maneuvered. "Guess we'll have to speed up the repairs and our planning before that meeting."

"No, I think not." Emilio arched her over one arm and leaned down, pressing a kiss to her exposed neck. "We could go with my idea. I go to Earth and kill Ramirez. I'll sneak away tonight and let you handle your parents."

She leaned forward and pressed a return kiss to the tip of his nose. "I say no. Remember, this whole deal would help us avoid killing someone who doesn't deserve it. You do that job and you'll never not be under Grecia's thumb. You and I both know selling oneself to anyone does nothing for you."

"You're right." He kissed her full on the lips, teasing her with his tongue. "Now, for five minutes, can we forget all of this stuff and enjoy the opportunity of being in each other's arms?"

The question startled her and she let herself relax. Letting him take the lead for one song turned into two, then three. From slow to fast, the moves he deployed and fancy footwork surprised her. She got lost moving around the floor with him, the severe focus in his eyes, the possession, the emotion present in his every gesture and gaze. He smiled at her, winked and made her feel like the only person in the room. Another song came on, a little dark and poignant.

"Follow my lead." Emilio whipped her from the left to the right, guiding with his arms. The dance style matched the musical notes from the guitar. "You should get out and dance more."

"I don't like the attention."

He nuzzled her neck again and she had to stifle a moan. "Well, all eyes are on us. Even your pal, Muscles, can't stop watching."

"Muscles has a name and he's a friend from childhood. Never took you for one to be jealous." She liked pushing against him with words and her feet. But he was ready for the little bit of resistance she initiated, moving around her, circling her. *Like a predator hunting prey.*

He stood at her back, pulling her against him, his arousal apparent against her backside, the slide of his hands encircling her hips. She let her eyes close, let herself feel. Turning her to face him once more, he lifted one of her legs to his chest and dragged her across the floor one, two and three steps.

She opened her eyes, tried to control her breathing. The labored sound came not from her alone, but them both. The song ended, and he stared at her, his eyes the shade of pitch. "If I'm ever jealous of anything you do, then I'd need to get my head examined."

They'd stopped right in front of her parents and he chose that moment to kiss her. It wasn't a simple kiss either. It was possession. A ravenous feast, where his lips demanded the ultimate surrender. She stood powerless against the onslaught, like a rickety shed in the fierce Mars winds. All she could do was give in. For her sanity.

Minutes passed by and finally he pulled away, whispering, "Well done."

Toni opened her eyes to everyone watching and the same heart galloping in her chest cracked at all the people staring at them, including her parents. She'd let herself get swept away, made a mockery of in the very place she'd been used time and time again. Without a second thought, she hauled off and punched him.

The crack of her fist hitting his jaw resulted in a collective groan from their audience.

"Satan's fire!" Emilio hollered as he moved his chin up and down.

Her punch hadn't done enough. She needed a pair of brass knuckles or... She spied a bottle in Eli's hands behind Emilio. Shoving Emilio to the side with a growl, she marched over and grabbed the liquor bottle. Eli never put up a fight.

"You wanted to light my match, then fine...let's add some fuel." She chucked the bottle at him. Emilio dodged and the damn thing shattered against the floor.

The smell of corn shine filled the air and Toni breathed in deep, anger still radiating through her veins.

"Honey, I stand by my words and I'm happy to light it up." Emilio grabbed a lit cigarette from a bystander and dropped it on the fuel. His eyes filled with mirth and pleasure. *He gets off on this, seeing me this way.*

The notion landed like ice on her flames of rage. That was when she absorbed the fact that everyone was staring at her, them. She'd done it again, put on some insane spectacle for the town of Frog Lick. Acted a fool, wild and manic. The looks on folks' faces were a mix of pity, dissatisfaction and glee. *Bastards.*

She needed to regain her dignity but found her throat dry and tight. Unable to voice anything outside of expletives, Toni stomped off. Across the dance floor, past the bar and out of the doors. Whatever mess she left behind her was one of his making and he could deal with the consequences.

Chapter Nineteen

Toni stomped all the way back to Gina, tears streaming down her face. He'd made her look a fool, reeled her in then deliberately sparked her anger. She entered the ship and marched down the hall from the entrance, past the galley where Dottie and Doc had a small romantic meal spread between them.

"Carry on," she hollered. Her problems didn't need to interrupt their wonderful evening, even though coming home topped the pile of worst ideas.

"I should have never suggested it," she muttered.

She'd stayed away all these years for a reason, even at her lowest when she'd had no income and no ship. Now, she'd falsely believed she'd be strong enough to maintain the new Toni. Except Emilio had proved her wrong. He sparked and butted against her as if trying to unleash the side of her she'd rather not relive.

The expressions of her amused parents and the men who'd gleefully stared at her mixed with the horrible memories of her past. How she'd been passed from one business deal maker to another, in the best interests of the family. How others had enjoyed when she got drunk enough to let them dance with her or when she'd pick fights.

She'd gotten herself under control since then and Emilio ripped it all away. She'd acted a drunk-on-love fool, letting him whisk her around the room, then his taunting and jealous farce.

Damn!

She almost went to their shared quarters but thought better of it, circling past the room and going for the one place she hoped to find refuge. She climbed into the shuttle, shut the hatch and took up a spot in the pilot's chair. The view was a nice respite – there was nothing as pretty as night on Mars. The sun sunk below the visible horizon lit the racing dome up in all its glory for the evening competition. The dust honeys and the racers were no doubt headed along the main road, whopping and hollering the entire way, though the sound-proofing on the shuttle protected Toni from having to listen to that false shit.

From behind her the shuttle door slid open. *Joseph's balls.* She knew who the hell it was. "Go away."

"Hell, no. I'm coming in to figure out how I messed up yet again." Emilio's angry growl rattled through the shuttle as he sealed them inside.

Then it got closer. "You don't want to look at me, talk to me, fine. But it seems odd, every time I think we're on the same current wave, you end up angry, flipping me off or hitting me. Part of me wants to know what I did to earn your reaction."

"You're an asshole. That's reason enough for me."

Emilio walked around the chair and she saw his waist, the belt, the clean black pants with a little Mars dust present and the zipper that hid his impressive tool. "Yeah, well, I never said I wasn't. In fact, I may have mentioned I'm a bad guy who likes bad things."

"Can you get your crotch out of my view?"

Instead of complying, he leaned backwards. "That's not what you were telling me you wanted last night."

She shoved herself out of the chair and pushed against his chest with both hands. "I'm telling you now. All of you fuckers are alike. A woman says no and because yesterday it was a different story, suddenly her change in opinion no longer matters. That little public display you put on in front of my parents, feeding right into the idea I haven't changed at all, got me in a less than charitable mood."

"That's not what I said, and I'd appreciate you not comparing me to those dicks in that bar across the way. I'm nothing like that. I merely said you liked what you saw last night. If you don't want it anymore, fine."

Her ire calmed a bit and she pulled back. "Fine, but that doesn't excuse the kissing and feeling me up or the acting possessive show. You wanted me to perform, like a slave girl on a string. Now they are just waiting for the wild, crazy Toni to show up, the one willing to sell anything for a drink and a good time."

"Maybe that's what we want them to think, but I don't believe you are that person anymore. But, if you were, I'd want you still. I want you whatever way I can have you."

She'd kept her eyes on his chest, not his face. Now she let those black-blue irises connect with hers. So intent, fixed—being the center of that focus made her want things all over again. "I don't get how me punching you and throwing shine on the floor is any bit desirable."

"*Hermosa*, from the moment I met you, it's all beautiful." He trailed a finger down her cheek. "I'm sorry if what happened over there made you uncomfortable, but you're not a bad person for going a little nuts sometimes. Besides, your parents would never fall for a perfect relationship, would they?"

"No, they wouldn't."

"Then this will keep them off the scent."

She turned away from him, moving between the two chairs. "You're a fool if you think they haven't planned for all contingencies."

"Am I also a fool because I can't stop wanting this?" His hand circled her arm and pulled her back, flush against his body. Her nipples pebbled underneath her blouse from the contact as his lips crashed against hers.

She pulled away. "If you're a fool, then I am, too."

"Then you still want me?"

Toni let her lips give her response, her anger transforming into something much more dangerous. Molten hot, like liquid metal in the fire pits right outside of town, the mere contact insane between them.

Coherent thought wasn't possible when he roamed his arms all over her front, peeling her jacket from her shoulders, working the buttons of her blouse. Both garments were discarded before he cupped her ass and moved to divest her of her pants, or at least get the belt out of the way. Guns clanked against the floor as he slid his fingers into the front of her panties.

Toni gasped, the sound cut off by renewed efforts of his lips, bites of teeth and swirls from his tongue, engaging in naughty imitations of what his dick could do for her.

"Yes. Keep going." She moaned the words in between desperately chasing the peak he pushed her towards.

Those skillful fingers of his sunk in and out, played with the nub at the top of her core and sought to drive her insane. Maybe if she just let herself go, she could get her senses back and sound a little less breathless.

"Oh, I will. Come for me, Toni." Emilio's words did the trick.

She arched onto her tiptoes, her legs tensing as her orgasm crashed over her, and she let out a high-pitched noise she never would have recognized. Instead of finding sanity, the reality had Emilio moving fast. He shoved her pants and his down, rocked her body back onto the dash, angled her knees apart and stopped right at her entrance, teasing her with the head of his dick.

Sex on the dash of a ship. She'd never done such a thing before. This equated to the wild, throw-caution-to-the-wind type of thing she should be against. Except the fire in his gaze and being surrounded by the heat and strength of him worked against rational sense.

"If you want me to stop, I will." He sealed the deal by bothering to give a damn what she thought.

She'd give him anything. Toni shook her head. "No. Don't stop."

Emilio leaned in, clasped her chin and kissed her hard. Taking this woman like this was probably a bad idea, but he had to claim her. An instinctual part of him cried out *Mine*. When she'd talked to that muscle-bound idiot in the bar and even when she'd punched Emilio in front of everyone, the urge had remained. Now, he stood with his dick angled to enter her.

He shoved home, releasing his hold on her face to grab either side of her hips. This mindless letting go inside her—if only she could feel his own emotions as he sought a climax for both of them. They chased happiness, and this was how he wanted her, free of inhibitions, her arching against him, hands plastered to the dashboard, breasts waving in the air.

"Mine. Tell me you're mine." The words escaped him, an accident brought on by the way she looked. He made her like this, drove her.

"I'm yours," she panted. Toni was gorgeous with her flushed cheeks and cries of pleasure. Before he could stop, his balls were tightening, ready to go over the edge with little provocation. He slowed himself, scooping Toni into his arms and sitting down in the chair to let her straddle him.

Her eyes glittered with understanding and his jaw dropped as she slowly sank onto his shaft, the act ten times more arousing than when he pounded into her. He watched her move and within seconds he was right back to where he'd been, near the exploding point.

Toni dragged herself up gradually, until the tip of him still hovered inside her center. Then she drove down, picking up such a rapid pace her breath stuttered. He chose then to meet her, to drive up when she came down and the magic of the mating, where they joined, reached supernova.

Elation surged through his body, chill bumps breaking out across his skin. She leaned down, biting into the soft flesh at the base of his neck, and he could no longer hold back.

He shouted her name, the sound echoing around the housing of the shuttle.

Emilio collapsed against the chair, his eyes blurring. "You're amazing."

"I love you," she replied, resting her head against his chest. The words made him freeze, his fingers gripping the armrests of the chair as if the hunk of metal was the remaining lifeline in the room.

Those weren't the words he expected, nor ones he knew how to respond to. No woman, besides his mother, had ever said those words to him. Sure, the one-night stands said they loved his dick, his scar or his prowess. But him…never.

Toni's post-sexual glow was disappearing fast. Her hands gripped his shoulders, nails digging in hard. "Did you hear me? I said, I love you."

"Yes." Fear, widespread and gut-churning, kept him from saying anything else. Hands gripping the armrests, he struggled to overcome the memories of being left behind. Of his mother, the old neighbor, his friends in the fields and even Manolo—all of them had left him. Those words, once uttered, to him symbolized the end. In that moment he realized she'd been too good to be true. A fantastic dream he wouldn't get to keep. "I love you, too."

Those words slipped from his lips, the match sure to send whatever lay between them up in flames. Except he couldn't lie to her. He felt deeply and wanted her to be with him forever, but that kind of good luck didn't happen to him.

She jumped off his lap, pulling her pants up and whipping that blouse over her to cover those gorgeous breasts. When she turned around, the smile on her face could have lit a universe in joy. "I would be happy to sit around here with you, but I think I want to adjourn to our quarters. Husband."

Oh, the happy times. He could see them souring within days. She'd turn from him, egged on by his inability to kill Ramirez or Grecia. The plan to attack the psychotic cartel leader was futile anyway. Even if Toni and her crew believed otherwise, Emilio had experienced Grecia's chateau fortress firsthand. The tall walls, within which rested numerous guards with automatic weapons and infrared sensors, meant the crew would all be mowed down before they got near the front gate.

"Great idea. How about you head there first? I'll swing by the galley for a little something to keep our stomachs happy after the exercise, wife." He loved calling her that. Missing out on what might have been would kill him. Maybe they could still have a chance if he got rid of the Grecia threat hanging over them himself.

Emilio stood and drew up his pants, tucking his dick away. He closed them tight and reached for his belt on the floor, entangled in Toni's. It was a big surprise that neither of them accidentally triggered a gun to fire. "I'll be no more than ten minutes, tops."

"Sounds good." She leaned up and pressed a kiss to his lips then headed for the shuttle door. She'd forgotten her belt, something he'd be thankful for later. He'd need the weapon. There were a few things he'd stashed in here months ago. Emilio moved to check them now.

Sure enough, the sharp shooting laser rifle he'd stolen off an APUP over a year ago was still tucked away in the spare compartment, along with an EMP pulse, spare bullets for his pistols and a few other fun toys. He had everything he needed to make the trip to Earth.

Checking the bone powder stores showed him there was enough to cover the entire trip. Here was hoping Toni didn't leave Mars with Gina before he finished the job. The com beeped.

"Sir, message from Toni." Gina's blue light dinged on the dash.

Emilio sat back down in the captain's chair. "Patch it through."

"Gina says you're still in the shuttle. What's going on?"

He didn't miss the note of concern in her tone, the worry. "Truth is, I care too much to lose you and it will happen sooner or later. I'm cursed."

"You're crazy. Come to our quarters and we can talk more about it."

Emilio flipped the switch to warm up the engine. Nothing could dissuade him from his present course. He had to remain true to his past, to himself. "You said it yourself, love is too risky and dangerous. I want you as you are, and there are parts of you that you would rather hide. In the long-term, we don't make sense."

He hated saying these things, each word like a poisonous stinger from an Earth bugger. Except someone needed to get them to wake up from this fairytale. He'd falsely believed they'd make it, but something would always have been in the way.

"You want me to believe that everything we've shared means nothing, after the days spent pursuing me? All the time you took to convince me it's more? The words of love, the times I've wasted saving your damn life? If you plan on launching that thing to Earth, damn it— You can't make a woman tell you she's yours and then leave." Her strong character dissolved into tearful sobbing.

He had to be stronger, for the both of them. "People can say silly things in pursuit of physical satisfaction. I've done—"

"Bullshit!" The echo of a glass shattering reverberated through the speakers. "I've been with men who only care about sex. You wanted more. I want more. We had a plan."

"Plans change. Your plan would get you killed and I can't live in a world where you don't exist." He tried so hard to sink into the role of villain, but hearing her in pain broke something in him every time.

"Then go! Leave and commit murder for someone who will turn you over in a heartbeat if it benefits them. I may keep your ship for you or Gina and I might take off to parts unknown."

He took a deep breath and focused on the pre-ignition sequence. Toni carried on.

"I want you to know you weren't the best fuck I've had. I said it to boost your fragile male ego. Oh, I've experienced plenty of mind-blowing orgasms and I'm sure there'll be more in the future. I needed a distraction of sex the same as you did these past few weeks. There's been enough bullshit to deal with so it was either a romp in the sheets or lose all the hard work I've put into being sober."

He finished priming everything and leaned over to secure Toni's belt to the other chair. Pulling her leather jacket to his face, he could smell her perfume. He tossed it into the seat. *Mother Mary, forgive me.*

"Are you listening to me, Morales?"

He rubbed the bridge of his nose, his vision blurring, as he monitored the fuel gauge. "I know you'll be happy, Toni. I'll fix this."

"You could fix this by fucking staying."

If he didn't leave soon, he would. He needed a firm resolve. No more discussion about love and how he'd lose her before they could enjoy any of it. "I can't, Toni."

"Stubborn bastard. Check the systems."

Grant me patience. He did as she asked and found a few surprises. "Looks like Sampson uploaded the maps and made some modifications."

"I asked him to. They'll help you," she replied. Toni, the woman of his dreams, everything he could ever want in a small package, but stronger than steel, even now when he chose to run away. She'd never believed him from the get-go.

"Thank you."

She sighed. "I just want to know why. Why play all these fucking games with me? I get think you're cursed, which is just an excuse for being scared. But people don't always hurt people they care about."

"They don't go in with that plan," he whispered. To prevent moisture from gathering in his damn vision, he had to summon every hateful thought towards the cartel that had enslaved his family, his mother, Manny and Grecia. "But you will, Toni. Everyone does. Look at your own experiences, your parents, Big Al. The offer, temptation of something better is waiting for you and your crew to cut a corner, to turn their backs. You'll say you're different, how you'd never hurt me and any words from me would be equally false. Similar to the idea you won't put your lips against a bottle one day when you realize how much time you've wasted on people who don't matter."

She sucked in a sharp breath and the silence in those following seconds did not chill him as much as the harsh whisper that followed. "I wish I'd left you in Sweet's and taken your damn ship for my own, runner scum."

"You may still get the chance, if I end up getting killed by Ramirez and his men. Otherwise, you can count on me coming back for Gina."

"Maybe I'll get lucky," she countered. "They'll pick you up when you enter atmo. We'll hold a celebration and maybe Eli will offer to comfort me."

Emilio slammed his hand against the dash, then strapped himself into his seat. The idea of someone else touching her... It wasn't his problem. "A musclebound freak to wipe away the memories of me. I think you'll need more than that."

The sob she let out wrecked him. Stomach in knots, he entered the launch sequence. "Be safe, Toni. Remember your parents want something from us, but I'm not sure what. Once I take off, you might stop being angry at me and worry about them."

"I'll do whatever I damn well please," Toni replied.

She always would, and he hoped she made good choices. He hated hurting her, but at the same time this was how he protected them from a horrible future.

"I hope you die out there." Her words were all righteous fury as she hung up on him.

"I hope you live."

Chapter Twenty

The worst part about having to do all this killing by himself was traveling alone. Four hours, compared to the thirty-plus days it had taken people to make a trip from Earth to Mars in the early years, was still a long-ass time. Auto-pilot engaged, Emilio got to prop his feet up, stare at the stars and rethink his last conversation with Toni.

Bad idea.

No, he wanted to forget the sound of her in pain and hurting, those last moments of abandon and joy before the words 'I love you' had ruined everything. Why did she say those damned words? Why had he encouraged them?

Yes, I'm a big idiot.

But he didn't want to love anymore, didn't want to hurt. Those were his thoughts as he drifted off to sleep. A steady beeping woke him and he gazed out of the main shuttle window to the Earth ahead of him. The sun was on the far side and everything was dark on the Western Hemisphere.

Home.

Funny how Toni's homecoming had happened a day or so prior and here he was headed back to the shithole he'd escaped. Most of his business on Earth kept him on the opposite side of the planet, nowhere near the continent where he'd struggled to survive, lost his mother, and had no clue if she lived or died. Emilio had no particular issues with the Ramirez cartel, but had been familiar with them growing up. Emilio respected this current Ramirez, since the man had done what Emilio and many others had dreamed of doing for so many years, killing the elder Ramirez for being a pedophile bastard.

Seeing the Earth from this angle brought back dozens of other memories. Few happy ones, and nothing worth recalling compared to his time with Toni and the crew. The same crew had been responsible for the detailed maps he could sort through right now, for the pre-programmed flight plan that would keep him out of Ramirez's radar and get him landing on Earth during the night. The entire group had put their grubby hands all over his life and ruined him.

How the hell are Gina and I supposed to keep moving forward? Focus on the mission or there is no Gina and me.

The shuttle landed without error and Emilio reviewed the maps once more. Maybe he'd enter from the back instead of trying the front entrance. They'd never expect that, if the cartel expected anything. Setting the landing boots in place and plotting his return course delayed things a little. The current solar time meant he had a couple hours to complete his assassination and get back to the shuttle without losing his nighttime cover.

Emilio moved to the rear of the shuttle to get the laser rifle. The damn things were more accurate, virtually silent and untraceable, one of the reasons the APU kept them from the open market. They enjoyed being the only ones capable of getting away with murder.

He strapped the gun to his thigh, pulled his jacket flaps around him and zipped up. Earth at night was cold, like Mars, a desert land with the matching vegetation.

He moved to open the shuttle door when a triple beep sounded from the dash. It rang again and again, continuous streams of triple beeps until he opened the communication channel. "Gina, it was supposed to be radio silence until I returned to Mars—"

"That's just it, sir. We're under attack on Mars. They've taken Dottie, Doc, Sampson and no one can find Lee or Toni."

Dread pooled in his stomach. Here he'd been thinking they were finally on the verge of good things, positive things. "Who did this?"

"Toni's parents and Grecia."

His throat got tight and his skin flushed but he managed to force out his next question. "Where's Toni?"

"Not sure. But Grecia's men spoke about taking her alive, said she would be a gift."

Slamming his fist against the console didn't help, especially when the entire right panel's electricity blinked at the amount of force. Grecia wasn't supposed to come after Toni or any of them, because he was going to kill Ramirez. In the time it took him to kill the cartel leader, Grecia would already have killed Toni.

"Gina, what about you?" He started looking at the possibilities of taking off now. It would be a few hours at least, if not longer. The currents were not in his favor now, but he didn't have very many options. Like a vulture flying overhead, the need to flee, to go after Toni, flooded every part of his being.

"I'm fine. I've powered systems down and contacted you to warn you to implement the manual override." Her speech core shuddered with the last word.

"You're afraid?"

"Yes, sir. I don't want to be used against you again." Gina's concern was touching, and it seemed Sampson had gotten those ethical subroutines into top shape.

Emilio laid in his course and launched. "I'll be there in four hours. Initiate the Big Brother Protocol and await my specific direction."

"Protocol engaged." Gina's voice disappeared faster than he could put the Earth out of visual range. As the planet got smaller, he let go of his hatred for it. Everything he'd learned, taught himself and discovered had come because of who he'd been on that planet. Now he'd use every last ounce of that knowledge to stop Grecia and save Toni.

When he reached an hour or so outside of Mars' orbit, Emilio reopened communications with Gina, but the damn ship, reactivated, would only send written messages.

How many men and what are their positions inside the ship?

Gina's response to his questions came in the form of a map. An outline of the ship with Xs to mark the spots of Grecia's hired guns. All the anger boiling inside him would be for them. There were still some flash bombs aboard the shuttle. It was time to stop playing fiddle to a madman's dreams and be the person he needed to be for his ship, his crew and his woman.

My woman. He liked the sound of that. Even if he didn't deserve her, even if she might leave him one day or stop loving him, loving her was something he could handle. It was a lot better than worrying about her. The torn-up feeling in his gut at the idea of Toni being gone was one he'd like to minimize.

Landing on the outskirts of Frog Lick, he powered down the shuttle and loaded up. Fully strapped with guns, flash bombs and a couple of knives, he was prepared for the fight of his life. Outside, he slunk through what shadows he could find among rocks and a few outlying buildings. The sun was edging close to mid-morning, testament to how delayed his travel had been.

If only he had Lee, but Gina could not confirm her whereabouts. With one thought of the devil, she showed up. Lee appeared a few feet away, skirting the backside of the Frog Lick bar.

"Psst," Emilio hissed, trying to get the damn woman's attention. He waved a hand in the air but before he could get her attention everything went black.

* * * *

"You better hope I don't get loose or I'll slit all your throats." Toni spat.

Grecia's goons, including the one who'd manhandled her, were in the Smiths' Watering Hole. Her parents were real pieces of work, with mother and father dearest negotiating some sort of deal for her and Emilio's ship in the back room.

She hadn't seen her crew since she'd headed back into the damn bar, determined to cause a little hell. After she'd wet her whistle with a lemonade—hell if she'd lose her sober streak for a man, not even one who broke her damn heart. Except the bartender had drugged her.

She'd woken trussed up in a chair and watching her parents walk away with Kain.

"Shut up, dust tramp, or we won't worry about the negotiations." This from one of the goons with no hair and a nasty boil on his forehead. The idiot cartel leader sure knew how to hire help.

She'd opened her mouth to retort when Eli tromped into the room. He didn't acknowledge her and headed for the back room. It seemed even her old 'friends' were in on the double-cross. Before she could continue contemplating next steps, the entire group walked out. Bones, Bebe, Kain, Eli and all the Grecia goons.

"Hey! I deserve to know what's happening."

Her mother shook her head. "You'll do as you're told. Stay put. Eli, watch her."

Her muscle-hewn betrayer sat down in a chair beside her and grinned. "It's good to have you back, Toni, but you should have known they'd want retribution."

"Yeah, and if wishes were fancy racers... Let me out of these ropes, Eli. Damn hemp is chafing." She batted her eyes and gave a sweet smile.

Eli frowned. "Can't do that. Bebe's promising me enough flash to get back in the circuit. Especially after I found the runner."

Fear snaked into her skin. "What runner?"

"The guy you married. Though Bebe says it's not a real marriage, not unless you did it in Frog Lick."

Toni had to escape. She started to wiggle her arms, attempting to loosen things. Ten seconds later, she decided on another approach. "I have to pee."

"Too bad."

"Yes, too bad you didn't let her go." Lee's voice echoed behind Eli as her arm appeared, knife in hand, shining against the light before she slit his throat. He gasped and slumped in the chair.

Lee marched over and cut Toni's bonds. "Well, I never thought I'd find you alive. Grecia's ship's already left the surface. They're long gone."

"Damn." Toni rubbed her wrists out of instinct at the pain caused by the rope. "What about Gina?"

"She's still in the same spot. I saw the rest of the crew bound out in front of the ship. But your dad and his mechanics are going to start work soon." Lee silenced her tirade, the echoes of boots trampling by outside.

Toni searched for weapons but found none. Lee tossed her a pistol and motioned for silence. The first pair of boots to walk through the door belonged to one of Bebe's guards. He'd barely taken five steps before Lee sent a whistling blade right into the center of his chest.

Her parents were the next to emerge.

"Don't kill them," Toni announced as she ran for her mother. Cocking the gun, she put the pistol straight to her forehead. "Move and I'll splatter your brains all over the wall."

Toni glanced at Lee, who'd already felled a second guard, and stood with a knife at Bones' neck.

"Drop the knife, you half-breed bitch!" Bebe screeched

Toni pushed the barrel against her mother's skin. "I don't think you're in a position to negotiate, Ma. You're going to answer my questions right quick or I give my friend permission to slit the main artery in Pa's neck. Got it?"

Bebe nodded.

Toni kicked the leg of the chair closest to her and her mother sat in it. Plopping her ass in the next one, Toni relaxed her frame but still kept the gun trained on its target. "Where are they taking Emilio?"

"None of my business where they're taking him. It's not part of the deal."

Toni nodded and Lee nicked Bones' neck. The older man hissed, a thin trail of blood winding its way down his neck.

"It's going to get worse if you keep avoiding the questions and I'm not playing games anymore. Where did they take him?"

Her crazy mother sat up straighter and wiped a stray blond curl from her cheek with a long fake nail. "To Grecia's place on Ganymede."

These two had obviously been misguided, in the worst way. "Why would you trade my husband to that bastard?"

"The deal was too good to pass up."

Toni scoffed, shoving herself out of the chair with a laugh. The urge burned to rid this world of people like her mother, parents who thought prostituting her to be the best possible way to show love and care. "Like the dozen deals you made with me?"

"Grecia claimed your marriage to be invalid. In exchange for Emilio, he'd give us the ship and regular shipments of shine and drugs we could resell. It was a good business deal, and a cartel leader in business with us...none of us would want for anything."

Oh, *Paul's hymnals!* "I love him, and you've sentenced the one person who cared about me to his death. I should take something you care about."

Lee coughed. "Toni, I think it's best if we get Gina back. Then you can let me kill this fool."

"Don't kill him. We'll do anything," Bebe stuttered.

"Give us the ship."

"Done," Bones hollered. "Now, call this crazy bitch off. I'll take you out the ship myself, call the gun hands off. All our own people, we did the hard work. Don't need any of those men dying. They do a decent job around here."

"He's right." Bebe nodded. "The best way is to let him do the talking, too."

They all walked out of there, through the crowd — most were unfazed by the goings on, but a few eyed Lee and Toni, armed women marching the leaders of their town out of the building after a big score.

Across the street, a crew was working on the outside of Gina, poised at various places along the hull and cutting into their gorgeous ship with high-powered torches. "Tell them to stop," she growled into her mother's ear.

"Boys," Bebe hollered. Then she yanked a whistle out from under her shirt and blew a loud shrill noise. Every man working stopped and stared. "It's lunch break — get on out of here."

They scrambled and left all the equipment in place, leaving the gunmen in the ship.

"Send in Bones first. He can call off the guns," Bebe suggested.

"Fine," Toni nodded at Lee. "Whistle to signal we're good."

Lee didn't respond, just shoved on Toni's dad's shoulder and led him to the shuttle hatch entrance. A sharp rap and the door swung open. The pair of them entered and she waited, each second another of agony.

"I don't get it." *Better to talk then stay silent.* The silence was wrecking her "Why would you pimp me out for business deals or flash? You treated me like trash."

Bebe laughed. "Trash? You lived on this world — the whole damn thing is trash. A shit-hole. I hoped one of those men would marry you, rescue you away from this damn place. But instead it made you tough. Look at you, able to handle anything. I bet even Grecia can't handle the fury you'll bring."

"Tough? You made me an alcoholic."

"That was you giving into weakness. I've always done what's best. On this planet a girl is worth one thing and time again you proved to be worth more, except those fools never saw things the same way."

The excuses and delusion made her sick. In fact, she got tired of waiting. Rage overtook her and Toni banged the butt of the pistol against the back of Bebe's head. Her mother went down like a ship without a slip drive, slumping to the ground.

Then she dashed to Gina's main ship door. Walking in, she scanned the room and found Dottie, Doc and Sampson over against one wall, bound in ropes. Lee wasn't in sight, and Toni called for her. But first, she needed to free the other crew members. Reaching Dottie first, Toni removed her mouth gag.

"Where's Lee?"

"That old man got away from her, took advantage of her checking on us, and she's gone to find him."

Next came Doc. "Good to see you again. They caught us by surprise. We weren't ready for them."

Finally, Sampson. "So sorry, Captain. Most of them should be in the ship's galley. They mentioned raiding the stores."

A shot rang out, along with a cacophony of voices, echoing through the ship. Toni looked at Dottie. "Get to the cockpit and start prepping Gina for takeoff. We're getting the hell out of here once I can toss or get rid of the gunmen."

Another shot. *Shit, at this rate Lee will leave dead bodies everywhere.* Dottie nodded her agreement and Toni took off, through the nearest corridor and towards the galley. As she got closer, Sampson's overhearing proved accurate. The thermal goggles she grabbed from the wall helped identify the numbers too. Three men remained.

Toni came in to find Lee wrestling with one of the men. Bones lay on the floor, blood seeping from a wound in his chest. "The other two are headed for the engine room!" she hollered.

Lord knew what they planned to do in there. Toni dashed out in the hallway, running for a smaller set of stairs that led to the engine room. The slip drive and trolling motor were the only things housed there, thank goodness. Gina's main computer was in the cockpit. A shot rang past her and impacted against the wall. She took aim and tagged the first one with a bullet right in the shoulder.

"Stop!" the other gunmen called out. "We surrender."

They both stepped out and Toni was surprised at how youthful the pair looked. Dirt-grimy faces, darkened white shirts and overalls of some material patched half a dozen times. The shorter of the two, the one Toni had hit, and the one who had no facial hair, spoke first. "We want off the ship. That crazy knife lady told us she'd have our guts out on the floor and we don't want such a punishment."

"Why were you here in the first place?"

"Someone hired us." This from the taller one. "But the job isn't worth the money they promised and everyone is near dead or off to meet the maker. We beg ya."

She considered the possibilities and found nothing horrible about letting them go. Releasing the hammer, she lowered her pistol and the taller one decided to do something stupid.

"Traitor!" The youth raised his gun and Toni did the same. Two shots. The one aimed at Toni didn't find its mark, but hers did. The tall boy fell to the ground.

Toni eyed the second one. "Do you want a bullet or many more years of life?"

"Life, ma'am."

"Get out of here." Toni followed the boy up the stairs and found Sampson at the top. "Retrieve the body below. Throw the bodies out of the cargo hold hatch."

Sampson nodded. "Aye, aye, Captain."

"You have ten minutes. If you need help, get Lee."

As she headed to the cockpit, desperation took hold. They were traveling toward the lion's den with no prep work. Emilio could be killed before she arrived, and her last words had been to hope he'd die. She leaned against the captain's seat. "Ready to go?"

Dottie sat in her chair, pressing the buttons and prepping for takeoff, Doc beside her. He was the one who answered. "The moment you give us a heading."

"Ganymede." Uttering the word, she fought back the tightness in her throat. She needed to believe Emilio could survive. If he didn't...

Dottie nodded. "I was afraid of that. Is this to snuff out life or rescue one?"

"Hopefully, both."

Chapter Twenty-One

Emilio lay there dreaming of a wild night, a bar brawl and sex with the one woman he'd ever want to be with. *Mother Mary.* He must have got hit hard, by the way his body ached, and the dryness in his mouth. He cracked open one eye, but his vision met pure darkness. Trying to move his arms... No luck. They were tied behind his back.

Where am — Then he remembered landing back on Mars, ready to rescue Toni, and getting knocked over the head with a pipe from that muscle-bound jerk, Eli. He regretted not having a gun at the ready or a knife for the sonuvabitch.

His whole body ached, no doubt contributed to by being tossed around like a sack of garbage. Now he hung trussed up, breathing made painful by bruised ribs, and he was pretty sure he was sporting a black eye.

The question remained — where the hell was he?

The gag in his mouth tasted like grime, oil and ugh. Wiggling his lips and chin, he worked the piece tied around his face down. Next, he wrenched his arms to see how tight the chains were.

Wasted efforts, resulting in agony, with him fighting to keep from crying out in pain. A light turned on overhead a second later.

"Ah, Mr. Morales, so happy you could join us." Grecia's voice was an ice-water bath to the face. Emilio wanted to sputter and protest.

"Where's Toni and my ship?" was the best he came up with.

He should have been focused on his own situation and safety. But in the end, he wanted her alive more than him.

"She's with her relations on Mars. They were more than happy to cut a deal."

A stone dropped in his gut. Had Toni betrayed him, given him up before the job could be done because he'd refused her? The situation would be fitting, except she'd wanted to help him. "Toni cut the deal?"

"It doesn't matter who did. The only thing you need to know is that you've been brought here to complete the debt owed to me."

"It matters to me." The words earned him a stiff punch from a big meaty arm, attached to a man he couldn't see. His eye ached at the contact and blood trickled from his lip. The taste of iron coated his tongue.

"Then take comfort in knowing anyone would sell you out. You're nothing compared to me. No one cares to support a flash-less, homeless betrayer."

"You're a bastard!" Emilio roared.

Another punch, this time to the gut, made his stomach grumble in protest.

"No, I knew my father. He was a wonderful man. Taught me many things, including how to inflict pain on people in horrible ways," Grecia replied as he stared at Emilio with those dead, soulless eyes. "I'm happy to share that knowledge with you and by the time I'm done, all those handsome traits you used to con people will be no more. You may not even have a voice."

Emilio fought against the fear—not of the man himself, but the pain. He'd faced a lot of bruises, cuts, shots and even blood. One thing he'd learned over the years was that he preferred to inflict pain versus being on the receiving end. If Grecia proved a true sadistic asshole, Emilio would endure more than what he preferred. Lights around the room clicked on one by one, revealing torture devices lining the concrete walls.

"I hope you like my room." Grecia circled around Emilio and stepped close enough for him to catch the scent of the grease in Grecia's hair. "I've had most of my toys commissioned based on devices used by my ancestors on Earth's Spain. A proud, great country that once executed many for crimes, using the objects in this room to do so. Most were used to extract confessions. In your case, the only confession I want is to know you are in pain."

"Fuck you! I won't give you the satisfaction."

Except he got the satisfaction of Emilio's grunts and growls as Grecia encouraged his peons to punch him repeatedly. Blow after blow delivered to his torso and face. Minutes ticked by like hours.

"One wonders what happens to a man who's experienced mass amounts of pain?"

Emilio couldn't answer Grecia's question if he wanted to. One eye was swollen shut and his lips were bruised. Throat on fire, he could barely swallow and everything ached. Grecia appeared far from done as he uncovered a table of reeds, sticks, and whips.

They started with his front, caning his abdomen, legs, arms, everything exposed. Then they took turns whipping him until his back flesh scorched and stung.

From there he was moved to another table, but to spray him down. The high velocity of the water spray stung his wounds and he tried to open his mouth for a drink with little luck. He tasted iron, blood and salt instead.

Grecia was toying with knives in a hot fire. Over and over he asked Emilio questions about storytelling. How much did Emilio value lying over the truth? How Emilio deserved a lash for each lie he told? And now, he couldn't make the effort to speak. *Praise be for small favors.*

A commotion, feet running, someone shouting. The light had started pissing him off hours ago, too bright in this torture room. Except he couldn't summon the energy to do anything but lie there.

"Honorable, honorable!" The shouts echoed into the room.

Grecia howled in frustration. "What? I'm in the middle of conducting business."

"We have a ship on radar. It's Emilio's vessel, Gina, and it's flying straight for the chateau."

Emilio's heart soared. His ship, Toni and her crew — they hadn't betrayed him, nor had she abandoned him. He prayed they didn't die in a futile attempt to save him. *Saints, please.*

The goon never got a chance to leave before a commotion got the guard at the door moving to secure the locks. "Boss, I mean…Honorable, we have movement in the courtyard."

The whirring sound, almost the distinct noise of a shuttle, then a bang. Multiple large concussions of noise shook the building, the floor. She was coming for him, to rescue him. *What a woman.*

A slow chuckle started deep in his throat and bubbled up, escaping his mouth with a good dose of blood and spittle. "She's coming, my wild and crazy Toni."

"Oh, you think so. Well, I have many men."

Those many men were shouting, squealing, crying out in anguish. Yes, what had started as sounds of men on the attack had become the pleas of the wounded and dying. It wasn't long until a knock resounded against the door.

"Open up, Grecia. We know you're in there. Time you faced me. I'm here to negotiate for Emilio. Or, Paul's hymnals, I'll bust this damn door down." Even muffled, only one woman spoke with such command and Emilio had some insane feelings towards her.

"We won't surrender!" Grecia yelled back.

Then all hell broke loose. The lights went out. Emilio heard the door crack open, the shouts, the stings and pings of gunfire. After a few seconds he was hauled to his feet with a knife at his neck.

"Halt or I'll slit his throat," Grecia shouted.

The lights came back on and, in the dim haze of weapon fire, Emilio could make out most of the crew. Lee lowered her knives, Sampson froze against the wall next to a control panel and Toni trained her weapon on the cartel psycho with a knife to his neck.

"All right, Grecia. Let's negotiate."

"What do you have to offer me that I can't get myself?" Grecia asked while he hid behind Emilio's body. *This poor excuse for a human being using my body as a shield.*

"I've got flash, bone powder and I've got a kid over there that can reprogram any computer system, hack any of the others. He's willing to trade some services for Emilio's release. Lee" — Toni pointed to her first mate — "is a trained killer. She's agreed to give you three assassinations at no charge. Name the targets. The one thing you have to do for these awesome rewards is free Emilio."

Grecia chuckled, a self-centered, ego-filled thing, and pressed the blade to his flesh. He'd experienced this before from upper trash folk who thought they were better than everyone else. Emilio's skin gave way to the pressure and blood trickled down his neck.

"It's a yes or no, Grecia. Decide."

Grecia smacked the flat side of his blade against his chest. "You don't call the shots. I do! I'm the person in charge and no one is allowed to tell me what to do, when to do it or make me look like a fool. The Honorable Alfonso Grecia descends from monarchs, rulers of ancient Spain."

Toni laughed, boldly. Emilio attempted to crack a smile in return, but the effort became too painful. Neither of them had a hell's chance in surviving this mess, but he was happy to see her at least one more time.

"No deal." Grecia's knife cut through Emilio's restraints and the bastard shoved him onto the floor. "I'll kill you both here and now."

Emilio had enough of an adrenaline burst to push himself up and hobble towards Toni. She grabbed for his arms as a smoke bomb went off. Pulling him roughly behind her, Toni forced Emilio to stumble backwards until he came up against a wall. Emilio couldn't see anything. Grecia's men started yelling, the noise of voices continued to increase and he was sure more of the goons were joining the fight. They'd never escape.

"You're safe. It will be okay. I love you," Toni yelled in his ear.

"I love you, too."

Then she left his side, charging back into the smoke. Minutes ticked by, with sparks of gunfire, large shapes falling to the ground and, when the gray haze started to clear, he saw Grecia with a gun pointed right at the woman he loved.

"Toni, behind you," Emilio shouted and pushed himself forward, trying to get himself between Grecia and his woman. He'd barely reached her before Grecia shot off a round.

His future, his love, turned and fired her pistol. The shot hit Grecia right between the eyes. When Emilio looked down, his shirt was stained with blood and that was when everything went black.

* * * *

For four solar days, Toni remained by Emilio's bedside. She didn't care if she stank so bad she'd be banned from the hereafter—no one could move her until her lover woke. At night she'd lie beside him, listening to him breathe.

During the waking hours, she'd help change his bandages, switch out fluid shots and even change the urine bags. Attractive, fun stuff, but anything for the man she loved. *Love...* The fact he'd returned her affection after being so against any future between them, the idea he'd be gone before he got to share in their love scared her to no end. He'd run a fever a couple of days prior, but it'd broken that morning.

She reached out and patted his hand. "You're an asshole, you know that? Said you loved me and got shot to prove it. I've had days to think about this."

"How is he?" Lee's voice startled her, and Toni winced at the sudden jerking movement she made.

She still had a few bumps and bruises remaining from the attack on Grecia's compound, but her injuries were minor compared to the suffering Emilio had experienced. Doc had healed his ribs and the fractures, but the bruising would take weeks to go away.

"He's still passed out. Doc's not sure what to make of it, except that a fever will make you sleep. Old man said different things happen to different people. But I need Emilio to wake up. I have so much to tell him."

Her friend walked into the room and dragged dragging a chair to the other side of the bed. Lee dropped herself in the chair and looked over at Emilio. "Never thought I'd say this, but I need him to wake up too."

"What's got you changing your mind about men?"

Lee held up a finger and shook it back and forth. "Now hold up. Wait a light-year. I never said all men. I said this man. Besides the fact his ship loves him and might hold a grudge against us?"

Gina's light flickered around the room and Lee continued. "He makes you happy, does a decent job in a pinch situation, and he got caught coming back to try and save you. That's more than I can say for most men. Hell, my husband never did any sort of thing like that for me."

The words filled Toni with even more love, if such a thing were possible. She wanted to talk to Emilio about it, tease him, ask questions. She'd settle for a little bit of knowledge for the moment. "How did my father die?"

"I killed him."

The words hurt less than they probably should have, but Lee explained everything about the situation. Her father's attempt to kill her and leaving Lee no choice but to defend herself.

Lee never took her gaze away, staring Toni down, owning her actions. The woman truly possessed a core of steel.

"I don't blame you. It was his fault, both of my parents' faults. They had a chance to make better decisions, but greed stole into their hearts."

A small, sad smile came to her friend's lips, along with a humorless half-hearted chuckle. "You are kind to say such things, but no one can absolve me of my sins except the devil himself. I'll pay for Bones' death and many more once I pass from this world. The problem is I stopped caring a long time ago how long the list gets."

A rap on the door signaled another visitor. Toni expected Sampson, who came by every day at least three times to check Emilio's status. *No change* was always the message and Toni turned, ready to let him know the fever was gone. The words died on her lips at the sight of Doc.

"How's the patient?"

"The same as earlier this morning. Time for vitals checks already?" Toni pushed out of her seat to get out of the way.

"No." Doc shook his head. "Dottie sent me down to get you versus having Gina page. Your mother is on the view screen. She wants to speak with you."

The devil woman must have heard them talking. Toni had yet to verbally confront her mother about how things had gone down on Mars. In a way, she never wanted to talk again to the woman who'd birthed her.

Outside of similar looks and sharing a last name, they held no likeness.

The woman had almost gotten the love of Toni's life killed. Time and again, Bebe Smith had proved she cared very little for Toni's beliefs or emotions. And where Toni would have made excuses in the past, she refused to now.

"I can't talk to her now. Emilio needs me."

Lee frowned. "You need to get closure, Toni. Don't let this linger. If this conversation is out of the way, you can focus on healing together once Emilio wakes up. Besides, she might want to apologize."

"Fine." Toni tugged on the hem of her shirt, a long-sleeved thing she'd found in Emilio's closet. Something to keep her warm. "But someone has to stay here, with him. In case he wakes, I don't want him to be alone."

"I'm here, you know," Gina chimed in.

"I know, but I feel better if he sees a face when he wakes. Sorry, Gina." They were still butting heads, and she questioned the idea of ever making peace with the AI.

Doc sat down in Toni's seat. "I'll stay. Go talk with Bebe. If he wakes, he can look at my ugly mug for a bit, at least until Gina starts complaining."

No more words were needed. Toni nodded and marched off for the cockpit. She could hear raised voices upon her approach—Bebe arguing with Dottie.

"Where in the fresh hell is my daughter?"

"I've sent someone to get her. I'm sure she's on her—"

"You could have paged her, a ship like that. What kind of messed-up operation have you been running over there?"

"I'm here, Ma," Toni announced as she stepped into the cockpit. She gave Dottie a kind smile. "You can go grab a cup of coffee or something. I'd like to take this conversation in private."

Rising from the chair, Dottie squeezed Toni's arm in understanding and left.

"Amen and thank you for that. Our family business ain't for everyone's ears, young'un. How many half-breeds does Emilio have running around his vessel, anyhow?"

Taking a seat in the captain's chair, Toni propped one foot on the edge of the seat and hugged her knee against her chest. "There are no half-breeds. Each member of my crew is a person, Ma. What can we do for you, since you called me?"

"I want justice for Bones' death. That's why I called." The words were said as if they were the sole reason for initiating contact. Not to ask after Emilio or apologize.

"What justice? He was killed in self-defense."

Bebe scowled. "Now you listen here, Antonia Beulah Smith, that half-breed assassin bitch praying mantis killed my husband. A woman like that can kill with nary an effort. Saw her work with my own eyes. So, there was no self-defense. It was cold-blooded murder."

No way her friend would end a person without provocation. Albeit not much, but still, Lee acted with precision if the situation required it. Lee had even sounded remorseful minutes prior, discussing what had happened.

"If you still want to be called my daughter, you'll take vengeance for me and kill the bitch where she stands."

The truth came to her when she stared into her mother's hardened gaze, blue eyes stern and pursed lips—that family didn't start with blood. In some cases, it started with friendships, bonds forged in the trials and challenges a person faced in their life. She shared more traits, opinions and appreciation for the people right here on Emilio's ship. The ones who cared about her enough to support her quest to not drink. To help her stay sober.

"Ma, I guess you can stop calling me your daughter. I'm not going to hurt my friend, who's like a sister to me, because she protected herself. And to be honest, it's better than what Pa deserved."

Bebe's jaw dropped and she put a hand to her mouth to cover it, glancing around as if looking for support. It took the woman a moment, but she came back in fine form. "We bore you, brought you into the world, gave you whatever you needed."

"Except love, support, protection… You sold me, got me hooked on booze."

Bebe scoffed. "You were crazy, a holy terror, from the day you were born. All your choices when it came to how you handled the world around you can be laid at your feet."

"Fine, then I'll lay at my feet my future decisions. If I've made my bed, so have you. I'm done." Toni didn't wait for her mother to end the transmission but called for Gina. "End transmission."

The screen went black.

"You're very brave, Toni." This from Gina, the words spoken with reverence.

Her vision blurred and some tears shook loose. "Funny how I don't feel it."

"You show it in your actions."

She wiped at her eyes, but the tears kept coming. "Yes, and I've come to accept my nature. I won't ever be someone who will please her, but Emilio seems to appreciate me as I am."

Gina's light blinked. "As do I."

Chapter Twenty-Two

Opening his eyes, Emilio blinked once, then twice. The tableau before him was similar to the one he'd experienced after the mishap with the folks on Ceres. Except this time, when he tried to sit up, pain engulfed his side, a throbbing, sharp stabbing sensation he'd not expected.

"Whoa, son. Take it easy." Doc stood and nudged Emilio's shoulders. "You need to stay as still as possible while that gunshot wound heals."

"Gunshot?" It'd been years since he'd taken a bullet wound. Most of his damage was cuts and scrapes from fist fights, knife fights… Grecia had shot him, he remembered. Toni had shot back, too. "The bastard is still dead though?"

"Yep, Toni put a few more bullets in Grecia than he did you. I got everything removed and sealed up the best our limited technological advances are capable of at the moment. No doubt if you'd been on Saturn or Neptune, they might have had a fancy gadget or special tank of goo to heal you up a little faster, but you were hit in the liver. Bullet embedded, but stayed intact. Used your fancy chem lab to work up some of that liver regrowth serum. Damn lucky."

He had limited knowledge of the human body, but typically a shot anywhere in the abdomen area was fatal. "Infections?"

"Had one, that's what's been keeping you asleep the past four days. Fever broke last night." Doc grabbed another pillow from beside him, motioning him to lift his head up.

"Toni," he said on a groan, as the extra pillow changed his elevation and made the throbbing sensation return. He needed to slow down a minute and focus on keeping his breathing steady.

Doc retook his position in the folding chair next to the bed. "She hasn't left your side this whole time, until about ten minutes ago. Woman's got a heart of gold and nuggets of steel."

"What happened ten minutes ago?" Were they under attack? Being boarded? A wave of frustration at his inability to assist came over him.

"Her mother called. Wants Lee's head on a platter. Not sure how well the conversation will go, but you can bet Toni'll be happy to see you."

He could hope. There were a lot of things he still hadn't said to her, a lot of apologies to make. She'd taken care of his wounded body, saved his life countless times since their escape from Casa Manolo and he had no way to repay her. If she still wanted her own vessel…he'd find a way to make it happen, but he hoped to convince her to stay with him.

Needed her to stay. For the sake of keeping the crew together, and because he loved her. *Screw curses.* He'd almost died and now he'd seek to get every moment for the rest of his life with her.

"Doc, I think some thing's wrong with my wound. Can you check it?" Emilio's heart pounded, nervous, jittery. Maybe the infection was back.

Doc spent the next several minutes inspecting the wound site, taking Emilio's vitals including his blood pressure and shaking his head the entire time. "Don't know what you're thinking about, but nothing's wrong with you. Not that I can see. Still got the stitches, nothing's pulled. No fever, no jaundice. You'll be right as rain in another couple of weeks. One more on bed rest and a second on light moving."

Except he didn't feel okay. His innards were ripping him up at the idea of telling Toni about the love he had for her, confessing his emotions. Then she was there. All bright, beautiful, hair still super short but her natural blond, standing in the doorway with a surprised expression, a dark-colored bruise on her cheek and a small cut on her upper lip. Seeing those injuries made him eager to jump up and attack whoever had attempted to hurt her, but he trusted his woman had already dealt retribution out.

She'd been crying, if the stains on her cheeks and the ruddy color to them were any indication. Having been present for previous crying sessions gave him knowledge of how she looked.

"Marry me," Emilio blurted out.

Doc took a few steps back, "I think that's my indication it's time to leave. Good luck to you both."

With the doctor gone and Toni coming towards him, fear paralyzed him. He lay there, scared shitless of being rejected. Not being used to losing, he planned to win this deal, too. *Or die trying.*

"I'm sorry. The words came out a little fast, but I meant both of them. I would like your hand in marriage."

She sat on the edge of the bed next to him, her face set in some unreadable expression—no sparks, no emotion. "Why the hell would you want that?"

"Because traveling space without you doesn't make sense. Love doesn't make sense if you don't share it with someone."

"This from the infamous Emilio Morales, who says people who love him will leave him," she replied, rolling her eyes.

True, he'd said that. Multiple times, many people receiving his preaching and cautionary words about love. "Those words weren't a lie. I loved you and I left you, but you came back...for me. That was the problem. No one ever came back, and you did."

She smacked him, good and hard, and he took the punishment. "It's supposed to be that easy. You almost died. I almost died. My strength has been tested to the brink and back these last few days. How do I know you won't decide I'm going to leave again?"

"Love comes with a burden of trust. I don't deserve you, but I'm willing to give it all to you if you can handle being tied to me." He rubbed his cheek and she leaned in and kissed the same spot.

"I'll marry you, but only because I love you and I'm not willing to let you go. Not yet."

More kisses came next, gentle ones, and all the exertion on her part. Emilio merely moved his lips, the effort to stay still difficult. After a few minutes of tongue twisting and sweet embrace, she groaned her own version of pain. They were both recovering from various hurts, making intimacy much more problematic. She pulled back and lay down beside him.

He flexed his arm around her. "I'm sorry I let myself get caught."

The visual of her storming in like some avenging enforcer still made his heart swell. He'd been surprised she was still alive, thankful, but devastated to know she'd risked so much to come for him.

"Well, it's not like we hadn't planned to go to Grecia's in the first place. The reasons multiplied, that's all." She fell silent, tracing a finger across his arm, brushing through the little hairs and making gooseflesh rise. "I almost thought I lost you. It was tough those first two solar days."

He brushed a hand across her hair. "The fever?"

"The fever, the bleeding. You lost a lot of blood. Sampson had to donate some of his for a transfusion. Then you were delirious."

His recollection ended at the gunshot exchange with Grecia. Nothing else, the subsequent days lost to him, but he'd been fighting for his life. "Well, I had to stave off the fever. Had to come back to you."

"Such a way with words, Morales."

"How it'd go with your mother?"

Toni sat and faced him. "Not so good. We won't be speaking for the foreseeable future. She wants me to kill Lee, but I can't kill family. Just like I couldn't kill anyone on this ship."

"So, we're family now?" Emilio asked with a smile. Such phrasing would have scared him in the past, but this was one group of dysfunctional folks he'd adopt without hesitation.

"We are. Come potential revenge seekers, assassin contracts, random jobs or whatever bad luck hits us."

Frowning, Emilio replied, "I hope not. I'm looking for a life of relaxation. Home and hearth, good food and stability."

"A wedding and a wife?" she asked with a smile.

Oh, that smile. It was the one he always wanted aimed at him. This was what he'd live for, looks like that and intimate moments to drown out the crap-filled solar system they lived in. "I'd have to say yes."

* * * *

Hands came over Toni's eyes and she tried to pull them away. "You're not supposed to see me before the wedding."

"It's not that the bride can't see the groom crap? Bad luck and all that? Serious stuff." Emilio refused to budge and so she stopped fighting it, let him hold her in this awkward fashion.

It'd been another two weeks of Emilio recovering from his wounds. Getting Doc's approval, only to have Emilio require additional stitches after straining his injury moving some cargo around. A few small odd jobs for them while dry docking on Callisto station and making repairs.

Sampson and Dottie had run most of that show, but Toni had helped and done some other things, too.

"Why are you here then?"

They stood, embracing one another, but he was the first to break their connection. "I came, not for presents or to induce bad luck, but because I wanted to make sure I had these vows right."

Over the last few days, they'd each produced two vows, things they would bring to the marriage and expected the other to bring. The goal was to recite all of them together, a true and equal partnership.

"Let's go over them. I still think you came to see the dress."

Emilio whistled. "I always dreamed about you wearing purple. The first vow, I vow to share in all aspects of our lives together. No crime, job or decision is decided by one half, but all are determined by the whole."

Stepping in close, she grabbed his hands, similar to how they'd be together during the ceremony. "I vow to love and cherish you through the good times, the bad, the scary and the fun. No illness, unkind word, frivolous purchase or mistake will drive me from you."

"Vow three." Toni leaned into Emilio's touch as he spoke. "I vow to put nothing ahead of our union. No material thing, no offspring, no object transcends what we share. Last, I vow to take care of you from this day forward until the day I leave this world for the next."

Twenty minutes later, they stood before a judge, the last thing Toni ever wanted to do. Getting married by said judge was even more insane. She glanced over at Emilio, decked out in his finest black pants, vest and white shirt combination with a pair of anti-grav boots that matched the ones she wore under her long purple dress.

"Do you, Antonia Smith, take this man to be your husband, from now until the sun goes dark?"

Toni nodded. "I do, your honor."

Oh, how I will once this ceremony is over.

"Do you, Emilio Morales, take this woman to be your wife, from now until the sun goes dark?"

Depriving themselves ended tonight. Doc had told them no funny business while they healed, but no way would she go on her wedding night without getting in this devilish man's pants. It'd been far too long since they'd engaged in anything other than a chaste kiss, for fear of Doc and undoing the man's good work.

"I do." Her reply garnered a wide grin from Emilio. It was damned strange how he smiled all the time now. How he found pleasure in spending time with her, even if that time was re-tooling parts of the shuttle or replacing wires in the computer systems. Yet his smile made her return the look. They were embarking on a future together. Something she'd never imagined.

"If anyone objects to this union, speak now or forever hold your peace."

Toni turned her head to glance out over their small group. Doc, Dottie, Sampson and Lee were their witnesses. A couple of guards stood at the back of the room near the door and another woman, the judge's assistant, sat in a chair next to Sampson. The assistant coughed, and Lee stood up from her seat. Everyone stared at Lee, tugging at the skirt wrapped around her legs. Why the woman had put on such an uncomfortable garment was beyond her.

"Lee?"

Lee looked up, darting her gaze between everyone. "What? Oh, sorry, the skirt. It's a damned pain." She sat back down, hiking the skirt up to right under her bum. "Carry on."

The judge sighed. "I now pronounce you husband and wife. You may kiss your bride, but keep it clean. This is a court of the Alliance."

"Did you hear that?" Emilio asked as he hauled Toni into his arms. "You can't ravage me here, just a simple peck, no tongues."

"I don't think that's me—" Her words were cut off when his lips touched hers and what should have been lips turned into a bit of something more. The judge above them cleared his throat and Emilio released his hold on her mouth, but not her body.

"Now, Mrs. Morales. I believe we are due on our ship."

The words, his name paired with hers, sent a thrill up her spine. She liked how she fitted against him, how they were joined in more than bodies—that it was legally binding. "Yes, and you'll be keeping the tattoo."

He winked at her. "Never saw a reason to get rid of it. Besides, seems fitting I'd get inked before we came before the judge."

Looking around, she watched the gazes of her adopted clan, her birth one still estranged. Ma and Big Al refused to speak with her, and would continue their dismissal unless she took out Lee. It'd never happen. Though Big Al had sent a private message that he might have some work for them, under the radar, if she was willing to risk their new, bad reputation. Word of Grecia's passing had spread like a dust cloud on Mars. Everyone had heard of what Emilio Morales and the crew of Gina had done.

Toni had politely turned her big brother's offer down. The opportunity for further reconciliation wasn't one she wanted to explore right away. Her primary objective was to discover more of her husband's body. So, she let said husband guide her away from the judge's bench and down the center aisle where they were showered with congratulations from their friends, their crew...their family. Doc and Dottie stood close together, beaming smiles. Where Dottie embraced Toni in a hug, Doc patted Emilio's shoulder. Sampson shuffled up to Toni and offered a small token, a rose twisted and turned from a couple gold leaves.

"You could have used this for other things. A new pair of boots, clothes."

Sampson shrugged. "Naw, making those from scrap metal was my maman's trade. Figured I'd give you a more valuable version. If we're ever in a tight pinch, this will get some bone powder or silence a uni."

Emilio embraced the young man, hugging his head to his chest. "Here's hoping we won't be needing to do that anymore. In the meantime, all of you are given shore leave for the day. Enjoy Callisto while the missus and I enjoy a little quiet time on Gina."

"Loud and clear." This from Lee, who stepped up and swatted Emilio on the ass.

"I can still shoot you."

"Shhh," Lee whispered. "Not in front of the judge. Would hate for you to end up arrested on your wedding day. The Callisto laws are lax, but not that lax."

Everyone laughed, even the judge behind them. Since Grecia, things in general had been lighter. Emilio had turned over multiple men who were still breathing, and Grecia's compound, which held a significant amount of drugs and illegal contraband, to the unis. The unis who'd showed up had given them a free pass, erasing Emilio's warrant and allowing them to leave Ganymede with no threat of retribution. Overall, life couldn't be better. Sure, they had no work, but there was still plenty of time to book jobs before they were dead broke. They still needed to decide what they wanted to do, because bootlegging was a thing of the past for Toni. She'd stay sober for the sake of her husband and the other people who'd saved her.

"Yes, well, test those lax laws on someone else, not me," Emilio replied. He swept Toni off her feet, literally, and she let out a sharp breath as one arm came underneath her knees and the other wrapped around her shoulder. "Okay?"

"With you, I'll never be better."

Chapter Twenty-Three

"You have too many clothes on. Take them off," Emilio demanded as he pressed the button to set the lock on his cabin door. He took in the breathtaking sight of his bride. Her hair was long today, curling waves of dark brown, not unlike his own color. He didn't care what color, shape or fashion she wanted it in – he just wanted her. A small scar trailed across her cheek, matching the one he sported, the last remaining visible testament of what Grecia had done to them.

Those first few days, weeks, of recovery had been awful. Not only had he been relegated to a bed, but unable to be near Toni. She'd recovered faster from her injuries, where he'd had to go through a regrowth of liver tissue – not a kind process – and though she'd come and visited him, Doc had refused to allow them to touch once they'd announced the engagement. It had reminded him of old stories of Earth-before-the-nuke and some of the practices uppers went through, not letting those to be married engage in carnal relations or even kiss until the wedding day.

Since then he'd been saying a bevy of words he didn't regret for a minute. Now, with the day behind them, the wedding official, the crew on Callisto and the pair of them ensconced in Gina on the Callisto docking station, they could do whatever they wanted. He wanted her naked.

"I think you're also still dressed."

"I can fix that," he replied, stripping the vest, the shirt, pants and boots in mere seconds while she toed her boots off, standing there in that dress. Another temptation all by itself. He'd always believed she'd look brilliant in purple and she did, like some sort of upper princess who deserved far more than he offered. "But you're still fully clothed."

She chuckled. "I figured you can do the honors."

"Oh, I will." He pressed his bare chest flush against the silk of her gown. He'd spent whatever he could to get this damn thing, messaged Akono Sweet for the name of a reputable clothier on Callisto. When they'd docked a few days prior, the damn thing had been delivered, along with a few other items. Everything fit perfectly, thanks to Lee helping him get Toni's measurements, since he would have given into a much more physical way of acquiring the information if he'd come within steps of her.

Now, that dress was a liability to his happiness. Gripping the fabric hanging loosely around her shoulders in both hands, he tugged and ripped the floor-length confection from her body. She gasped, her pale skin covered in a white lace under-corset revealed to his eyes. Her breasts lifted, nipples pebbling in the cold air.

"Looks like you need someone to keep you warm."

"I do," she replied on a breathy sigh. "I think I know just the person who can meet my needs."

Any closer and those breasts would touch his chest, but he wanted to get a view of her. Gently pressing against her shoulders, he gave her a playful shove and she fell back onto the bed with a *thump*.

"You're gorgeous. Before you tear into me for those words, let it be known that I have to say them. You take my breath away, have from the moment I first met. A part of me despised how you affected me…and now, I'm learning to embrace it."

Toni held her arms up and motioned to him with one crooked finger. "Less talking, more action."

He climbed onto the bed next to her and supported his own weight by resting his elbows on the mattress. Nothing separated them. Every part of him touched every part of her. "Can't I do both?"

"It's been too long. I need you," she replied, clutching his shoulders, and pressing her body against him.

"My wife must be obliged." He gave her what she asked for, sinking into her heat. She was more than ready for him, and they found their own dance. The primal mating he'd enjoyed with her before meant so much more now. This would be the last woman he joined with for the rest of his life. She'd be the one to bring him to the height of pleasure and vice versa.

That knowledge alone made those moans and cries escaping her lips all the sweeter. He'd do his best to be creative, to coax every possible noise from her over the coming years. Years…together. They'd have time to do so much, since they were giving up anything to do with illegal contraband.

Her body tensed around his, so close to release, and he drove into her as hard and fast as he could. She didn't beg him to stop. No, her words were the exact opposite.

He'd never be able to say no to her. Not after the vows they'd exchanged. His commitment to her involved giving her everything she needed, in the bedroom, in their relationship and in life. He grabbed hold of her hips and pounded himself into her slick channel. She met him stroke for stroke, wrapping her legs around him until they both fell over the edge of reason, the edge of everything.

Pleasure, pain, fatigue, love—all those feelings blended together. He rolled off her and, lying beside her, he sighed.

"Husband… Interesting how that word rolls off my tongue."

He smiled. "But you like saying it?"

"I love saying it." She rolled over onto her side and rested her chin on his chest. "Are you happy?"

"Never better. Just wondering what we'll do next.'

"I wouldn't worry too much. We've a talent for finding trouble." Her words were accompanied with kisses, and the domestic feel of the moment was something he'd enjoy, similar to their companionship.

"I'm ready for it, if you are."

Want to see more from this author?
Here's a taster for you to enjoy!

Bad Boys of Space:
A Gamble Among Sheep
Landra Graf

Excerpt

Caterina Genovese still loved gambling, even after it had brought death to her life over and over. She enjoyed the sounds of cards shuffling, dealers calling out winners or losers, the clink of glasses and the smell of tobacco smoke that left random clouds over tables. A good spin of a roulette wheel only added to the atmosphere. Her appreciation for all that was why she'd closed her tattoo shop, crossed the street and entered the establishment of her father's competitor.

Daddy dearest had competitors in every city on Callisto, but for some reason unknown to her, The Sweet Spot, with its red and gold color scheme, was the one Daddy worried about. Evidence of that was her brother's threats mere hours ago, after she'd wrapped up her work for the day.

She took a seat at a pontoon table, pushing her long ponytail behind her shoulder, the tattoos on her arms visible and gaining a few side glances from a couple of guys already seated. No sense in covering up her personal advertisement for her current profession.

"Ante in," the dealer announced.

She pushed forward a chip before cracking her knuckles.

"I don't think I've ever seen a Genovese in this place before."

Fatch. She'd been recognized. "Surprising what a loaded gun will do."

The dealer laughed and dealt the cards. She chuckled along with him, for appearances' sake, even as her brother's words replayed in her head.

Luca had laughed too. *'You're a regular peace-loving spacecase here and your mourning is over. This is about business, and doing what's right for the family. Our family. If you don't want violence, you'll march your anti-killing ass over to that fatching club as I've requested. I'll meet you there and we'll have a nice evening.'*

'Or?'

Luca had pulled out his gun, the shining surface glaring against the halogen beams overhead. *'Yash's wife and kid are going to find making ends meet a bit difficult if Daddy is no longer around to pay the bills.'*

Her stomach curdled as the other players received their cards. This visit wasn't for her pleasure. Familial obligation laced with the threat that her tattoo shop boss would die. More people killed because she wanted to be rebellious. Their deaths would lie at her feet. So, she shoved down the disgust, heaped bricks of anger on it and focused on the cards.

Rina tipped up the corner of the face-down card. A nine. Then came another nine, face up. She glanced at the three other folks sitting at the table. Each took their turn betting or folding against the dealer's face-up ten. When the dealer, an older man with a bit of paunch, pointed to her, she flipped over the other nine. "Double down." She threw a couple of extra chips into the growing pot in the center of the table.

Play continued and the dealer busted. She won on nineteen with both hands. The pile of chips tripled her original amount. And so it continued, the shuffle, the deal-out, the betting and finally the outcome. She kept playing, winning some, folding on others. Rarely did she go the full way unless she was sure she'd win.

Like riding a hover cycle.

She lit a clove cigarette, taking small drags. In between rounds, she glanced out over the crowd at the other tables, taking a gander at the faces of the gamblers. She could tell which ones were from ships, hardened by a life of never living in one place for too long. There were the women hanging on the backs of the high rollers, most of them house women, sent out by the club's owner to entice patrons to invest their winnings via sexual escapade in the rooms somewhere at the top of a spiral staircase.

Rooms only the women working the floor could take clients to These housewives worked the gambling area and the bar, as well as cutting a rug on the dance floor.

Rina kept watch over everything, something she'd honed over the years she'd spent in her father's club, as first an observer then as a manager.

"Bet's to you." The dealer's voice got her attention back on her cards. She had an ace of spades showing and a queen of hearts underneath—the same as a pair of her tattoos. Instinctively, she reached up and touched the right side of her neck. Then she flipped the cards.

"Twenty-one. The winner is the painted lady."

The patron beside her moved out and someone new sat down. A man, full suit, nice hat, rich brown skin, hazel eyes a gal could get lost in and full lips with a thin goatee. "Quite a run you're on."

"My day is definitely looking up." She'd pack away a nice little sum for her first trip to this place. *And I'm keeping every last leaf.*

"Mind if I join you?" he asked, all half-tilted lips and already moving the seat up to the table. He extracted a stack of chips from the inner breast pocket of his suit jacket and placed them on the table.

"A little too late for me to object and it's not my club, not my choice. Though I question why you're sitting so close."

He winked at her. "Hoping some of that good luck might rub off on me."

I got something you could rub.

The round started anew, the cards falling. Rina was well versed in the addition of players to the table. It meant the cards she would have gotten were going to someone else. As she stared at her three and the upturned five, she grew envious of the showing ten her handsome stranger enjoyed.

Shit, have to fold.

Her new chair companion stayed in and, at the last second, she decided to stay with him. No extra betting had been thrown. She would see what the next card was. The dealer rounded the table and she noticed how the man played, not calling for a card. *Staying. Yes.* They faced off against the dealer, not other people like in Hold 'Em poker, but still she wanted other players to bust, to lose. That way the club manager didn't feel the need to switch out the dealer. How many times had she watched a table switch dealers to kill the players high on lady luck and keep the money flowing to the business.

This was the only time in her life Rina had wanted the majority of the money in her stack. At the very least, she wanted to beat this man who'd woken up her libido by sitting next to her. She tapped the table, signaling for a card.

The dealer flipped it. "Eight of clubs."

A sign. The eight was the date she'd been born on, the club matching one of the cards on the left side of her neck. She threw some chips into the pot, raising the amount of play. The two remaining players and the gorgeous suit next to her followed her lead. Then came the dealer, who ended with twenty, to the groans of the two other players, but she flipped her twenty-one in delight. The man next to her tied with two tens.

"Impressive playing."

Rina was aware of this suit as a man, a good-looking one, but at the same time, she wasn't here for flirting. She'd already caused enough death…her dead fiancé was proof of that. So she played it cool.

She lit another cigarette, inhaling deep. "Yeah, you too."

"Anyone ever tell you that you have some amazing-looking skin?" He smiled, looking her over like a prize animal.

Another one.

She sighed, sticking her cigarette in her mouth and rubbing her hands down her arms. "Yeah, I'm told it would look better without all the ink."

He frowned. "Well, whoever said that is an idiot. The ink tells your story. Like ancient civilizations did on Earth-before-the-nuke. They'd mark up their skin with tales of adventures, courageous deeds and the battles they'd won."

"I've haven't been in any battles."

"You sure about that?" He looked over at the dealer and gave a nod. "You didn't get those without a reason. Each one tells a part of your story."

She'd done what she came for...except getting noticed sat at the bottom of her list. "It's not an interesting one. I can promise you that."

"Table's closing. Please cash in your winnings at the counter or continue play elsewhere." The dealer made the announcement and started tucking away the cards and dealer chips in a drawer beneath him.

"Looks like it's time to go." She scooped up her chips, stuffing them into the pair of pockets on her vest before moving to the ones on her pants.

"You don't have to go."

Oh, but she really did. Especially since she'd figured out exactly who she was talking to. It was one thing to enter the enemy's lair, but another to flirt with him. "I do, especially since you're Akono Sweet."

He grinned again. "I like it when you say my name."

"I'm sure you do. I can imagine you like of lot of things if it lands you a beautiful woman in your bed."

"How about we take this conversation to the bar and you can tell me more about what you like… Is that the offer you're used to receiving?"

She shrugged. "Not sure. I've haven't been in a position to receive offers as of late."

A low profile was what she'd aimed to keep for the last six months. Something to separate her from the person she'd once been, to strengthen her new role as untrustworthy, wayward daughter to the biggest cutthroat business owner on Callisto.

"Well, let me be the first to extend an offer."

She took a long drag. "I think I'll decline and finish my cigarette."

"I heard smoking kills."

Rina smiled this time. "I'll quit smoking the day I find something worth living this life longer for and that will be a cold day in space—"

"Just the two people I was trying to find."

What the hell is he doing here?

Sweet didn't take his eyes off her, but they narrowed and looked more suspicious than she'd seen them. "Do you know this woman, Luca?"

Her brother sidestepped Sweet and put a hand on her shoulder. "I do. Since the day I was born. She's my sister."

Akono Sweet had sat at the table planning to play a few hands with the sexy tattoo parlor owner from across the way. He'd seen the woman plenty over the last several months. She'd caught his eye with her pale skin covered with tattoos. From cards on her neck to the intertwining infinity snakes on her upper arm, he found each tat alluring, in its own colorful way.

So of course, when she appeared in his club, he needed to take advantage of the opportunity and investigate. *Strange how she suddenly appears here for the first time when she's lived across the street for months.* And she wasn't new to the game. Her stack of chips showed as much. Add in her sexy black pants, black vest, white T-shirt, her long brown hair…a bundle of woman that drew his attention.

Except…she turned out to be the sister of his biggest competitor. An enemy.

They'd infiltrated easily enough, and while he'd expected this day to come, he wasn't ready for it.

Akono stood up from the chair, straightening to his full height, which was an inch or so taller than Luca. A good gander between the siblings and the similarities between them started to stand out. Hair color, eye color…though she wore the pale skin better than Luca, who looked a bit sick. "What are you doing here?"

"Came to chat. See you're already talking to my sister." Luca clenched his palm against the woman's shoulder, but if he intended to hurt her, the sister didn't give any hint.

"Say whatever you need to then get the hell out of here." Akono gave a signal to Willie back by the wall. The guard headed toward them, gathering one of the others, Zeke. Akono would have Luca thrown out, the sister too.

Send a strong message.

"I don't like the idea of conducting business out in the open. Better we take this to the back. To talk privately?" Luca had sent spies in before, but never his sister. She'd disappeared six months ago.

If Akono had known it was her across the street from him… "Say what you need to here and now or get out of my club."

Luca grinned, "But it's not really your club, is it?"

"The hell you say." No way would he confess to anything.

Luca shoved a piece of paper in front of his face. Akono skimmed it, taking in the most important parts, the name of the man who'd sold him this place and Vincent Genovese's, both clear as day.

Akono folded up the papers then motioned for his guards. "Fine. Come this way."

Luca looked down at his sister. "You'll be joining us, too. Should have known you'd wait for me at the tables. You could never resist a good round of Arcas Hold 'Em."

So the sister had been a plant. Sweet typically didn't come out on the floor much anymore, with so many of his future plans being focused on ventures far away from the club. But when he'd seen the gorgeous woman on his holo-screens, he'd been unable to resist the temptation. He should have known she'd be a trap. Even worse, a Genovese.

The Geneveses had the moon at their feet, heirs to their father's fortune of clubs and businesses spread across Callisto like an infectious disease. Akono didn't bleed his clients dry, not like that family did. No, those clubs took everything a patron had one way or another. He'd heard the horror stories from other folks who'd worked there and barely got out. Employees paid less than a decent wage, indentured servants bought from the space stations and house women force-fed drugs. *Disgusting stuff.*

Every instinct in his body screamed in opposition to taking these two snakes deeper into the world he'd created. A world he'd once deemed to be safe from these people. *Lies.* "How long is this going to take?"

Akono left the gaming area first, heading towards a set of velvet curtains. He nodded to his guards so they would move in behind Luca and the sister.

"Only a few minutes," Luca replied from behind him.

Through the curtains, up the wrought iron circular stairs to the second level, and only twenty steps away from where his office sat. Select clientele could head down a separate hallway to venture into the house women's entertainment area.

"And you need closed doors to deliver bad news?" Akono kept a steady pace, pulling on the key ring on his belt. A pulley system let the chain extend under pressure. The heft of the keys in his hand seemed more poignant, as if this might be the last time he'd have full control over them. The beginning of the end.

"Closed doors to discuss the nature of what comes next."

He unlocked the door to his office and walked in, flipping the switch to trigger four different lamps to illuminate the room. The paintings, the desk, the chairs…everything in here he'd won or traded for. He couldn't lose all this to them. Refused to.

His guards took up position on either side of the office entrance. Of course they frisked Luca, then the sister. Luca's sister was an enigma. Akono still didn't even know her name. *I shouldn't want to know.*

Except an urge to dive head first into whatever she'd give him still hovered there beneath his skin. He'd heard of her through the years. The ball-busting woman who managed Geno's largest club. At least she *had*, until some mess with an assassin who'd almost killed her father. If she'd been anyone else, he might have summoned an ounce of sorry for her situation, but it was hard to muster up caring for people who gave no hells about him or the people in his enterprise.

Genoveses were greedy, nasty beings. By extension, so were those they associated with. He'd learned over the years to expect the worst from them.

Willy held out a hand for her cigarette.

"What the fatch do you want, a tip?" She spoke right around that damn piece of smoke, like it had melded to her lip and wouldn't let go.

Akono waved Willy to stand down. "There's no smoking in my office. I prefer to leave the smell of shit out here, but it seems like tonight I'm making a lot of exceptions."

She opened her lips, touched the tip of her tongue to the filter and the offensive thing dropped to the floor. Defiance burned bright in her eyes as she squashed the lit end with the tip of her boot, smashing the embers into his carpet. He knew his guards would have someone take care of it, but the disrespectful action wore at his already thinning patience.

Once they were all inside, door shut, Akono stalked to his desk and leaned against it. "You got your privacy, Luca. Say what you need, but this document is going in front of the authorities for verification."

Luca grinned. "The Callisto government seal is imprinted on the bottom. Plain as the stars in the sky. We got the thing in triplicate if you want to keep that copy."

"But I bought this place outright. How in the hell —"

"He never owned it. Not truly. Guess the old fool always figured he'd be too small potatoes to attract our focus. Except you're not running a small business here. And per our contract, we deserve a piece of the action, if the number of patrons coming in and out of here matches my guy's numbers."

Akono frowned, scrutinizing the contract once again. "How much action?"

"Half."

The sister, who'd taken up residence in one of his high-backed office chairs, laughed, throwing her head back in such a way as to expose the column of her neck. Three initials were inked in big script under her chin, and he wondered what they meant.

"Dad wastes no time."

Luca stepped back, lining up with the chair, and looked down at his sister. "Rina, shut up."

Rina…her name sounded a bit blissful. He liked it as much as he enjoyed her saying his. She was so off limits and yet she called to him. A siren in tattoo ink.

Akono set the contract on the desk. "Here's the situation. We can agree to half, if it means I keep my business afloat, but who is going to act on your father's behalf and ensure you get the full amount? I mean, last time I checked, Luca, you were in charge of running the rest of the operation here in Arcas."

Luca touched Rina's shoulder and she tensed. "My sister will."

TOTALLY
BOUND

Home of Erotic Romance

Sign up for our newsletter and find out about all our romance book releases, eBook sales and promotions, sneak peeks and FREE romance books!

About the Author

Landra Graf consumes at least one book a day, and has always been a sucker for stories where true love conquers all. She believes in the power of the written word, and the joy such words can bring. In between spending time with her family and having book adventures, she writes romance with the goal of giving everyone, fictional or not, their own happily ever after.

Landra loves to hear from readers. You can find her contact information, website details and author profile page at http://www.totallybound.com